Transient of the Stars
A Seven Lights Novel

Angel Fuentes

Edited by Ivonne Falcón

Based on the characters created by
Angel Fuentes and Ivonne Falcón

To the memory of my grandparents Pedro Menéndez Cruz and Angela Rivera Rojas.

All your wise lessons learned.

All your loving words remembered.

You are with me forever.

CONTENTS

ACKNOWLEDGMENTS

Dear Haley's Comet: You are my favorite comet. See you in 2061.

If you haven't read *Violet Descends* before this book, don't worry. You don't need to. This story stands alone and you'll be able to get all the necessary backstory you need in the prologue. So go ahead and start reading. Once you're done with this, if you'd like to know more about the world of the Seven Lights, you can always go back and read Violet's tale any time. There's a larger story developing in these novels. You'll catch a few unresolved plot threads that hint to the overall arc. This story is about Blue, the angel of science and progress and an astronaut named Yan Fan. The other angels show up too, but this is mainly about those two.

After writing Violet Descends I was undecided on what story to write next. I tried creating several short stories about the seven archangels to see if I'd get inspired to continue developing any of them into a novel. One of these stories became chapters 2 and 3 of this book. It was called Cosmonaut Blue, and it dealt with the idea of facing the unknown. I thought it'd be cool to mix up angelic mythology with alien lore. Basically, it tried to reconcile the idea of God's existence with aliens traveling the cosmos. This is what this novel touched upon for me... at least when I started writing it. But then the characters took over and it evolved into something else. I'm not telling what, though. You'll have to discover it by reading this book.

Thank you, Ivonne Falcón, for joining me throughout the fun ordeal of making sense of this angelic mythology we're building. Not only with your beautiful artwork, but with all those long phone calls we've had ironing out every detail of these stories. I can't wait for us to sell the movie rights and share our millions 50/50! I love our friendship and you're a super talented awesome and beautiful woman. There. I said it!

To the real Yan Fan, a good friend I met here in New York City a few years ago. You always gave me such great advice. I hope you get a kick out of this brave and 100% fictional character I named after you.

I also wish to thank the following people whose contributions help make my persistently fantastic novel writing indulgement possible: My family: Yussef A. Fuentes (my awesome son); Alex Fuentes (world's best brother!); my lovely mother, Carmen Ada Menéndez; my beautiful niece Elora Fuentes and her mother and my sister-in-law Merary Gutiérrez; my crazy cousin Isabel Sierra and to all my other cousins and uncles and aunts and such; Special shout out to the Seven Lights' number one fan, Steven Sierra! My friends: Jorge Berríos, Elisabet Díaz-Cintrón, Zamaly Díaz, Joe Clemente, Milo Adorno, Adile Kahraman, Bill Álvarez, Emily Parsons, Carlos M. Mangual, Maite Acosta, Claudia Blanco, Vivian González, Cindy Papp, Silvio Olivares, Cindy Marín, David Arroyo, Natalie Blandino, Carolina Zapata, José R. Román, Yuliet Méndez, Le-Andrea Sylvester, Leticia Díaz, A.C. Osorio (taking the world one ass kicking at a time!), Éricka Lugo, Josué Acevedo, Wilfredo (Wilfo!) López, Josué Oquendo, Mitch Hyman, Juan Lapaix, Yaritzys Cassidy, Samuel Figueroa, and Rikky Carrión. RBA Illuminati: Luis S. Ramos, Ivy Beth Gladstone, Ozzy Fernández, Guillermo Martínez, and Rangely García.

Special thanks to Felisa Disanto, Rebecca Hehl, Rachel Mahler, Jessica Kesselman, Branon Sardine, and NYU Langone.

There are three very special people that were crucial in making *Transient of the Stars* a reality and elevating its narrative quality: Sally Blue, Amy Joscelyn, and Tom Mortensen. Please read the Afterword for more on them.

If you'd like to keep up with news on the Seven Lights saga and other publications of mine, follow @panicomundial and @rbacomics on Instagram; @emoangelviolet and @theangelfuentes on Twitter; and Facebook.com/Angels of the Seven Lights. Please also visit www.panicopress.com

Hope you enjoy the story.

PROLOGUE

You need to know that angels exist.

Every night, when you go to sleep, they fight your demons and monsters back into the dark. They shape your hopes and fears; they feed the world around you; they tweak the cogs of your technology; they wink at you with small miracles; they watch your birth and how you choose to live; and then they hold your hand when you die. Everything that you are able to perceive and everything you cannot, they make possible. I know this because I've seen them. They know my name and I know theirs.

There have been many contradicting accounts of angelic encounters throughout written history. Some describe these presences as merry winged infants; others have seen perfectly beautiful and regal glowing beings. We have written of fiery spirits, savage warriors of God, multi-limbed and multiheaded deities. The truth is that in the past there were as many kinds of angels as there are human races in this world. Ophanim, Erelim, Hashmallim, Seraphim; all of these angelic forms, or casts, either perished or vanished during the first war of Heaven and the fall of Lucifer. Only three forms survived the devastation: the innocent and playful Cherubim, inexperienced students who were forced to take over the duties of all other extinct casts; the Seraphim militia, ordered to descend to Earth and guard it from demonic attacks; and the leading form Elohim, the Archangels.

Archangels; seven angels that wield great power, each granted a light, a ministry that protects an aspect of our universe. They were born during the early days of God's creation when the universe was first defined under the golden light of miracles, the white light of life, the emerald light of nature, the blue light of invention, the scarlet light of freedom, the violet light of emotions, and even the absence of light, the blackness of death. Known as

1

the Seven Lights from the top of the highest truth spiral towers in Heaven to the lowest and murkiest recesses of Hell, these seven guardians have closely guided humanity's destiny in the absence of God.

The world was created in seven days; its age, roughly six thousand years since the days of immortal lovers Adam and Eve. Everything that happened, that is happening, and that will happen is chronicled in the Bible and apocryphal books. However, these tomes were written by men, and men often lie.

The idea of the end of the world, for example, as a single prophesized catastrophic end to our planet is not something that will happen on only one specific day sometime in our future. It transpires again and again every single day. The prophet Abinadi referred to it in his writings not as end of days, but as days of end. The war between Heaven and Hell is relentless and Earth has been too close to the brink of its demise so many times. These events are secrets not meant to be seen by humanity, but if for some reason it is inevitable that we do witness them, we are all made to forget them. Only a few unfortunate remember these crises. Those who try to warn the world are deemed as deranged individuals that need to be institutionalized, others find each other and secretly organize. I prefer to write things down for people to read when they are ready.

Case in point: Last year our world almost came to an end when the archangel Uriel, the violet angel of emotions, abandoned her ministry. With no control of humanity's emotional range, we all became chaotic irrational creatures. In her defense, Uriel was possessed at the time by Beelzebub, or Envy of the Deadly Seven arch-demons. I was asked to perform an exorcism on Uriel, but even after we succeeded, it was too late. The world had already fallen under siege by Hell's demonic legions.

In a final battle that took place in New York City, we all became minutes away from the utter eradication of Creation. Archangel Raphael was given the task of resetting reality; and so humanity woke up the morning after with no recollection of what occurred.

…But I remember.

In my lifetime I've witnessed six such extinction events. I have researched many more recorded in ancient manuscripts that I've had the opportunity to acquire. The common thread is the presence of the Seven

Lights and the hand they play to protect us.

If you are reading this, you should know the names of our secret saviors. From what I gather, three rosters of this group have existed, each marking important periods of our time. The first Seven Lights, the ones given their ministries at the beginning of Creation, were Gabriel, white angel of light; Abaddon, the first black Angel of death; Jophiel, evergreen mother of nature; Zadkiel, blue angel of invention; the enigmatic shepherd Metatron, wielder of the violet emotional light; the warrior Michael, scarlet angel of freedom; and the aforementioned Raphael, golden angel of miracles. Theirs was the first age of Creation, a period marked with constant turmoil, the birth of supernatural creatures, and of which very little is known or written.

The second age arrived right around the time of Ramses II's rule over ancient Egypt. Two new archangels replaced the angels of death and emotions respectively, black angel Azrael, and violet angel Uriel. The second age set the evolution of humanity at the forefront of our recorded history.

Finally, last year, during Uriel's emotional breakdown event, I believe a third age commenced, one that is too early to define, but that includes two other new archangels after the demise of Michael and Gabriel. They are Isophie, the new red angel of freedom, and Ricadel, white guardian of life.

· · · · · · · · · · · · · ·

Before I begin, I need to admit that at the time of this writing, I may be somewhat inebriated, but that doesn't make any of the incidents I'm documenting untrue. I clearly remember waking up that night to yet another world ending event. Barely opened my eyes and tasted my foul dead rat breath as I tried to assess which parts of my body were in pain. My breath reminded me I needed more Jack Daniels in my gut. I reached to grab some of the bottles on the floor, but they were all empty. Forced to get out of bed much sooner than I sought, I cursed my mother for birthing me and this world for being an utter mess.

The TV was still on since the previous day and it blasted breaking news reports about explosions and cities being invaded. I ignored it, thinking it was just a movie, and headed to the kitchen. I opened a bottle and sat next to the window. It was already dark. My neighbors' car was gone. There was trash everywhere on the street and I even saw a mailbox lit on fire.

An enormous dark figure stood still on my neighbor's lawn unmoving and facing my way, but I wasn't entirely sure he was looking at me. I kept drinking without taking my eyes off him, waiting to see if he'd leave. He took a step, and then another. When he walked under the post light I was able to see he wasn't a he or a she. It had no face; no eyes, no nose, no ears, no mouth. Its head and the rest of his body was of a humanoid-shaped being of gelatinous colorless skin. Its hands were four-fingered. Step by sluggish step, this giant got closer to my window. I no longer doubted that the faceless unreal thing knew I was staring at it. It tried to communicate with me, but it made an unintelligible sound, like loud TV static. I stepped away from the window. It moved away back into the dark immediately after.

In this world of angels and demons, of werewolves and vampires, of witches and immortals, I never thought that aliens could exist. Yet there was one outside my window. And I knew right then and there what the sight of it meant for me. It was going to be a long night, and I needed more whiskey if I was to write all of this down.

God dammit.

> — From the secret journal of Father Anselmo Duarte.
> September 18. Ortega, Santa Cristal

1 1986

Yan Fan had a dream in which a glowing cobalt space saucer landed on a giant red star. When the craft's door slid to the side, she found herself standing next to its frame; sometimes wearing a full heavy silver astronaut suit and other times being completely in the nude. Her thick hard boot was about to take a step out into the fiery sun. She felt elated. Her bare foot planted itself on the heated gases; engrained on solid mass which felt hot without scorching her. It was an impossibility that did not escape her even in a dream, but still she took another step. Yan was standing on a star.

Everywhere she looked through her helmet she saw red flames briefly taking the form of her loved ones' faces just before they dissipated. The tears of joy in her eyes dispersed too. She danced and ran and did cartwheels in this new red paradise she found for herself. She passed her fingers through floating crimson sparks just before the space ship behind her took off, leaving her stranded. She was not scared. She knew she was meant to be on that star. Yan followed the blue saucer with her eyes as it reached the atmosphere. Suddenly, the craft exploded in a bright white flash. She kept her eyes on the fading remains of the ship as they fell in arched trajectories like a million shooting stars. When she realized she was left alone and completely naked on that red star, Yan Fan took off her helmet. Then she chose one of the many fired pieces of the ship falling from the sky and made a wish.

. . . .

Waking up to another fantastic and senseless dream was something that

Yan was getting used to. The young baby-faced Asian woman scratched her head and combed her straight long black hair with her fingers as she tried to remember the details of her absurd subconscious adventure. One moment she was on another galaxy, the next she's back at her uncle's apartment in Bay Ridge. It was pointless to try to find any meaning to her dreams other than a graphic mental reflection of her anxiety as the launch date grew closer in her calendar. Yan took off the turquoise blue large jersey shirt she used for sleeping and slipped into her tight jeans and pink t-shirt before heading to the bathroom to freshen up.

Her uncle was already up. She could hear him screaming at the TV in Mandarin and broken English. "Yan! Yan, come look this guy! He crazy!"

She was still brushing her teeth as she stood at the corner between the hallway and the living room. Yan's uncle Chen, a fifty-something overweight man, sat on the lazy boy recliner with his feet up and laughed while he watched a morning talk show, *Wake Up, Brooklyn*. It had a simple closed set with the host, a blonde woman in her fifties with an odd-looking facelift and a blue dress; and another younger craggy looking and poorly groomed male in his late twenties sitting next to her, with only a coffee table between them. The woman made mocking faces at the TV camera as the male obliviously discussed his point.

The host interrupted the young man to address the TV camera. "For those of you who just woke up, we are talking with self-proclaimed xenologist Matteo Tsekalo. You are also an alien historian, which is to say, you study alien phenomena throughout human history, am I correct?"

"That is correct Darla", Matteo Tsekalo declared, "There's evidence of alien contact that dates as far back as the time of the cavemen, with hieroglyphics of men fighting what many mistake to being huge birds when in fact these are aliens. And in the Bible, we see it in the Old Testament, there are many passages about this. Prophets often described the arrival of angels to Earth as winged warriors descending in horses and chariots of fire. How silly and close-minded these people were! Clearly, these were early sightings of alien space crafts."

"So you negate the existence of God and the angels in favor of extraterrestrials?"

"Oh no, there is a God and angels do exist. There's massive proof of that too. What I propose in my new book *Satan Has A Rocket Ship* is that this is not an either/or type of situation. The undeniable truth, the one masterfully hidden by our government, is the co-existence of aliens and angels, who have kept in contact throughout millennia to plot the course of humankind."

"I see..." Darla rolled her eyes.

"It all began way back at the beginning of Creation, when God cast Lucifer and his legion of fallen angels to Hell. The devil was stranded and needed a way to ascend to Heaven and exact his revenge on God. That's when an alien space craft the size of a football field crash-landed on a volcano in Hawaii. Satan saw this as an opportunity and ordered his demons to attack and possess the bodies of the alien crew. We're talking about a group of peaceful scientific aliens slaughtered so that Lucifer and his legions of the dark could take over their ship. But the problem is, Satan could not get the ship to start. All this time, the prince of darkness had been trying to jumpstart the space craft. But the technology needed to accomplish this was just not there. Lucifer had no other choice but to push humanity into evolving its science at a faster rate that it was meant to so that we could develop the tools he needed to launch his space ship. He and his army of demons have successfully infiltrated the highest ranks in our governments trying to conceal that fact. Make no mistake. They are walking among us right now."

"They are?"

"It's all in my book, available in hard back at your nearest bookstore."

"Okay. How exactly did you come by with all this information about Satan and the aliens?"

"Well, some of it came to me in visions, but you will see in my book that I've travelled around the world amassing evidence to my claims. And listen, it all comes down to the upcoming launch of the Defiant in a few weeks. The research doesn't lie. I've interviewed all my contacts in NASA and we all came to the same conclusion. In this computer era, we have reached the point in our advanced technologies that the devil needed to be able to fly to the stars. I have foreseen that Satan, Lucifer himself, will make his presence known to humanity on the day the Defiant launches into space."

"Alright, well, how nice! Why not add the existence of Santa Claus and we can all have a tea party!" Darla said.

Matteo stared directly at the camera slowly zooming in on him.

"Laugh all you want, Darla, but I urge the crew of the Defiant to prepare themselves. To Yan Fan and all involved, beware: Satan is real and he's coming for you!"

"Hoo! Satan come for you!" Uncle Chen teased.

Yan Fan shook her head and slipped back to the bathroom to spit the toothpaste drool.

"Where you going?" her uncle asked. "News coming now!"

Chen switched the channel on his remote control and a sixty-year old Caucasian scientist appeared behind a podium at a press conference. NASA's logo was seen covering the wall behind him. A graphic on the TV screen under the scientist read: *Dr. Edmund Peale – NASA Head of Project Defiant.* Press people faced the doctor and competed within a loud barking of questions. As the rumbling of voices died down, Dr. Peale began to speak.

"Good morning. As you all know, Halley's comet will be visible once again to mankind in just a few months after seventy-six years from its last passing. The data we expect to collect is invaluable and we are prepared for the event. A couple of years ago, we sent super satellite Emersyn to orbit the Moon and record the comet's passing. However, four months ago, satellite Emersyn reported failures in its video recording equipment and transmission sensors. Our mission is clear. We are currently constructing a new ship with improved and faster engines that will allow us to reach the Moon in record breaking time. Ladies and gentlemen, we will complete the satellite repairs. Space shuttle Defiant will launch come hell or high water. Our staff has worked tirelessly and we want to thank them, along with the ship's crew who have trained very hard for the last few months. This includes miss Yan Fan, the brave young New Yorker of Chinese descent who is about to become the first civilian in history to travel—"

Yan Fan stepped into the living room and took the remote from Chen. She pointed at the television and clicked it off.

"Hey, hey!" Chen complained. "I'm watching!"

"That's enough of that. Are you thinking of getting ready to work any time today?"

Yan pulled her uncle by the arm out of the recliner and gently pushed him all the way to the bathroom. After closing the door behind him, she picked up her almost empty book bag from the top of her desk and carried it on her right shoulder. Then she grabbed a banana from a small fruit tray on the kitchen counter, and locked the apartment door before heading towards the elevator at the end of the hallway.

. . . .

The young woman arrived at Fort Hamilton High, the school she had been teaching for six years before she was recruited to the space program. When she saw students and faculty gathered to pay tribute to their science teacher, she smiled and acted pleasantly surprised. She was given a bouquet of pink roses and a plaque with an engraved message of gratitude for representing their school and the city's five boroughs on an important space mission. Yan Fan spent most of the day in a huge auditorium catching up with her peers and responding to any questions about the galaxy that the kids came up with. When she got a small break, the teacher went over to her empty class room and searched around for any possible changes since she left. Everything was pretty much the same. Yan hung up her plaque on the wall behind her desk. She sat down and slid her palm across its cold smooth surface just to get herself reacquainted with it; at least for a little while. Feeling tired, she rested her head on the desk, using her arms as pillows.

Yan noticed a girl, a fifteen-year-old African-American freshman, walking away from the classroom door. She must've been staring at her for a while, Yan thought, but she didn't remember her from any of her classes. When the bell finally rang and the students left the school, Yan sauntered towards the bus stop. She saw the same girl sitting at the bench and decided to accompany her. The girl did not pay attention to Yan; her eyes never stopped looking up at the sky. The young teacher raised her eyes, following the student's gaze.

"That's a full moon in broad daylight." Yan said, "In a week's time, I'll be waving back at you from up there."

The girl remained motionless, looking up at the white moon.

"Are you okay?" Yan asked, "Do you need help?"

As Yan touched the student's hand, the girl turned her gaze towards her. Her face started to mesh into its own flesh. First her mouth, then her nose, then her eyes. Yan Fan was terrified as she stared into a blank face. She began to hear a sound that grew louder every passing second; a sound that echoed loud confusion and fear into her mind. Yan Fan screamed.

Yan jumped from her seat spooked by her nightmare. She was still sitting at the desk of her classroom embarrassed while she wiped a string of saliva from her lips. She felt anxious, but she composed herself and thought it was time to go home.

. . . .

Taking the N train that afternoon was a welcome change to Yan Fan. Setting the flowers next to her corner seat, she took out the banana from her bag and opened a book that she began to read. After spending almost a year in training at Cape Canaveral she didn't mind riding space craft simulators or floating in anti-gravity chambers, but it was being under the constant spotlight of the public that got to her. There were so many smiles and hand waving she was able to give before going nuts. And answering the same questions over and over again got old fast. At least the anonymity of the subway gave her a bit of time to herself. She focused on reading Carl Sagan's Contact as she ate her banana.

"That's a good book. It tells it like it is." A familiar male voice spoke to Yan. "No mention of angelic presence in this universe, but it's a nice portrayal of how humanity's first contact with an advanced extraterrestrial species will be like. I've seen it."

Yan Fan turned to seek who was pulling her away from her moment of solitude. Sitting right beside her was a young man wearing a white shirt with sleeves rolled up to his elbows and baggy brown slacks. His face was one she'd only seen on Television before.

"You're that guy, the one who wrote that book - what was it - Satan's Rocket, right?" She asked.

"Satan Has A Rocket Ship. Matteo Tsekalo. I'm glad you know of me." He offered to shake her hand, "That makes what I need to say a bit easier."

Yan abstained from greeting him. "Sorry. My hands are messy. How did you find me?"

"I knew you'd be on this train, I foresaw it."

Yan stood up from her seat alarmed. Matteo noticed an error in tactics approaching her.

"Okay, look, it's not like that, I'm not a stalker." He tried to explain. "Just listen to what I need to say. I'm trying to help you. It's about the Defiant."

"What are you talking about?" Yan asked with clear discomfort.

"Thing is... well, Lucifer is going to be on that ship. He's going to kill you all. I'm not sure why he wants you dead, but I know this is just the beginning. I think he made contact with an alien civilization and he's going to bring them here. You must not get on the Defiant. That ship is destined to be destroyed. Just stay home. There'll be a backlash from the press, sure, but at least you'll still be alive."

Yan Fan was stunned.

"Stay. Away. From me," she warned Matteo.

"Miss Fan, I'm not crazy. This is not crazy talk. I have seen-"

Matteo was not able to finish his sentence. As soon as the train stopped at the next station, Yan hurriedly stepped off and merged with the busy peak-hours crowd. The young man moved over to the corner seat. He picked up the roses Yan left and smelled them with gloom in his eyes.

"Now I have to see you die all over again."

. . . .

Days before the launch, the entire planet watched news reports about the lives of the Defiant's crew members. Yan Fan was spotlighted among the crew and became a worldwide sensation as everyone saw themselves flying to the Moon through her eyes. She was the "average joe" achieving what so many had dreamed.

On February 8, 1986, at 11:32 am, the Defiant took off with a crew of five men and two women. Yan Fan, wearing a thick blue jumpsuit and heavy boots, carried her white helmet across a tall launch pad that appeared when the metal platform elevator doors opened. Out of everyone in the crew, she was the only one that stood in awe at the sight of the Defiant. It seemed that the vastness of the starship would go on towards the heavens and beyond. Yan swallowed hard and was just short of panicking when she saw the crowd of people gathered at a distance cheering, photographing, holding up signs with kind messages. She breathed deeply, smiled and waved to them.

Many families sat in their living rooms glued to the live transmission of the countdown to the Defiant's liftoff. Cameras followed the perfect trail of white smoke left behind by the ship, which went straight up until it disappeared in the clear sky. After the rocket left Earth's atmosphere, people celebrated while the crew took turns to radio their hellos to families and friends. The last person to hit the speaker was Yan, who nervously slurred most of her words in Mandarin.

On the third day of the journey, the Defiant's passengers had reached their destination. Satellite Emersyn, orbiting the moon, was coming straight ahead and it was time to make repairs. Yan was invited to step into the void of space by Malcom, an engineer, and Hannibal, an expert in orbital mechanics. They helped her put on a bulky space resistant suit and helmet. As soon as the Defiant aligned itself close to the Emersyn, the three astronauts hovered over to the satellite's hull. Yan Fan found herself floating in massive nothing. She could see the stars from all directions; under her boots, above her helmet. There were too many and of many bright colors. And she could see the moon so close. Its rough topography was so crisp to her eyes, she felt it was not real; more like a painting or a sculpture laid in front of her. And she could see Earth…

"Yan… Yan." Hannibal called.

"Sorry." Yan snapped out of her beautiful distraction.

"It's fine, lass. Pass me the PGT." He smiled.

Yan Fan handed Hannibal the pistol grip tool and saw him unscrew bolts from a couple of panels. While he checked the video cameras, Malcom ran diagnostics on the satellite's computer. An hour passed without any eventuality. Yan was done admiring the universe around her and was eager to return to the ship and take her suit off.

"I think we're ready to test the video feed." Malcom said, "The system is rebooted and I changed the floppy discs on the drive, too."

"I'll go tell the guys," Yan said.

The young teacher propelled herself towards the Defiant as she slowly retracted the cable that harnessed her to the satellite. Once she reached the ship, she unlocked a hatch that lead to a small chamber. Yan immediately suspected something was wrong when she saw the red lights of the compartment did not change and there was no gravity on the ship. That made it impossible to take off the bulky space suit. She could have managed to take off her helmet, but for some reason she chose not to. Yan went through another hatch to the next area where she was horrified to see the body of Laura, the physician, floating lifeless, her head bumping on the ceiling. The doctor's skin was colorless; blood tearing from her black eye sockets. Yan screamed and swiftly dragged herself through the narrow metal funnel towards the cockpit. Both pilots were dead and strapped to their seat. A quick glance to their faces showed they died in the same manner as Laura. Something drained the life out of them in just minutes, maybe seconds. A virus, maybe? Yan was glad she kept her helmet on. And where was Captain Alex Kraus, the commander?

Yan Fan tried to contact Malcom and Hannibal. However, the controls of the Defiant were almost completely shut down. There was no power at all on the ship. Yan knew she had to go to the engine section and restore it. She felt her hands shake through her thick gloves so she took a brief moment to try to compose herself. Holding on to the handles of the chute, she slid upwards until she reached the engine room. Alex, wearing a white shirt under his opened blue jumpsuit, faced the rocket engine with his back towards her. Yan wanted to call out to him, but something inside her stopped her. She felt dread overcoming her.

Alex calmly stood there. He was not affected at all by the lack of gravity even though Yan had to hold on to anything to avoid having her head hit the ceiling. The captain took a step closer to the thruster and then looked over his shoulder. Yan saw that his eye balls had turned black, with only his iris showing a gleam of white. Whoever this was, he was not Alex. He smiled at her, and simply touched the engine with his open palm. The entire space ship shook and Yan spiraled backwards. A huge burst of fire quickly surged and filled the chamber. Yan went back through the chute, crawling as fast as she could while trying to escape the blaze that seemed to follow her like a shark sniffing blood.

In a flash just before she died, Yan Fan briefly saw a stranger. He was a male in an odd cobalt space suit standing towards the back of the ship. The flames that swiftly engulfed the Defiant moved right through him. Their eyes locked for a hundredth of a second and she could feel his fear. He was not evil, that much she knew. He was nothing like Alex; on the other hand, he seemed to be exactly the same kind of individual that Alex was. He was much more than just a man.

The hull cracked behind the blue clad stranger, tearing everything into the darkness and for a quick moment, the man in the cobalt space suit was the only thing that stood between Yan and an infinity of stars. He opened his mouth just about to speak, but the fires reached her first. The Defiant exploded and its debris destroyed satellite Emersyn along with the two astronauts repairing it.

And that was it.

It would take the Defiant three days to reach the moon's orbit, but once there, it only took forty-two seconds for the hopes of billions of people to turn into tragedy. According to official reports, an explosion in one of the engines of the Defiant caused a rupture that reached the hull of the ship in rapid chain reaction. The spacecraft increasingly fell apart piece by piece, causing instant death for its seven team members. No one would ever know what really happened to the ship's crew. There would be no record of the black-eyed thing that Captain Alex Kraus became, nor of the stranger in the metallic cobalt suit that appeared to Yan Fan seconds before she died in the flames.

The world mourned the loss of its emissaries, particularly their fifth grade teacher whose face became the banner for the media outcry that demanded an explanation from NASA. An investigation ensued. After many rounds of complicated technical verbose and futile finger pointing on administrative negligence, it was discovered that some contractor who knew about faults in the ship's engines greenlighted the mission out of fear of losing money for his company. He got tried and convicted.

The damage, however, was already done. The few countries that could afford space travel development backed away almost entirely as governments cut much of their funding to refocus on more "immediate concerns" like the arms race and war with other countries. NASA was disbanded and the space program got shafted. Eventually, the world turned its eyes away from the stars and delegated the Defiant's crew to a heartbreaking footnote in humanity's history.

2 MOON WALKING

For every click and swipe and save and selfie, for every text and call and tweet and like, for every uber called and subway taken, for every new drug and prosthetic limb, for every robot puppy and 3D gaming console, invisible airwaves of cobalt faith unite humanity. People constantly reach out and attempt to make each other better. They find in each other's mind an endless source of upgrade. In a world that runs on its devices, prayers to the Archangel of progress and invention never end. And the more the masses pray, the more they all agree:

"God, kill me nowww! Why is this taking so loooong!" Archangel Zadkiel complained as he kept swiping the hologram controls of his floating light-based monitors.

It was a windy afternoon at the very top of the Burj Khalifa, in Dubai. The spire-shaped tower with an impressive total of 211 levels (if you count the maintenance floors) rose at a whopping 2,722 feet, above not only all the other buildings in the United Arab Emirates, but the entire world. It represented a great technological achievement for mankind. And that was what it was all about for Zadkiel, also known as Blue.

Blue's chromium bubble-craft, Matilda, as he eventually got around to name it, hovered silently over the building, undetected by any human eyes or any radar invented. Matilda was a small spherical ship with a single chamber within her hull. The compartment was a dimly illuminated sitting room, fully rugged with matching curtains. One big divan occupied most of the space against the wall while several ottomans were placed around it. A couple of cube-shaped pink glowing tables were lighted from inside giving the room a modern neon look. There was a pimped minibar, too.

The Burj Khalifa was Blue's place of solace. It brought him a fresh perspective on the future as he kept himself busy tending to his ministerial duties. He had immersed in non-stop work since his last gathering with the rest of the Archangels in Sao Paulo. Saving the world again from its prophetic doom did not feel like a happy ending at all for any of the angels of the Seven Lights. It just felt repetitive.

Truthfully, what affected Blue this time around was the disturbing revelation that his favorite sibling Jophiel, the angel of nature also known as Evergreen, had pledged her servitude to Lucifer in exchange of resurrecting a human male. The blue angel felt powerless to protect his beloved sister. Evergreen did not come to him for help and instead chose to make a deal with the Devil. Feeling betrayed, he took a break from the other Archangels to escape the family drama and to avoid seeing Evergreen for a while. He tried ineffectively to get his mind off it, though. He couldn't stop thinking about her and the fact that she only had a handful of years left before her contract with Lucifer came to effect. As soon as the human died, Evergreen would be bound to Hell.

"All the variables are in. How much time will it take for this damned update to complete?" he asked.

"Several factors cannot be analyzed at their current state—" Matilda's GPS-like voice announced.

"Work around it. Ballpark it. How much time?" Blue demanded.

"Estimated time for possible loophole conception is—"

"Fifteen hundred years…This sets me back fifteen hundred years—" Blue dropped back on his navy velvet couch and took a breath.

"She should've told me," he lamented.

Blue was failing miserably at solitude.

And he had other concerns of his own. There were still many parts of the world that had their science thrown back to the stone age as a result of the demonic outbreaks. Worldwide communications, transportation, energy, and medical technologies, among others, all needed to be improved.

Mankind's scientific growth would not course-correct by itself.

The blue angel did find some time to upgrade his look. A brand new metallic blue and dark gray armor protected him from neck to toes. It felt lighter and more flexible than the last one that got damaged in a battle against the arch-demon Sloth in New York.

"You have thirty-six messages," Matilda informed him.

Blue saw a blinking light on his hologram control panel. He sighed and tapped it. A long list of unheard messages from the archangels appeared on screen.

"First message from... Uriel, archangel of emotions," the computer announced.

The voice of a teenaged girl spoke through the ship's speakers. "Hi, yeah. Blue? It's Violet. My tablet's kind of acting up and stuff. So I was wondering if you could take a look at it? Or, hey, maybe you could give me a new one? Or not. I mean, if you can. Whatever. Also, are you okay? I'm getting some bad emotional vibes from—"

Blue rolled his eyes. "'What-ever'...Ignore."

Matilda continued. "Twenty routed prayers. First prayer from... S.Jobs, spirit."

S. Jobs' prayer came up. "If there's someone listening, I've had a lot of time to think on this and I believe it's possible to develop an application that allows chat or maybe even vid-face from the afterlife between a soul and its living relatives. We could revolutionize—"

"Oh, hell no!" Blue groaned and swiped left.

The next four messages came from Evergreen, which Blue thought was a feat in itself considering his sister wouldn't bother to use a cell phone or any other type of what she called hi-tech abominations. He considered listening to the messages, but decided against it. He was not ready to listen to her voice just yet.

The remaining messages came from other angels: Ricadel, Raphael, Isophie, and even Amion II, leader of the Cherubim Council. They all left a few voice-mails concerned about Blue's well-being. He was not in the mood to speak with any of them, so they had to wait. Blue chose *Ignore All* on his holo-screen. The voicemails swiftly began to slide away until he noticed the last one.

"Wait a minute. Don't ignore this one," he ordered Matilda.

It was a message from the angel of death.

"Azrael?" he asked, genuinely surprised.

Azrael, the Black Angel, was not one to ever leave messages, much less one to Blue. Blue's relationship with his sister had always been... aloof. Like distant relatives who'd only meet at family gatherings and have nothing in common at all; nothing to talk about except the weather. Blue loved his sister very much, but he always thought she was a little creepy, with that *Nightmare Before Christmas* look she had going on. A day or two at the beach wouldn't hurt her complexion, he thought. He knew her to be kind-hearted, though. He could tell she cared deeply for all the souls she collected and escorted to the afterlife. Strange that she had reached out to him. Was she concerned about him like the other angels because of the whole Evergreen debacle or was she there for another reason? Was this perhaps his time to die? His thoughts raced. He stared at the blinking Vid Mail notice from the Black Angel for a few seconds, then he pressed play.

The Black Angel appeared in one of his holo-screens. The pale angel with the physique of a seven year old girl in a tattered dress and what seemed like a spinning black hole of a halo. She beamed a cute innocent smile and waved hello from what looked like an airport field. Blue could tell that she was standing on an expanded runway or platform of some sort. Black Angel turned the camera sideways, and for a moment, the sunlight took over the video image making a bright white blot. As the she kept walking, the sunlight receded and Blue saw that the Black Angel stood in front of a vast gray-walled hangar. Its main entrance opened and Blue saw a huge white rocket-ship resting inside it. The hangar walls were labeled NASA.

Blue realized the Black Angel was not just calling from any field, she was at Cape Canaveral in Florida. Suddenly, the angel of death held the cam to her face and as she continued smiling, she signaled with her index finger for Blue to come to her. The video message ended.

"What is that girl doing over there? Whose soul is she going to collect?" he asked himself, confounded.

Blue scratched his short blond hair and took a moment to consider things.

"Hmm, I don't know…What do you think, Matilda? Should I go?"

"Please state your request."

"You useless bucket of ice-cold apathy…Oh, what the heck. I'm not feeling productive today anyway. Take me to Cape Canaveral, Matilda."

"Setting course," Matilda replied.

Blue's cobalt crystal visor placed itself in front of his eyes. The angel pressed a few holo-switches and buttons. He took a break to see what was trending on the many social media sites. Matilda hummed slightly as the bright blue laser bubble ship quickly took flight to the clear skies.

…………..

Hundreds of people lined up to enter the visitor's area of Kennedy Space Center, a miles long museum that hosted the last remnants of a bygone age. Because angels are invisible to the human eye, Blue and the Black Angel walked among the crowd unseen by anyone. Blue grinned when he saw many different types of antique spacecraft models lined up for public display at the Rocket Garden exhibit. Skyrockets he helped design decades ago as cutting edge technology for a strange new uncharted field of space exploration were now obsolete vintage curiosities of the campy future flying car variety. The angels skipped the ticket booth and went right through the entrance of the Astronaut Memorial building.

"This isn't what I pictured at all, snow face," Blue said to the Black Angel, "If you'd told me you just wanted a day at the museum I would've stayed home. You know I'm not one to dwell in the past."

The Black Angel grabbed Blue's hand and pulled him towards the special exhibits hall. He stopped at the entrance and sneered.

"Really? The Defiant exhibition? Do you enjoy rubbing past failures in my face or are you so morbidly obsessed with the dead that you think this is an amusement park ride to you? You go in, boo. Knock yourself out. I'm out."

Blue let go of his sister's hand and began to walk the opposite way of the hall. The Black Angel frowned and ran up to him. She pulled his hand

and pointed at the exhibit.

"My God, how exasperating can you be?" the angel relented. "Fine!"

Both angels entered the exhibit hall. The walls were filled with small artifacts and blown up photos of the Defiant, its crew, and the crowd of people that gathered on the day of the launch to witness the ship's takeoff. There were four flat screens that displayed heartwarming interviews with family members of the crew in looping. The main piece of the exhibit was placed in the middle of the room. It was an exact replica of the cockpit of the Defiant that people were allowed to enter and photograph. However, what caught Blue's attention was a photo of seven people dressed in astronaut jumpsuits posing as a group and smiling. He stared at one specific face.

"Yan…" he whispered.

As Blue stared at the group photo of the space crew, he found it surprising how painful the memories continued to be for him after so many years. It had taken the angel more than thirty years to try to steer mankind back into space travel research. He once considered it to be their destiny to find and colonize hospitable planets and to embrace the vastness of Creation. These last few decades, though, any progress on this field was so little and so slow that he had seriously come to doubt humans would ever be able to reach Mars. However, his biggest pain came from humanity's loss of hope. He faulted himself for that. Yan's face reminded Blue that in his drive to push the world to the next step of its technological evolution he had failed to watch over them.

The Black Angel tapped Blue's cobalt armor to get his attention. She pointed at a picture of Yan Fan handshaking President Reagan. Then, she directed him to a sign by the entrance of the exhibit hall. The sign read: *Lost and Found* with an arrow next to it.

"Lost?" Blue asked, "Yan Fan is lost? You know, this would all be so much easier if you took the time to learn sign language…"

The Black Angel placed both hands on her chest.

"Her soul is lost…" he said. "But she died thirty years ago, how could you know—?"

Blue remembered that just after the recent war against the demon horde in New York, the Black Angel and Ricadel, the white angel of life, worked together to determine which souls were truly intended to die and which were meant to live during that catastrophe. It was a sort of soul census, one that had not been done since either the great flood or the bubonic plague; Blue couldn't remember which, but it didn't matter. He supposed that the Black Angel must have been made aware of Yan's soul gone missing during the count. But still...

"What does any of this have to do with me?" he asked the Black Angel. "The dead and fate of souls is your ministry, I—"

The Black Angel interrupted Blue by pointing at another picture on the wall. It was a photo of the Moon. He finally realized what the angel of death was asking; it made sense that she came to him. The restless soul of Yan Fan meandered somewhere on the Moon. She needed to be recovered. Even as fast as they could fly, it would take angels many tiring weeks to reach the Moon with nothing but the fluttering of wings to take them there. The angel of progress was the only one of the Seven Lights with space travel capabilities. He had Matilda.

"It's okay, I'll bring her to you."

Black Angel smiled and hugged her brother.

"I'm going to the Moon!" Blue exclaimed. "It feels a bit retro, I have to say. It's all about Mars these days, but I'll take it."

Blue sprinted out of the exhibit hall and then the building as he headed towards his small sphere-shaped ship. The prospect of traveling to space was an exciting one for him. He had fitted his ship just in case it was ever necessary to go into space, sure, but up to that point, Blue had never actually tested her. Now there was a reason to take Matilda out for a spin. A soul was at stake, and not just any soul; it was the soul of Yan Fan. Of course there would be much planning to do. He couldn't just leave his demanding ministry unattended, but he could easily monitor things remotely if he made up a few apps. This could work, he thought.

Matilda slid a door open for the blue angel, which only he crossed while singing in his best Sinatra voice. "Fly me to the Moon. Let me play among the stars. Let me see what spring is like on -ah-Jupiter and Maaars..."

The Black Angel stood outside. Blue sneaked his head out the door.

"Are you coming?" he asked.

Azrael gave him a sad smile and shook her head. The ministry of death wasn't one that could be handled from a tablet.

"Okay. You can just stop talking. I get it," he told her.

The angels waved goodbye.

. . . .

Matilda only took six and a half hours to reach the Moon at 92,000 kilometers per hour. Blue studied the possibilities and concluded that for Yan to be a ghost haunting on Earth's only natural satellite, the debris of the Defiant must have crashed on its surface. It most certainly should be buried deep within some crater for the humans not to have noticed its whereabouts yet. After calculating the Defiant's position before the explosion and the trajectory of the wreckage, he landed the ship on the edge of a hollow bowl-shaped gap the size of ten football fields. The crater was too dark for him to bring Matilda closer to the bottom without risking her, so he needed to descend by foot.

Having landed on the dark side of Luna, Blue put on his helmet and left his ship. Everything on his periphery was pitch black. The darkness lapped his suit's long and short range lights, giving him no clue of his surroundings. He was still determined to relish his first steps on the Moon, but he just needed to step carefully. The angel felt the rocky terrain incline little by little as he walked downwards for many hours. On occasions, he thought he heard faint whistling sounds, but as he turned, there was nothing but darkness and silence around him. When he finally reached the bottom, he felt relieved. His fear of treading the hill gave in to a safer feeling as his body was more in control at the flat bottom of the canyon.

He had an idea.

Blue pumped up the music on the settings of his suit to *Smooth Criminal*, his favorite Michael Jackson tune, and improvised many of his dance steps including his famous forward incline and, of course, the moon walk. As his little dance number came to its climatic end, he held his crotch and pointed to his front while screaming "Wooooooh!" The angel saw in the corner of his eye that a figure stood very close next to him watching. He quickly turned towards the apparition, but the person was no longer there. Blue spun around to try to catch the figure again, but he saw no one.

"Yan? Are you here?" He spoke pointlessly, knowing no sound could be heard in space.

Blue stood in that spot waiting for a response that never came. After almost twenty minutes, he decided to move on. His suit sensors showed that there was a large concentration of titanium close. Surely, it belonged to the Defiant's wreckage. He walked in a straight line, following his readings, and found himself at the entrance to a cavern. It was a huge dark opening that looked like a giant belly button, if the Moon was the belly. He studied the rocky path in front of him. It was the markings or tracks left by something big that seemed to be dragged or pushed as it headed deeper into the cave. Blue cautiously ventured in and his suit let him know he was getting closer to his target.

"And here it is," he stated.

The tech-armored angel stood right in front of a huge scorched chunk of the Defiant's engine and part of its carapace. There were a few sections of the ship that were covered in a thin layer of ice or shiny dust. Blue walked through the rubble, inspecting it closely and touching it a few times with a bittersweet sensation.

"You were such a beauty... You still are. Sorry I failed you," he whispered to the chunks of scrapped metal.

Suddenly, Blue felt a rumble that made him back away from the ship. He saw pieces of the spacecraft, small pieces first then bigger ones, levitating in the space above the terrain. The entire engine slowly rose from the ground. He then saw the dark figure he'd noticed before hidden in the shadows at the other side of the floating wreckage. The figure stepped forward. It was an astronaut with a big round helmet and an old bulky white space suit with ash burn stains all over. As it approached the angel, it flickered intermittently in and out of existence. The specter moved in small slow motioned hops that seemed affected by the low gravity.

Blue sighed. He stepped forward and tapped his helmet, signaling the ghost. The angel pointed his arm at the astronaut spirit and the wrist shooter in on his suit fired a small metal chip that adhered itself to the ghost's helmet. The force of the shot tilted the astronaut's head backward a bit.

"Ow…" Blue heard a female voice from his suit. Good, he thought. His speaker was working.

"Cut it out, Yan. You're embarrassing yourself." Blue said. "And quit the Neil Armstrong bit. You don't have to leap all the way here. You can drift. Gravity doesn't affect you. You do know you're dead, right?"

"I've seen you before… You-you're him, the man I saw on the Defiant, right before… Who are you?" Yan Fan asked terrified as she took a couple of steps back. The floating rocket's scraps slowly dropped back to the ground.

"Call me Blue. I'm an angel and the guy taking you home."

"A what?"

"Look, I'm not going to hurt you." He took off his helmet and smiled. Yan stepped back. The angel put it back on.

"You can take yours off too, you know." He extended his arm to shake hello.

Yan froze. The angel could tell she was panicking.

"It's okay, baby doll," he said warmly. "Go for it."

It took some time, but eventually, the astronaut ghost removed her helmet. The young Asian woman's face was dead pale. Her eyes and mouth were wide open as she laughed nervously. Her long hair floated outwards, free from captivity.

Blue reached his arm again to her. "Don't leave me hanging now," he smiled.

Yan Fan backed away from Blue. There was fright and tears in her eyes. She locked eyes with Blue and moved her lips, enouncing soundless words. Blue tapped his helmet again and shook his head. Yan felt embarrassed and put her helmet back on.

"I'm sorry. It's been…It's been so long since I—" she whimpered.

"I know."

"How long?" She managed to ask.

"Thirty-one years give or take."

She stepped back further. Both hands on her mouth and eyes wide. She fell on her knees. "Oh, mother…"

Blue got closer and touched Yan's shoulder. "We should go. There's someone who's waiting to meet you."

"I–No. I can't leave the- huh- the Defiant. Not like this." She moved her shoulder away from his hand.

"Oh, trust me, she'll be fine. I'll come back for her. But just wait 'til you see Matilda."

"Matilda?"

"Like the musical. Come check her out."

Yan Fan pushed Blue aside and sped out of the cave.

"Hey!" the angel yelled and followed suit after the astronaut ghost.

The pair made it all the way through the valley and up the crater. Yan zig zagged aimlessly, flashing in and out of existence. They both noticed how the darkness went away; they were able to see the light gray rocky surface with thin layers of sparkly foggy dust that made everything look magical on the Moon.

"Where do you think you're going?" the angel asked as he followed her.

The ghost of the woman floated several feet away and then stopped as she stared upwards. Blue caught up with her.

"Thirty years…" she mumbled.

"Yan Fan, give me your hand. It's time for you to rest in peace," Blue told her.

"It was all for nothing…" Yan cried.

"Say what?"

"My life…did it mean anything? Did I make a difference?"

Blue refused to reveal what Yan's death meant to the world.

"Do you regret getting in the Defiant?" he asked.

Yan turned her eyes to Blue.

"When I was alive..." She said, "I tried teaching my kids that there's so much more we don't know about this universe. I thought maybe I could spark something in them, some curiosity to motivate the next generation of innovators. But all I did was bore my students to death. How was I supposed to make them understand? To them, it wasn't science. I was just teaching fantasies... But, God, when the space program happened by, I applied. I applied because I thought that I'd make everything real not just for me, but for them. They could look forward to experience something unforgettable that would put everything in perspective, you know? This was going to be an adventure for all of us. My kids watched me on TV as I flew to the stars... But instead they saw me die."

"Yan-"

"Now you tell me, if you're an eleven year old watching your totally radical science teacher explode in space for no good reason at all, are you getting inspired yet? Are you lining up to become the next great astronaut? I died... for nothing. And that... I just wish this wasn't it... I'm sorry, I'm just rambling. I should've never..."

Yan Fan fell silent and kept looking upwards. Blue joined her as they both quietly stared at an Earth that looked astonishingly close and full of intense blues and greens and browns and whites. Peaceful, quiet, still; that was their home planet magnificent above them.

The blue Archangel rolled his eyes and grinned. "You know, if you don't want to go home right away, just say it..."

3 COSMONAUT BLUE

Stepping into the futuristic glowing blue sphere made Yan Fan feel that she was living a Spielberg alien movie like Close Encounters or E.T. But the inside of the space craft was the real surprise for Yan. She expected to be in a room full of complex-looking switches, lights and screens. Instead, she felt like she was in a neon-lighted VIP lounge. It was a small flying lounge with no cockpit. The control panel of the ship was a floating hologram that followed the angel to any corner of the room he went. If any passenger wished to get a view outside Matilda, all they had to do was swipe on any wall of the ship and a window would open.

The blue Archangel had dimmed the lights and gave the ship an oral command to set course to the Andromeda galaxy.

"E.T.A. to Andromeda: two point five million years, nine months, one week, three days, one hour, and twenty-seven minutes," Matilda calculated.

"No, you silly thing. Launch the wormhole app and then set the course." Blue corrected the ship.

"E.T.A. to Andromeda: three weeks, four days, seven hours, and forty minutes."

"That's more like it. We got time some to kill, let's get this party started!"

The astronaut ghost hovered quietly by a corner next to a large curved-shaped blue couch.

"Oh, don't be such a square. How about some music?"

"Music! All that quiet for so long… Yes! Yes, please!" Yan Fan exclaimed as she approached the armored angel.

Blue kicked things off with a dance mix of Elton John's *Rocket Man*. He boogied his way through hits of the late eighties, nighties, two thousands and beyond. Yan observed the angel with a smile on her face and listened to the songs with thrilled curiosity. She paid most attention to the artists she knew, like Prince, and Aerosmith, and how much or how little their music had evolved through the years. She absolutely loved Madonna's *Ray of Light* and Alanis Morissette's *Jagged Little Pill*, and asked the angel to play them again a few times. They challenged each other at karaoke with Beastie Boys, No Doubt, and U2. As Peter Gabriel's *I Grieve* came on, Yan noticed Blue became teary-eyed.

"Pancakes!" Blue yelled.

"What?"

"Oh, just ignore me. Pancakes is my emotional safe word. I say it to get myself out of a funk when I'm a little choked up."

"Got it!" Yan laughed.

As time passed, talk about music turned to talk about artists. From Michael Jackson's heartbreaking last years, to Kurt Cobain's music revolution and eventual suicide, to the tragic deaths of the Notorious B.I.G. and Tupac Shakur, to how much the world still missed John Lennon, and so on.

The conversation transitioned into movies; Blue wouldn't stop bragging about his uber-high definition and eardrum-wrecking hyper holo-cell-tech home theater. They watched Titanic, a few Batman movies, The Twilight saga, Up, The Social Media, and Argo, among others. Then, he showed her news footage of historic and current events, such as the death of Princess Di, 911, the war in Iraq, President Obama's election, Trump, how technological improvements like the internet and smartphones bred the millennials selfie generation, and the recent re-classification of Pluto by astronomers.

"A dwarf planet? Poor Pluto…" Yan remarked with true concern.

"Indeed. That's messed up, right?" Blue replied, "It went from being one of the nine planets of the solar system to one of hundreds of astral bodies or so that fit with the definition of a dwarf planet in our system. Epic Fail!"

"So sad..." she sighed.

"What? Are you going to cry? It's just a piece of rock."

"No. Ha! Of course not! But, it's just... in a way, it kind of makes me feel a bit smaller. I don't know why."

"Really? You're adorable! Listen, sweetie, Pluto will be fine. We'll all be fine. I'm sure Pluto will still trend as the star of the dwarf planets. It's still our Pluto, okay?"

Yan smiled and nodded embarrassed.

Three weeks alone in space with nothing but music and movies was more than enough for Yan Fan and Blue to bond and become very good friends. Eventually, Matilda interrupted their trip into humanity's memory lane to announce the proximity of the Andromeda galaxy. They saw three immediate planets on the floating holographic screen. The closest one was a small red planet. The two bigger ones farther away were mustard yellow.

"The red one's mostly got carbon dioxide gas layers. It's the safest to walk around for a bit. We could cruise the other two and have a look," Blue let Yan know. "But I got readings of high concentrations of methane in their atmospheres; not to mention sulfuric acid, so bad for my suit. You're about to go where no human has gone before and probably will not go, at least until the next one hundred and eighty-two years by my calculations."

Yan Fan nodded and put on her helmet. In her excitement, she shook her body slightly in a quick kick and hop dance.

"Let me know if you can hear me through the speakers I set in your helmet."

"Loud and clear!"

"I meant, once we're off the ship, wise ass."

. . . .

"This place is amazing!" Yan grinned wide-eyed as she stared through her helmet's visor at the brick red, peach, and white multi-colored sands that covered the planet's surface like frosting layers on a cake. Even with the dusty wind that blew on the red world, the curvy rings of sand on the ground remained separate from each other all over the barren deserts. Smooth red spiky rock mountains rose sporadically from the surface and reached hundreds of feet high into the sky. A nearby star provided permanent daylight to the side of the planet they explored, but Yan Fan could still clearly see the two big yellow planets waiting for her in the firmament. She took a moment to look around her while listening to Train's *Drops of Jupiter*, which Blue played for her from the ship.

"You get the honor of naming the planet." She heard Blue's voice through her helmet.

"Roger that," she replied. "But shouldn't we hold off until we make sure there's no other intelligent life forms here that may have already named their home world?"

"Yan, if you're looking for aliens, I'm afraid you're not going to find them." Blue interjected, "It's creationism a go-go, honey. We live in God's universe. And by 'we', I mean humanity, divinity, and demonity (is that even a word?). Anyway, that's pretty much it."

"So why create a universe so vast if the only life forms in it live on Earth?"

"Because," the Archangel answered with a slightly brash tone, "God said unto Abraham that his children will count as many as the stars. Do you know how many stars are out there? Yeah, there's going to be a time when humans will need to look for apartment space on the other side of the galaxy."

"That's very disappointing, man. I refuse to believe the notion of Earth being the only place where life was made possible."

"What is so disappointing about having the entire house for ourselves? There's still a myriad of miracles the human mind has never even conceived."

"If we'll ever manage to reach them…"

Blue's tone changed to admiration, "That's why you are so important. I truly believe that because of people like you, no corner of the infinite will remain without conquering. And us angels will be there to guide you"

"Okay." Yan Fan rolled her eyes, "Well, I guess I should name this place for the sake of our future realtors… Cai Shen. Welcome to Cai Shen."

"The Chinese deity of wealth. Nice."

"Just a small reminder there are many ways to envision the idea of God" Yan explained.

"As many as the stars…" Blue winked.

Yan Fan and Blue explored more of the planet. They stumbled into a valley where there were many flat ramp-shaped red rock pillars that the angel thought would be a skater's paradise, so they called that area Skater Heaven. They found other peculiarly shaped areas that they playfully baptized according to their form, like Swirlyville, Cock-a-doodle Crest, or Angel Wing Mountains. Yan took advantage of her ghost state to fit into places living humans would have trouble getting into. She collected rocks she felt could be studied and found a small one in particular that had seamless undulated lines. The astronaut ghost thought maybe it could be a petrified shell. A quick probe by Blue's scanners showed it was just another eroded pebble, but Yan decided to keep it anyway. After staying on Cai Shen for the next few days, they moved on to the next planet.

The closest mustard yellow planet was easily twelve times bigger than Earth and fifteen times the size of Cai Shen. Hostile weather made Matilda shake a few times. The entire planet's atmosphere was plagued with loud thunder, acid rains, and thick coffee-brown clouds that obstructed the view of the travelers. Stepping off the ship was out of the question, but Blue pondered if it was even worth the risk to descend to the surface just to get a look at it. Against his better judgment, the angel ordered his ship to drift merely thirty feet above ground to give Yan Fan a good glance of the terrains. The dark brown rocky grounds were brutally perforated by sulfuric acid rains. The levels of erosion and decay on the surface astonished the ghost astronaut. If they were to label each distinct area they found as they did on Cai Shen, they would probably come up with horrid names like Vomit Road, Bad Acne Valley, or Dog Shit Mesa.

"Hell Part Two," Yan said. "That's what I'm calling this planet."

"Hell Part Two? Not New Hell, Hell's Square, or Little Hell?" Blue asked.

"I think this place is a direct sequel to my imagined vision of Hell."

"I have never been to Hell, but I know some angels who have. I'll be sure to compare notes," the angel said.

Suddenly, Yan Fan's eyes focused on a spot at the corner of one of the holo-screens. "Wait! What's that? Turn back!"

"What? What did you see?"

"I think I saw something moving at the hill we just passed."

"Matilda, replay to minus fifteen seconds," Blue commanded.

The holo-screen showed footage of the view just as the ship was about to pass the hill. Nothing unusual was seen until the hill was about to disappear at the right corner of the screen.

"There!" Yan Fan pointed.

A blurry shape moved between some boulders at the top of the hill.

"Looks like a reflection. Is that a rock?"

"No! Look! Look! It moved!"

It was hard to see it clearly at first as it seemed to have the same brown color as the rocks, but the movement allowed to distinguish its legs. It was a bipedal haze. After a second look, the angel realized the creature's skin was not so much the same color of the rocks, but it reflected their color, like a water drop distorting colors and shapes around it. The creature was translucent. Nothing more could be assessed from the recorded visual, but it was enough to disturb Blue.

"Matilda…" the blond Archangel hesitated.

"Awaiting orders," the ship replied.

"You said there was no life on other planets. What is that?" Yan Fan inquired.

"It's impossible, it's what it is." Blue responded astonished.

"But this is a wonderful thing!" Yan yelled, unable to contain her excitement. "Oh, man! We gotta get down there! Let's first contact the shit out of this mother! E.T. phone home!"

"Yan, Yan, sweetie, you can't even imagine how terrible this is!" Blue exclaimed as he sat nervously on the big couch.

"Come on!" Yan turned towards Blue. "This is such a great honor! We get to be ambassadors of Earth!"

Blue dreadfully lifted his head and locked eyes with Yan.

"Baby doll, we are opening a cosmic can of worms here! God made humans, man from dust and woman from his rib. He designed a divine plan that solely revolves around humanity's salvation and its purpose to inhabit the universe. If we have aliens running around, what role do they play in God's plan? Are they a threat to humanity like demons are or maybe something even worse?"

Blue pulled his blond hair with a new realization dawning on him. "And—and never mind all that; look at me, I'm an angel! We're beings of higher power and closeness to the universe's secrets with one mission only: We are here to protect God's Creation, its beauty manifested on Earth and its people."

Blue grew more excitable. "So, after dedicating ourselves entirely to the wellbeing of mankind, all this time we have been ignoring other beings out there for who knows how long? How could we have been so blind and deaf to not even suspect this could be happening? And how do these aliens work? Are there other alien angels out there looking over them? Are there alien demons? Did God just decide to omit a whole section of His divine plan to keep us unaware of their existence or is there more than one God, each with their own separate plan? Either way, everything we've based our decisions for thousands of years is a damned lie!"

"Okay, okay, I get it, Blue! Calm down!"

The angel took a breath. "It's... If they exist, then why do we?" There was uncertainty in his voice.

Yan stared at him.

"Awaiting orders," Matilda said.

"Hey..." Yan cautiously approached the angel of science and placed her hand on his shoulder. "We need to make sure. We need to go after it."

Blue pondered.

"This is a mistake. Just go back and scan the area for whatever that thing was, Matilda," the Archangel finally ordered.

The ship spun and headed towards the hill. It circled the area for a few minutes until it pinpointed the halcyon creature running to get cover from the sulfuric acid storm.

"Look how fast it runs!" Yan Fan exclaimed. "Go faster! You're losing it!"

"Why? We catch up to it and then what? We abduct it? That's not going to happen."

The astronaut ghost was not paying attention to Blue at all. She stared intently at the holo-screen.

"That's weird. It's about the same size as a human being." Yan noted, "With the gravitational pull of a planet this huge, the creature should be the size of a giant for its body not to be crushed. Do you think something unique to its anatomy allows for a different mass density or-"

"I don't know, Yan. I can't even process what I'm looking at. Don't make me think right now. My head hurts!"

The translucent humanoid being quickly entered a small crevice at the base of a mountain. This time, Blue zoomed in on the footage and got a good look at a gelatinous transparent humanoid with arms and legs that moved just like a jogger. The creature also had a human-shaped head, but it was entirely see-through and faceless. Yan noticed something lodged inside the thing's torso. It was difficult to define it from the light reflections on its skin, but it looked like some sort of fleshy embryo or an unborn infant in fetal position.

"Is that a...baby? It sure looks like one. So, is she the female of the species?" Yan Fan asked.

"Maybe, but that's a question I will need to deal with later. I need to speak with the other Archangels about this. We're done here," Blue replied. "Matilda, let's go home."

The blue bubble ship changed its course and started to ascend.

"Wait! Hold on just a second!" Yan shouted, "We can't just leave now! We need to land the ship and see this through!"

"I'm not going down there! We've risked the ship enough under *El Niño Acido* already." Blue replied, "The alien is not your problem anymore, Yan, adventure time is over. Time for you to move on."

"Well, I'm not going back," she replied. "I'm staying here. We need to learn more about that alien. You need someone to keep an eye on it."

"That's not going to happen."

"I'm not asking for your permission," Yan said. "And I don't need you to land the ship. I'm a ghost, remember?"

Yan put on her helmet and focused on phasing down through the floor of the ship as she waved Blue goodbye. As she descended, her body seemed to be swallowed by the thick rug until it disappeared.

The angel swiped all the holo-screens and saw the astronaut ghost hovering down towards the ground. She still faced the ship and knew Blue was watching her. She tapped her helmet with her index finger. The angel immediately switched on the communication link.

"—hear me?" Yan's voice asked through the speakers.

"Yanhua Victoria Fan! What the hell do you think you're doing?"

"Victoria? Really?" Yan laughed as she kept levitating downward, "Blue, just think about it. How many decades will it take mankind to reach this hostile planet all the way here in Andromeda? And you are a busy angel, sir. You don't have time to study that alien. You need to go back and prepare the world for this. If this wasn't in God's plan, then you need to start working on a new one. On the other hand, I have all the time in the world. There's nothing back on Earth for me but oblivion, man. That can wait."

"You don't know that." Blue replied concerned. "You don't know what that thing can do to you."

"I'll be careful, I promise."

"God…" He paused, "Please be careful, girl."

"I will. I will. And hey, you get to test the long range of your super

36

awesome com-link, right?"

"Oh, I know it'll work. There's- ah, there's also a little red button on your left glove." Blue blubbered teary-eyed, "It's a tracker. Use it if for some reason you, um, if you get off planet for some reason. I will find you. And I want to hear from you every night."

"I will call, dad."

"I'm serious. And if you need for me to come back to get you for whatever reason, just—"

"I'll be fine, Blue. And thank you for everything, okay?" She waved her gloved hand.

Blue cut the feed for a moment and held his head, worried.

"Tell me this is all a big fat joke, God. Please let this be some sort of cosmic prank," he prayed.

Blue let himself drop on his big cushioned couch. He stared at his floating holo-screens and watched as Yan Fan reached the surface and entered the crevice. He turned the audio back on and waited patiently to hear Yan's voice again. Matilda had already left the planetary system and was on her way back to the Milky Way.

. . . .

Black Angel returned to the airfield at Cape Canaveral several nights later. She watched Blue return from the stars and back to Earth's soil. As Matilda landed, the angel of invention came out of the blue bubble craft with a somber look. He hugged her sister and pointed her to the ship.

"There's something you should see. I'll wait outside. I need some air."

His tone worried Azrael. She boarded the small ship and immediately shifted her attention at the floating holo-screens. They all showed the looped footage of the alien humanoid running and sneaking into the crevice at the base of a mountain. The visual had some static due to the acid rains, but the contents were undeniable. Azrael, the Black Angel, covered her mouth and opened her eyes wide in shock.

"Blue? Come in! Hey, I found them!" Yan Fan's voice came through the speakers.

The Black Angel turned her attention to the com-link light.

"There's so many of them! Millions! You should've given me a camera to shoot this! And listen, remember the baby fetus inside the alien's torso? They all have one inside them! For the life of me, I can't tell which ones are males and which are females, but I'll keep observing them closely... Blue? Are you there?"

The Black Angel opened her lips, but no sound came from her mouth.

"..."

"You're-you're not Blue..." Yan's voice shuddered from the speakers.

An awkward silence followed between the angel of death and the astronaut ghost.

"What I'm doing here... This is important for myself, and for the world. Please... give me more time."

Black Angel looked back at the looped images of the alien creature on the screens and considered the request. She nodded in agreement.

A short while later, the Black Angel departed the ship holding the shell-shaped rock Yan brought to study from Cai Shen as she approached Blue.

"It's just a rock."

Black Angel glanced at him confused.

"My thoughts exactly."

Blue threw another rock, Black Angel kept holding hers. They both looked up at the starry night and he pointed up in a specific direction.

"That's where she is." He said.

Black Angel tapped his chest to get his attention. He lowered his eyes to meet hers.

"I'm okay. Just thinking of something Yan said to me about Pluto. I finally understand a feeling she had. That sudden realization when things are not really what you always believed they were. It kind of makes you feel...small."

Blue strode back towards Matilda.

"Just wait until I tell the others. That'll be all kinds of fun... You need a lift, snow face?"

Black angel nodded. She slid the shell-shaped rock in her front pocket and followed her brother back to the glowing sapphire tinted ship.

4 THE AFTERLIFE ADVENTURES OF YAN FAN...IN SPAAACE!

(Start Recording)

Day 01

Hey, Blue. So, I was thinking if something happens to me; not that I'm saying it will, but if it does, I'll be recording these transmissions... Hoping this gets to you somehow. It's been almost 24 hours since you left this world. I've been combing a twenty-mile radius from the lifeform sighting. Still no sign of the creature we saw. I'll have to expand to other areas.

For now, I just thought this would be as good a time as any to say thank you. Thank you for rescuing me from exile on the moon. Thank you for giving me a second chance at having the adventure I never got to experience when I was alive. Also, thank you for going against your judgement and trusting me with this mission. I will not let you down.

I meant it when I said there's nothing for me back on Earth. I'm used to being by myself. I was never big on family. It's just not the kind of person I am. Never married. Never had any kids. My mom died birthing me, and my asshole of a father toured state prisons like they were hotels in Cancun. I did live with my uncle Chen, and though I admit that once in a blue moon I may wonder what became of him, I have no doubt he moved on pretty quickly after I died. Our relationship was- I always thought of us more as roomies than relatives. He never tried to get to know me better, and I never cared to let him. That's fine. He took me in when I was 14 because he had to, but he did take me in...

I barely ever felt alone when I read about the stars, though; fiction or otherwise, it never mattered to me. I may have not felt part of humanity at times, but I always knew I'd help make the universe complete. I just never knew how. I belong in space, Blue.

I am the astronaut ghost.

Okay. Yeah, I know that's just a handle you gave me for fun when we talked through the helmet communicator, but I take its meaning seriously. Astronauts are travelers, discoverers. I get to roam millions of light years away from Earth with literally an infinity of possibilities to explore. This, to me, is to be truly free.

And then there's the ghost part. Believe me, it freaked the hell out of me at the beginning. So many questions hounded me. Why did Alex destroy the Defiant? Why was I the only one of my crew to become a ghost? Are there others like me out there? Also, randomly flashing in and out of reality is not fun at all. But you know what? I had more than thirty years to figure out and accept what I'd become, and I learned to handle some of the strange gifts that came with being a spirit. I ended up levitating scraps of the Defiant; I phased through crater walls, and ultimately, I was able to bring along small pieces of rocks with me. And by the way, when we met, I did know how to hover. I just thought I'd try to give you a scare.

Anyway, my point is, all those years stranded on the Moon, learning to accept myself as a ghost helped me realize that any prior ideas I had about death were just that, conjectures. Suddenly, the afterlife had become another item in my long list of phenomena that I aim to decipher.

...And then to top it off, you landed your spaceship on the moon and told me you were an angel.

So not only ghosts exist, but angels and demons, too! And again, oh, man! Talk about throwing preconceptions out the window! You moonwalked on the Moon! Where is that written in the Bible? Blue, you are very human to me; not at all like some divine emissary of the light or whatever, even though you keep insisting that you are. In life, I used to be an agnostic. In death, I sang karaoke with an archangel in the lounge of his spacecraft and held my own. There is so much I want to learn about you...

Listen, I know how disturbing it was for you to discover the existence of other life forms. I saw the look in your eyes when you stared at that monitor. This goes against everything you believe in. But you are the angel of science and invention and there is a mystery here that needs explaining. When you asked me to come with you, I took a leap of faith into your world. You should do the same when it comes to extraterrestrial life. Don't be afraid, Blue. Embrace the unknown, even if you don't understand it.

Alright, enough rambling. Back to the mission. Here I am, about to take my next leap into infinity again. Who knows what wonderful things I'll uncover? I'm ecstatic. I owe you, sir!

. . . .

Day 22

Blue? Come in! Hey, I found them! There's so many of them! Millions! You should've given me a camera to shoot this! And listen, remember the baby fetus inside the creature's torso? They all have one inside them! For the life of me, I can't tell which ones are males and which are females, but I'll keep observing them closely... Blue? Are you there?

. . . .

Day 29

It's been a while since we talked, Blue. Is everything okay? This weather has not been helping at all with the signal. You're probably working to fix it as we speak. But still, I can't help feeling ignored.

There is nothing pretty about Hell Part Two. Between its mustard-yellow rivers of crackling acid waters and muddy landslides that spread down the mountains like chronic diarrhea, I feel like I'm inside a large intestine. The yellow lightning storms are getting worse... And now we are getting earthquakes, too. I'm afraid this planet is becoming too dangerous for the faceless.

It's very frustrating not to be able to study one up close. I know you want me to stay safe, but I'm really fascinated by their biology. And just so you know, I'm referring to them as faceless until I come up with a proper name for them. Calling them 'aliens' or 'monsters' just doesn't cut it for me.

42

I've mentioned before that it's hard for me to tell one from the other because they're all identical. About ten-feet-tall, colorless viscous skinned andromorphs with invertebrate bodies and a very simple cardiovascular system. They have blue bio-luminescent veins that grow like weeds from the fetus in their torsos and spread throughout their bodies. It looks to me like the babies floating inside them serve as some kind of hearts maybe? They're quite stunning to look at once you get the shock of their existence out of your system.

They don't eat, or at least not the way we do. I suspect that, like amoebas, they absorb whatever nutrients they need from their surroundings into their membrane flesh. But I'll need a sample to corroborate this.

At first glance, their daily activities are restricted to moving from one place to another trying to find safe havens from the planet's hostile climate. They are big fans of living in caves, but I guess there's so many of them, they have to venture the elements to find more places to stay. The faceless migrate mostly when the weather allows it. They move in clusters of five to ten, one behind the other and each moving in perfect synchronicity, very much like ants. There has to be some way they communicate among themselves. I still can't catch how they do it, though. They are so quiet and devoid of tactile contact between each other. Maybe they congregate by instinct, or perhaps they got some sort of telepathic abilities?

By the way, I'm having trouble with the music player. I keep tapping my space helmet trying to fix it, and I played around with the wires a bit. Every time I flash in and out of existence the song that plays skips to another random tune without finishing the last one; from Def Leppard's *Rocket*, to Soundgarden's *Black Whole Sun*, to Genesis' *Land of Confusion* and so on. It's driving me nuts!

Lately, not only am I shifting, but I'm doing it at a fast rate. If you blink many times and fast enough, you'll probably get a slight idea of what I go through. When I disappear and come back, I see reality around me skip a bit. Things move just a little out of place. Like in those moments when we watched those old laser discs you were showing me. It gets to me sometimes, the fear that I may never come back once I shift out of existence; that in the blink of an eye, I become nothing…

. . . .

43

Day 37

Blue, you are going to kill me… While in pursuit of the faceless across the planes, I came across a strange looking specimen. This guy was separated from the herd, but it didn't stay too far behind the rest of the group. It had two heads, one hung behind the other, right under the back of its neck. And it had an extra limb with another four-fingered hand coming out of its back. It was a Siamese faceless!

To say I was intrigued by this phenomenon would be the understatement of the century. I'd been spotting faceless for a couple of weeks. How could I have missed this one? I was hiding behind some rocks up on a hill looking down at the Siamese from afar. I needed a closer look. I slowly hovered down the mound, staying behind boulders and making sure I was out of its sight at all times. It marched at a different pace from the other faceless; slower, heavier. As it followed its posse that by that time were almost out of sight, I moved laterally to keep up with him. I studied his features, looking for any particular difference from the others, but I found none.

Well, that's not entirely true. I think I saw something; I'm not sure if I did see it or if it only happened in my mind, though. If it did happen, it was in a split second. Looking at his fetus I swear I saw its head divide into two and then stare at each other. But then it merged back together. I don't know, I think that's what I saw. I winced to focus my eyes on the baby, trying to make sense of what I witnessed. That's when the Siamese head that hung from behind turned my way and it discovered me.

I tried to be careful, Blue. I really did. But I guess this was bound to happen. We wondered if the faceless were capable of seeing spirits like me. Yeah, mystery solved.

As soon as I was made, it growled at me a deafening continuous sound. Like the humming of a broken air conditioner. The front head heard the back head's yell, and it immediately looked in my direction as it joined in its screaming. The Siamese ran towards me quite fast, slightly wobbling side to side with uncoordinated leg movements. I just panicked. I didn't know if this two-headed faceless would be able to touch me, but I was not about to wait and find out. I ascended to the hill top as quickly as I could, trying to get my mind off from the fearfully hypnotizing noise it made. I could hear its feet crunching the soil getting closer to reach me.

By the time I managed to hover all the way to the top of the hill, the loud sound was fading until it finally stopped. I peeked downwards from the high edge. I didn't see the Siamese anymore. I saw two distinct creatures sprinting back down the steep knoll. The Siamese had divided into two!

Suddenly, all my fears subsided, and the science nerd took over again. I just witnessed another amazing discovery! I laughed overjoyed, staring at those two faceless running downhill to rejoin their group. One word slipped through my lips almost like a whisper, and it was the only word in my mind at that moment; an important key to unlocking the secrets of these creatures' biology. I said it again, even more excited.

Mitosis!

. . . .

Day 45

I keep flashing out of existence, Blue, and it's getting fucking scary! The worse this damned weather gets, the more frequent the flash outs from reality are. Either the acid rains or the electro-magnetic fields from the thunderstorms are affecting me, I don't know. I just don't know anymore.

Today I was studying a group of faceless when I went through an abrupt flash out. By the time I returned, the band I was following had already left for miles. I must have shifted for at least two or three hours! Fuck! I hate not being able control this!

…Okay, sorry. I'm sorry. Let me start over. This has been a very s—

. . . .

Day 48

Dude, guess where I'm at? Dog Shit Mesa! Hahaha! The faceless band I followed led me all the way back here! I did a little exploring of the caverns, keeping myself out of sight between the pillars and staying in narrow pathways. The deeper I went, the darker it got. The lights from my suit helped, but there's so much they could manage. No worries. I'll make do. This place is massive! Turns out, this may not actually be a mesa after all.

The mountain is void inside with an empty center big enough to harbor most of the faceless population. A mountain this hollow makes me think it could have been a volcano long ago, maybe.

I have a feeling we'll be staying here for a while. It's just too dangerous for all of us outside. There's a superstorm the likes of which I've never seen before punishing the region non-stop. The lower plains are getting flooded with streams of acid fluids and there's more landslides because of it. I've been seeing a colossal movement of faceless bands migrating from all over to Dog Shit Mesa seeking refuge from the storm. If they're smart, they won't be heading out any time soon.

I'm staying put too. I'm not risking anymore flash outs if I can. Somebody has to keep an eye on the faceless. Anyway, I'm waiting to hear from you. You know where to find me!

. . . .

Day 52

I believe this terrible weather is affecting me more than I care to admit. I don't know if I'm slowly becoming desperate or downright irrational, but I feel like I've making so many impulsive decisions... I'm not sure if ghosts can go mad, but if they can, I'm ready for the looney bin. Today, for example, I got in direct contact with the faceless again. And it was sheer madness. I'm still a bit rattled…

There was one faceless running through the caverns and it seemed to have just come into the cave from the tempest outside. Its body had acid dripping over its shoulders and torso that sizzled through its translucent skin. It carried something between its arms. It was hard for me to distinguish what it was in the dark, but it looked like a bulge the size of a small cantaloupe. The fact that this faceless was alone and away from the others caught my attention. I sped behind the creature as it descended deeper into steep passages of the caverns that culminated into a huge hollow crevice.

I was taken aback by the chamber. This was an area of the caverns I'd never seen before. It had the look of a naturally built sanctuary. Its granite ceiling formed the shape of two joined four-fingered hands with their palms facing down. Several holes spread throughout the cavern ceiling allowed acid to stream down. It gave me the impression that the curved stalactites descended from Heaven to protect whatever resided underneath.

By the time I caught up to the faceless I saw it drop to its knees. Its movements were weaker. It placed the bulge it held among a heap of other similar bulges. I reached closer into the cavity and got a better look. The bulges were thousands of dead curled fetuses stacked on top of each other. Shocked by what I saw, I let out a whimper and quickly shut my mouth, hoping the faceless hadn't heard me. I was horrified by the imagery, but was also fascinated at the same time. I couldn't stop myself from getting closer to observe the discarded babies. Most of the corpses were putrefied, giving me the impression that they had been piled up for a long time.

I turned my attention to the faceless in the room waggling a few feet away from me. It was on its fours, barely able to support itself. Acid drops perforated severely into its body, burning through its veins and slowly liquefying its gelatinous body mass from the inside out until it fell on its belly. The sight overcame me with unbearable sadness. I felt so helpless watching it die. I'd seen other faceless die before, but never this up close.

I snapped out of my trance and moved closer to the creature slumped on the ground. At that moment I didn't care if the faceless could grab or hurt me. If I couldn't help it at least I'd keep it company. I kneeled next to the faceless and using levitation, turned it on its back. The weary faceless extended its melting four-fingered hand at me and hummed a buzzing sound similar to what I heard from the Siamese, but less violent. I wondered if seeing me in my astronaut suit was scaring the creature. I took off my helmet and gave it a sad smile. Its call weakened and then it stopped altogether.

The faceless' see-through body was inert, but I could still see the infant's chest subtly expanding and contracting. My ghost hands went right through the transparent gelatinous skin and touched the feeble baby it had inside its body. I phased it through the dead body and held it in my arms. As soon as I did that, the colorless body melted completely into a liquid stream.

I kept the fetus close to my chest, being extra careful not to drop it. Its breathing became slower and erratic until it rested motionless in my arms. I froze, distraught by the baby's passing. My first thoughts were guilt-ridden assumptions that I somehow tampered with the faceless and that by lifting it I may have killed it faster. But then I remembered the acid rain that pierced through its skin and logic offered me a bit of relief. The planet was the true culprit of this and many faceless' death, not me. I couldn't understand how it was possible that these indigenous creatures had not yet adapted to the dangerous conditions of their home world. Acid erosion would eventually destroy the cavern systems. That much I knew from many leaks that permeated above my head. Where would the faceless be able to seek refuge then?

That was when I heard a faint buzzing sound from far away. Uncomfortable humming increased to a loud chorus that reminded me of New York's echoing subway trains passing each other or deafening construction machinery on the streets. Dozens of faceless became hundreds, swarming through the chamber's entrance and heading towards me. I put my helmet back on and stood up with the baby's corpse levitating in my arms. I could have left it there, come back for it later, but please don't ask me why; I just didn't want to let go of it. My first thought was to run, but I forced myself to calm down and ponder my options.

If I was alive, I would have had to run at least twenty yards in any direction between me and the cavern walls before the band of faceless got to me. I'd need to find a crevice to fit through and hide from the creatures following me. If the faceless had caught up to me, they could have trampled me or maybe killed me with their bare hands; I didn't know for sure.

But I was a ghost. I had just phased my arms through a deceased faceless' skin. It wouldn't be a problem to cross right through the incoming creatures. But the baby I carried was another thing entirely. It usually takes some concentration on my part to levitate something or phase an object through a wall. To keep the baby, I'd have to do both. And I was so scared I wasn't completely sure I could focus.

They were running very close towards me at this point; savagely mobbing and raging at me. The noise bounced louder from the walls until it was useless for me to try to hear beyond the sound of a thousand trucks about to run me over. I gambled and stood silent facing the incoming faceless horde. Struggling to control my fright, I held tight to the dead baby. When the incoming faceless where only a few feet away from me, I closed my eyes and thought of the baby: levitate and phase.

I opened my eyes again and found myself immersed in a nightmarish river of flowing specters. The cave around me looked distorted; I saw everything through the translucent bodies of the faceless. The creatures ganged up everywhere around and within me, and their hands swung straight through me again and again. They yelled their abstract calls and waived their arms savagely, trying to grab my body. I felt nothing at all.

Noting that it was safe, I levitated over the faceless crowd. They stretched their arms up as much as they could, but I kept myself floating a few feet higher from their reach. I suddenly realized I didn't feel the baby in my arms. I checked my hands to see if I'd dropped it, but the hands that I saw were the baby's tiny pudgy hands. My entire body was gone because I was now the baby, or rather my spirit inhabited the infant.

Blue, I possessed a baby's corpse.

I will give you a moment to digest that.

A floating fetus phased and levitated through the faceless. They were looking up at me, their TV static chorus chanting at me. Imagine if you saw a luminous human brain or heart hovering over you. Pure madness! Blue, you may want to know what was going through my mind at that moment. That's easy. I just wanted to get the hell out of that cavern. I was more interested in knowing what those poor creatures were thinking as they saw me, to tell you the truth.

I flew over the faceless crowd towards the entrance of the chamber as if I was some sort of totemic baby god. Once I reached the pathway and distanced myself from the faceless, I concentrated on getting myself out of the fetus. This was all new to me, but I figured that maybe it was worth a shot to try to repeat the same thing I did before. Focus. Phase. Levitate. Eyes closed.

Eyes opened. I felt a great relief to see that my hands were mine again and the baby's body safely levitated between them. But this break only lasted for a moment. Echoes of buzzing noises followed me in the darkness. The faceless were coming after me. I moved faster and phased through thick pillars, trying to lose the creatures behind me, but carefully making sure I would not drop the baby I carried.

Eventually, the loud sounds behind me faded. I wanted to think I managed to lose the faceless mob through the caverns, but I was too afraid to look back. I kept pushing forward, not trusting the silence. "This is stupid. They can't hurt me." I said to myself.

I yielded to my Orpheus complex. As I mustered the courage to turn around, my eyes immediately aimed upwards. A faceless stood just a few inches behind me, looking down at me and holding a dead fetus in its arms close to the chest. Another creature stood behind it, and then another in an endless single file of faceless beings that extended beyond my sight. All of the creatures stared at me and they all carried rotted babies picked from the mountain of stacked corpses; just like me. At that moment, I did the only thing I could think of. I tried to—

. . . .

Yan Fan had to wait until the worst part of the storm had passed after three long weeks before she was able to go outside the caverns and reach a mountain top. She found a good spot to lay back and floated face up just a few inches over the ground as she stared directly at the thick brown clouds that made it hard to contact Blue. Suddenly, a familiar voice came through her helmet.

"Breaker, breaker. This is light bulb calling the astronaut ghost. You read?"

"Loud and clear, you trucker cliché," Yan responded through her helmet speaker. "Dude, it's been 63 days! Where've you been? This shitty communicator needs serious upgrading."

"Don't knock the technology, Yanhua. I've been pulling my hairs all this time expanding the signal. I'm so sorry it took me so long. I was so worried about you."

"I know… It shouldn't come as a surprise that reception from Dog Shit Mesa is not always the best. And by the look of those clouds coming my way, it'll easily be another month before we can talk again. Anyway, I'm so glad to hear from you."

"Oh, baby doll… Are you okay?"

"I'm super. Thanks for asking. Listen. Have you talked to the other angels about our see-through buddies?"

"Yes-ish… It did not go well. But that was expected. I mean, I just mentioned it to them in passing and-"

"'In passing'?"

"—And we're convening for a gathering tomorrow. You don't know my kind like I do, Yan. I need to prepare them. And I need to give them something more than just a big foot sighting on another galaxy. Anything you can give me will be appreciated."

Yan sat up straight. A few acid drops fell from the sky. Some of them dripped right through her spectral body. She didn't feel anything, but she was interested in observing if these drops were enough to set her on a random disappearing phase. They weren't.

"It's been— there's so much I want to talk about. They're definitely a handful. They can be pretty violent sometimes. They got very agitated when they saw me-"

"They saw you! Don't you think you should've start our conversation with that tidbit?"

"It's no big deal, Blue. Listen, I've been recording my findings in detail. I'm uploading to you now. Let me know if you don't receive the files. But in a nutshell... I got good news and bad news," she said.

"Oh, God. I can't take the stress. Bad news first."

"Great. So the good news is—"

"I said bad news first."

"So the good news is that I've learned quite a bit about the faceless."

"You mean the aliens."

"Come on, Blue. I'm on their planet. If anything, I'm the alien here."

"Yes, okay. I see your point."

"Anyway, these beings are asexual. They reproduce through mitosis. And they do it in industrial quantities, my friend. I don't know the exact number, but it's in the thousands for sure; and that's every few days. Think of them as rabbits of cellular level replication. I only caught up to their high multiplying rate of after staying at Dog Shit Mesa. With very few exceptions, they mostly stay in the caves when they reproduce to avoid complications with the hostile environment outside."

"I see. That's so interesting."

"Yeah, and it's a needed trait for them, too, because they have a very short life span. Like a week, week and a half before they die."

"Oh, that's sad."

"Now, most of this I gathered from observation. But a few weeks ago, I got a hold of one of their fetuses. You know, the babies they keep inside their torsos?"

"Yan, don't tell me you dissected a baby!"

"Does that gross you out?"

"Of course, it does!"

"What can I say? I'm a science teacher. I used to open up frogs like nobody's business."

"Ugh!"

"Again, all fetuses are identical to each other on a genetic level and it's safe to say that because of the way these creatures reproduce. At first glance, judging by its weight and length, the fetus looked like a human baby in about 30 weeks gestation. But when I studied its internal organs, it was way underdeveloped. I found a heart that pumps a weird milky substance to the infant's body and all the way to its external membrane through their glowing blue veins. And the heart, it's very similar to a human heart, but with only one atrium instead of two, one ventricle instead of two, and one pulmonary vein; that sort of thing. The same pattern repeated in all the other organs. One lung, no stomach, no reproductive organs. And get this, they have brains similar to a human infant, but they deteriorate at a faster rate than the rest of the other organs."

"They go braindead before they actually die… Maybe that explains their short life spans."

"Exactly. To me, the faceless seem like they have their own genetic makeup working against them. They are born to this hostile world they're ill equipped to survive, they reproduce, they live briefly for only God knows what purpose, and then they die. Like organic shooting stars."

"Ah, that sounds tragically poetic. But you know, we need a better way to refer to them than faceless. I bet you can come up with a better name for our biped friends, can't you?"

Yan stood up when she noticed the rain surge and stepped over to the edge of the peak. She looked down at several clusters of faceless running towards the caves for cover. Some of them did not make it as their translucent skins liquefied, leaving only their fetuses to struggle under the killing water that poured to the ground. Other faceless picked them up on their way to the caves as much as they could. This reminded her of the faceless she encountered at the cavern sanctuary and how even in its death throes, the creature managed to reach the large chamber to make sure the dead baby it carried joined the others. Do they believe in the afterlife? Yan pondered. These beings, she thought, as short-lived as they were, as biologically challenged as they were, still tried to find some worth to their existence.

"I have. I named them transients," Yan said.

"Transients..." Blue repeated. "Works for me."

"It's starting to rain again. We may get cut off. The thunderstorm's electromagnetic charges mess me up."

"Are you flashing out more often?"

"When it gets very bad, when the storm hits long and hard, I could find myself flashing in and out for hours. And when that happens there's nothing I can do but wait it out. "

"Nope. No way. You've done enough. I think you've been on that planet too long. I'm sending Matilda to pick you up."

"Don't baby me, Blue. I knew the risks. I can take it."

"Aren't you afraid that you won't shift back?"

"Yes, I think about it all the time... Okay, I agree it's time to leave. Send Matilda. My preliminary research is almost done, anyway. Thing is, if what I suspect is true, I think I won't be the only one that needs to leave this planet."

"What do you mean?"

Yan fell silent for a moment. She looked up at the dark clouds showering over her and she followed the rain all the way down to the gravelly ground in front of the tip of my boots. The astronaut ghost saw the drops land on the rocks and make multiple needle-thick holes through which more acid liquid went in, widening the gaps little by little. She sighed.

"Okay, so the bad news," Yan continued. "This is just a hunch; I can't prove it yet, but I've been comparing the intel you collected on Hell Part Two with the meteorological conditions I've experienced in the past two months and I think this planet's climate is increasingly becoming unstable. With every passing week, super thunderstorms get more destructive, each worse and longer than the one before. We're getting earthquakes now too; entire fields swallowed by landslides. And don't get me started on those acid rain torrents. As the acid seas levels rise, the damage they cause to the transients' ecosystem is getting too severe. Blue, if this keeps up as I suspect it will, in a matter of months these creatures won't have anywhere to hide from the rain. They will all die."

"You want me to get the Transients off that planet," Blue said.

"Yes, thank you. The sooner the better. And we need to find somewhere that can sustain their life conditions. Not Earth, of course... We're not ready for a close encounter like this yet. Maybe Cai Shen? We can start there. I mean, a universe this big, there must be somewhere we can fit them in."

"Yan... no."

"What? What do you mean no?"

"I can't do something like this without an agreement from the Seven Archangels. And I already know what they're going to say. No."

"Why not?"

"Because our mission is to protect humanity. And anything we do to help these transients or faceless or whatever they're called, the Archangels would see it as putting humans at risk."

"Why the hell would they think that? You can convince them of the opposite, can't you?"

"I don't think so, Yan. I'm not sure I disagree with seeing these beings as a threat."

"Blue, we have a responsibility to protect this species! You can't just let them die! If you had no interest in helping the transients, then what the hell have I been here for? ...Please. Just show them some of the recordings. There's some good stuff there we can use—"

"Be honest Yan, you've stayed with them longer than anyone in this universe. Can you answer me unequivocally, what's the purpose of the transients?"

"That's not fair! The same can be asked about humanity. You can talk all you want about divine plans and sanctimonious destinies, but none of it matters unless humanity decides for itself the path it will follow. Why can't we give the transients a chance to do that too?"

"I see your point, but... I don't know... What you're asking... We would need the help of all the Archangels to get this massive exodus done..."

"Let me talk to them, Blue. Let me make a case for the transients. If you're so worried for humanity's safety, at least let a human speak on this matter."

"You don't stop, do you? You'd dare speak to seven of the most powerful beings in the universe?"

"If it means saving the transients..."

"Alright... I'll speak to my sisters tomorrow and call you back."

"Okay...wow...I can't believe I'm going to meet the seven Archangels from the Bible..."

"Believe me, baby doll, keep your expectations low. We're a hot mess of a family. Just hold on tight and don't do anything brash. I'll call you tomorrow."

"Promise?"

"Well, maybe I'll leave a couple of days go by. Wouldn't want you to feel like I baby you..."

"Jerk."

. . . .

55

Day 126

Nine weeks have passed since you and I last spoke.

I don't know where I am.

I don't know if this damned communicator works at all.

I don't know if we'll ever see each other again, Blue.

I'm sorry if I'm not sounding… well. Everything becomes a blur when I try to remember. I'm just trying to put together the pieces of how things happened…

It started with the climate. Lethal weather conditions worsened exponentially to the point we were forced to permanently remain under the cover of Dog Shit Mesa's grottos. But even the caverns became increasingly dangerous to the transients.

Acid stream leaks grew into small waterfalls of deadly liquid that blocked our paths and flooded many of the safe chambers like the dead baby sanctuary. The ground underneath shook viciously from time to time. As we moved deeper into the mountain, less light was able to come through until everywhere was pitch dark.

I tried my best to keep thousands of transients together. I appeared in front of transients and they ran after me. Terrifying echoes of loud buzzing vibrated throughout the cavern ways calling onto me. But I kept hovering into the darkness, leading the transients and hoping to buy them some time from the certain death sentence that was their home world.

Hundreds of transients lost their lives; some walked over edges of cliffs, many others got burned by acid falling from above, while some got crushed under falling spikes. Sudden tremors opened the ground beneath us swallowing dozens of transients into bottomless pits.

Those were the longest of days of never-ending surviving. I hoped that you hadn't abandoned us and that you and the rest of the angels would come rescue us. I tried calling many times, but the thick solid mountain walls cut out any possible signal. And I would not dare to go outside without risking the ferocity of the superstorm shifting me out of existence forever. The only answer was to keep penetrating the mountain and wait for you to come.

At one point, everywhere around us got illuminated. The cavern pillars and walls lighted up in a white-blueish electricity. This was immediately followed by a supremely loud boom. Thousands of transients that were close to the walls were instantly fried. As swift as these electric surges appeared they disappeared, leaving the dead mixed with the living in total darkness once again. It must have been a massive lightning bolt that stroke the mountain and electrified the place as only lightning from a thunderstorm so vast would most likely use elevated peaks as rods.

The transients were rattled. The ones that lived carried dead fetuses as they kept perishing. The lurid noises they made transformed into a sad screeching. Even though it broke my heart, there was nothing I could do to soothe them. I just kept seeking their attention and leading them deeper into an unknown destination that I prayed would not be a mass grave.

Eventually, I was able to gather most of the transients at a large cavity that I believed may have been the center of the mountain. The ground felt reliable and mostly smooth and there were no acid leaks from the ceiling. Once there, I hid between pillars, and observed the transients' behavior. Almost all of the creatures stood still in silence. The ones that carried dead fetuses walked to the middle of the cave and deposited them, each on top of the other, forming a pile of dead babies similar to the one in the sanctuary. Overall, it wasn't perfect, but at least I was glad that maybe we had found a moment of peace in the nightmare situation we were in.

Very little time passed until peace was interrupted by another tremor. The ground loosened under the transient's feet, making them uneasy. They began to scream their shrieking chants. I kept holding on behind the pillar, not wanting to make the situation worse by revealing myself to them again. But the unending quakes amplified until a large chunk of the ground underneath the transients gave in and thousands of the creatures fell into a void. I tried to save them. I quickly extended my arms and aimed at about thirty of them. I caught them mid-air with my levitation gift. It required a lot of concentration to try to move the creatures towards safe land with the remaining transients, but then I saw my arms slightly blink intermittently.

I begged the universe to help me. I asked to be granted just a few more seconds to save the transients. Just a few more seconds...

The rest of my body followed. I shifted out of reality and back in. In just a mere blink, I was looking at the thirty transients floating in the air almost about to reach the ground, but immediately after I just saw empty space... The group had fallen with the others. I damned myself for failing them and I cried.

I turned my attention to the surviving transients. They were still a large number and I was determined to keep it that way. I moved right through them and across to the opposite cavern wall in order to keep them away from the edge of the precipice. They yelled at me and waived their arms to clutch me. I succeeded in keeping them focused on me, but it didn't last.

There was a golden light that crept through the holes on the ceiling and the walls. The area became illuminated and a deafening bass sound of horns was heard from outside the mountain. The transients moved away from me and followed single file in a path, guided by the sound. I kept screaming and waving at them, but the transients completely ignored me.

I followed them through the path, moving among them as they walked like cattle. The transients were being led out of the caves, out of the mountain and into the storm through a different crevice I had never seen before. Fearing for their deaths, I hovered through them trying to cut them off.

When we reached the outside rim, I saw that the light and the loud blowing sound of horns came from a massive flat cylinder-shaped golden space ship that drifted next to the mountain. The craft reminded me of Matilda, but it was twenty times her size.

I first thought we were being rescued. I was so relieved that I screamed and cried out of joy. I wished that you were on that ship, Blue. I remembered you told me there were no other ships at the angels' disposal apart from Matilda, but I hoped that since the last time you and I spoke maybe the Archangels built another.

The transients lined up in single file and began to board the vessel. A few died from the acid rains before reaching the star ship, but most of them made it. When I got closer to the ship, I saw someone. I yelled your name. But the closer I got, the better I was able to see this luminous being. It became clear to me that it was not you. It was a transient; a strange looking golden transient with no legs, but a fish tail, like a siren. It had wings that allowed it to float at the entrance of the ship and its arms were open to welcome its brethren to their salvation.

I was confused and afraid. I didn't know what to do. Was this winged transient another smarter kind within their species? Maybe their leader? Who knew what its intentions were? And to what unknown corner of the universe we were being dragged to? I thought of staying and wait for you, but the end, I felt responsible for the transients and opted to sneak among the millions marching into the ship. At least this way I could keep an eye on them. After I moved into the light, the star ship launched into space. I don't have the faintest idea of who this golden creature is or where we're heading to.

I'm at a loss here. I don't know what to do. I'm praying to you, Blue... Where are you?

(End Recording)

5 BLUEPRINTS OF PROCRASTINATION

"Morning, Matteo. How was your night?" the nurse said to the old man while fixing his pillow.

Matteo Tsekalo was sick again. He felt weak as he lay on his reclined medical bed. His head hung heavy on his frail body. He couldn't feel his legs. He looked at his wrinkled hands, shaking, but still with his five fingers. When Matteo looked around, he recognized the room he was in. His spacious penthouse apartment bedroom had a 360-degree view of Manhattan through fancy glass walls and doors that connected to a nice terrace with an outdoor jacuzzi and pool chairs for sun bathing.

The adjacent room displayed a decades long collection of awards he'd won for his recorded prophecies; a trajectory of honors for his published works and other media: movies, an Amazon original series, and video games based on his books. Looking at the trophies and medals from that room next to him made him feel accomplished. His career started with *Satan has a Rocket Ship*, a book that took him almost four years to write and nobody supported. But after the release of his second book, Matteo went from being regarded as just another conspiracy lunatic to become beloved by the masses as America's Clairvoyant. He had a successful life indeed. And after leaving such a legacy to the world he felt he was almost ready to die. There was one more book to complete, one last prophecy, before he could let go.

The nurse, a tall handsome dark-haired Indian with a friendly smile, stood close to Matteo and carefully placed a tiny plastic tube up Matteo's nose.

"You took off your breathing mask," he said to the old man. "Did you have another one of your notorious dreams?"

"N-Not just dreams…visions."

"Yes, yes, sorry. I believe you."

"No, you don't."

The nurse sat next to Matteo. He cleaned the old man's drool with a soft wet cloth and wiped off the sweat from his bald head.

"Well, these things you see are real enough for your millions of fans, enough to pay for your retirement ten times over. And, hey, I love your books, too. They're very imaginative. *Journey into the House of Feathers* was such a vivid depiction of hierarchic angelic presences in—"

"Hiran, I'm… thirsty."

"Here," the nurse answered, holding the glass of water close to him and slowly pushing a straw into his lips.

Matteo took a few sips, then turned his face away.

"Are you going to eat today?" the nurse asked.

"No. Your soup tastes like salty garbage."

"You need to eat something, Matteo."

"No."

Hiran stepped back and crossed his arms.

"Okay, then I'm not going to write down your dreams anymore. No New York Times best-selling book for you."

Matteo shook his index finger at Hiran. "This is elderly abuse!"

"We had an agreement. You eat, I take dictation," Hiran reminded him. "Let's make things easier for each other. What do you say?"

"…Okay," Matteo relented. "But these are not… Dreams."

"Visions. I get it."

"I'm a prophet…"

"Yes, you are." The nurse shrugged. "You're also a guy with many ailments at eighty-two, including a broken hip. So how about it? You want to start with the rice pudding?"

Matteo nodded. Hiran placed a tray on a small table he rolled closer to Matteo. There was a small bowl of soup, a carton of orange juice, and the rice pudding on the dish. Hiran sat on the edge of the bed and began to feed Matteo.

"So, what did you see this time?"

"Not sure. It was… the end of the world…but it was not this world."

"What world was it?"

"Not sure. But there were people…"

"Will this be another book about aliens? It sounds like a return to your earlier works."

Matteo refrained from eating the next spoonful Hiran served. He stared at his hands and in his mind saw something else instead of his five fingers. He touched his belly and in his mind, he saw something that should not be there, something that he could not explain. And that disturbed him.

"Hiran… I think… I think I finally know the truth…"

"You do?"

"Please put the food aside. Get your note pad. Listen carefully and write down what I say before I forget."

Hiran stood up and looked at Matteo skeptically.

"Yes, I promise I'll eat everything on the tray, including your shitty excuse for a soup," Matteo said.

. . . .

Matteo Tsekalo was healthy again. Even though he was unable to see himself in a mirror, he was doing things he had not been able to do in decades; things like running. He found himself running scared in an endless city of perfectly symmetrical black domino-like edifices.

Fear was the only emotion Matteo could muster, even though his mind tried to explain his situation. *Why am I afraid?* he kept asking rhetorically, until he looked around. The sky was red, and clouds were black. Thousands of fire balls fell from above, destroying upon impact every building within a thirty-mile radius. Each blazing meteor came closer to destroying Matteo as if God was specifically aiming at him with a supernatural shotgun.

Matteo dodged debris that soared at him. He jumped over rubble and pushed his way through thousands of people running from being incinerated. Clusters of individuals disappeared into red-hot fragments as fireballs landed on the multitude. He could feel their fright, and this emotion connected everyone in the moment like terrified bees fleeing from a hive repeatedly pounded by a stick. Fear was the only message he could convey and receive from the people that fled alongside him. *But these are not people*, he thought. None of them had faces and their skins were colorless. He tried calling out to them. Maybe together as a group, these non-people could find a way to survive the catastrophe. However, the clatter that came out of his throat was not his voice. There were no words heard, only white noise.

Matteo kept running as he eyed his see-through four-fingered gelatinous hands with luminous veins connecting his innards. And his entrails, that was even more shocking to him; there was a child curled up inside his torso and he could see it through his skin. He panicked. This was not his body. And this world that was ending, burning fully into mountains and fields of black ash, this was not his world.

These are not meteors, Matteo thought. As he got close to the scorched rubble of a blasted ancient building ruin, he saw the dead body of another non-human ignited in flames right at the center point of the explosion. This one did not have legs, though. It had a fish tail. Matteo raised his head and watched hypnotized at the meteor shower, realizing it was a rain of burning fish-tailed non-humans falling from the sky. He asked himself what all of it meant.

A thunderous sound from another nearby crashed corpse snapped Matteo from his momentary trance. He resumed his running and followed a crowd of non-people, hoping they would find somewhere they could hide. However, everything around him had become a lump of charred coal. Hot ashy winds picked up and Matteo had trouble breathing. Taking cover was impossible.

Further ahead, there was a gravelly peak that the running mob climbed, and once they reached the top, the non-people seemed to jump off to the other side of the hill. Matteo tailed them, puffing his way up, rock by rock. When he made it to the highest point, he saw a lake of red water that extended to the horizon. Fish-tailed non-humans on fire kept falling from the sky while the bipeds threw themselves at the lake. Matteo froze, resisting other non-humans that pushed him from behind. He was afraid to jump, but he did not want to go back down the hill. There was nothing else he could do but dive.

The viscous lake splashed when Matteo went into it. His body quickly sank into the endless well of liquid red. He turned his head to see dozens of other non-human bipeds forcing their way up to the surface. In all the confusion of bodies around him swimming upwards, he managed to grab someone's leg, but was immediately kicked away. Matteo's terror increased. He instinctively paddled his limbs upwards until he found his way to the surface of the red water.

He noticed the non-people swam towards the lake shore, where he saw a figure hovering and staring down at the bipeds in the water. It was a fish-tailed non-person, but this one was different. The infant inside it glowed with a bright golden light. Matteo was not sure if it was the light or the huge membrane wings on the flying non-person's back that attracted him, but he needed to go to it. Just staring at this glowing fish-tail eased away his fears.

Thousands of four-fingered hands tried to reach out and touch their messiah in eerie unison and Matteo was one of them. He needed to hold and worship this special being. He made his way through all the other bipeds in the water, sometimes forcibly, and when he got close enough, he extended his hand.

Matteo yelled for attention, but more white noise hummed from him and every other biped in the water. It was a buzzing that increased to the point that it was hard for Matteo to hear his thoughts. Still, out of everyone in the crowd, the flying fish-tailed non-human hovered towards him and grabbed his arm… and Matteo grabbed his. The faceless non-person with the golden light tilted its head slightly and stared directly at Matteo as he pulled his four-fingered hand up. Through the deafening buzzing noise, Matteo was able to hear the glowing golden fish-tail's voice mumble to him:

"Hrm…"

. . . .

Matteo blinked and flinched a few times. He could not explain it, but for a second there, Hiran was not sitting beside him in his luxurious bedroom. But when Matteo opened his eyes again, there he was, sitting on a small stool next to his bed and writing down the last words he had dictated. Matteo felt ashamed that his senses had been failing him at his old age. It was not the first time it had occurred to him. The important thing, though, was that Hiran was there with him, and he was safe. He opted to ignore his latest episode and move on with his work.

"Why fear?" asked Matteo.

"Excuse me?"

"I remember… fear was the only emotion available to me in my vision. I saw people die. I saw civilizations end. Why wasn't I angry or sad? The entire time I felt… incapable of feeling anything other than fear."

"Do you want me to write that down?"

"Yes—no… Just make a note of it, but don't include it in the narrative. I need to think."

"Did you see anything else? After the flying fish grabbed you from the crowd at the beach?"

"It wasn't a beach. It was a lake of blood. Get it right. And no, I woke up after that. That was my most intense vision in years. I think this is it…This is the last of my prophecies. I can feel it."

Matteo lifted his eyes and saw no one on the empty stool beside his bed.

"Hiran?"

The old man scanned the entire room and the balcony outside. There was no one in his apartment. No. That did not ring true for Matteo. He felt he was being watched. He turned his eyes to the corner next to the door and saw a thin shaggy-haired teenager with pajama pants and a grey t-shirt slouching on the floor with legs wide open and his head leaning against the wall behind him. His big hairy feet could barely fit in a pair of scruffy brown crocs.

"Who are you? How did you get in here?" Matteo asked.

The teenager mumbled and dozed off. "Hrm…"

"What did you just say?"

Matteo recoiled on his bed as he saw the bedroom and the apartment around him melt into another room; a much smaller and oddly familiar room. Empty white walls with no furniture or decorations, just his medical bed and a small table next to it, where a large collection of pills and a plastic glass of water were placed. It was the room they had him stay in for years. He was at "the home," he slowly remembered. This is not my home, he thought.

Hiran, who sat again on the stool next to Matteo's bed, put his palm on the old man's shoulder.

"Oh, don't even bother. No one ever knows what he's saying, if he's even talking at all."

"Hiran? What's going on here?" Matteo asked confused. "Who is that young man?"

"That, my friend, is royalty. You are in the presence of one of the seven princes of Hell. He's the arch-demon Belphegor. One of the seven cardinal sins, you probably know him better as—"

Matteo panicked. He shook the bed when he tried to sit up. Hiran pressed his chest back against it.

"Sloth!"

"Yes, that's right! Now calm down, Matteo. Remember to breathe."

"Why is he here? Is he here to take away my soul?"

"Don't be ridiculous! Not at all. Relax. He just needed some information from you. Our master needs to know what you know; the things you see. That's important. He sent Lord Belphegor to do a little scooping. That's all."

"But—"

"If you don't calm down, I'm going to have to leave you alone with him. Is that what you want?"

"No."

Hiran kept his hand softly placed on Matteo's chest until he felt him slowly calm down. He tugged him in bed and put back the breathing tubes up the old man's nose.

"But why spy on me? Why not just read my books? All my visions are written there."

Hiran pouted his lips and lifted his eyebrows.

"Oh, gee. I'm so sorry to tell you this...Well, it turns out that after your first book, you did not actually publish anything else."

"I don't understand! What did he do to me?"

"Okay, so... How can I explain this? There's a Norwegian proverb; 'the lazier a man is, the more he plans to do tomorrow.' You know, like when you know you need to do something, like, let's say, write your book, but you think too much about it? In your mind you paint a detailed picture of how your book is going to be like, right? And you start mapping out how great your life is going to be after you finish your book. You already see that it's going to be a hit and you imagine yourself lauded by your peers and you start making up acceptance speeches for awards you've never received. Because— doesn't it feel awesome to indulge yourself in daydreams? And those thoughts, they're so exhausting, they keep you from sitting down and writing your book. Then the moment passes, and you didn't even write a single word. You tell yourself it's okay and that you'll get to it later. But you never do."

"I... never wrote my prophecies?"

"Not. One. Word. And those fantasies, those little jerk off thoughts you had, those are the blueprints of procrastination. Sloth is the king of those. He feeds on them. He amplifies them. That's his power. He's the puppeteer of string-less puppets. No strings, no movements."

Matteo held his mouth. His heart beat faster as he continued to remember his real life.

"I've been... in this bed for..."

"You've been in that bed for twenty-eight years. You did not live a life of success until you were in your eighties or anything like that. I'm afraid you are not America's Clairvoyant. Ha! No. That was all in your head. By the way, you're not even eighty-two, you're fifty-two. So that's good news, right?"

"Oh, God! Are you a demon?"

"Me? Goodness, no! I'm just a nurse in this home. But I'm also a Satanist and a worshipper of the cult of the deadly seven arch-demons. Also, I think I died at one point and became a poltergeist? But I'm not completely sure about that last part. Anyway, it's been such an honor to serve lord Belphegor, and it's also a real pleasure to have taken care of you these past years. But now that we know all of your prophecies—"

"Are you going to kill me?" Matteo was terrified.

"Nothing like that. The master doesn't want you dead. He probably has something planned for you. No, he just wants Belphegor to keep an eye on you and make sure you never get out of this room. Please get comfortable in that bed because you'll be there for a while."

"Hrm..."

Hiran briefly turned his head towards the teenager on the corner floor and nodded. He then returned his attention to Matteo.

"Oh, I'm sorry. I stand corrected. There is one last thing Belphegor needs from you..."

. . . .

Lord Belphegor, fifth of seven princes of Hell; Sloth of the Seven Deadly Sins, snored as he rested on Matteo's medical bed. His long hairy legs extended beyond the cot. He was exhausted. It had been another long hard day for the demonic teenager. Doing nothing for all eternity takes a lot of skill, charisma, and self-control. Sloth deserved the recliner bed.

"Hrm..."

Matteo curled up on the floor next to the bed. He was cold, afraid. His body felt sick, but he wondered if his illnesses were just in his mind. He stared at the door and imagined how easy it would be to run through it and escape. He would tell the world his story; how he'd been kept prisoner at a home for almost thirty years by the forces of Hell to keep him from revealing his visions. He would be a hero.

Nurse Hiran knelt next to Matteo and covered him in a warm sheet.

"Hey, are you comfy? Listen, now that I've realized that I'm a ghost, I think I've been feeding you salted sewage water all this time. Ha! My bad. No more soup, okay?"

Matteo stared at the door intently.

"Are you thinking of running out that door?" Hiran asked.

Matteo needed to reveal his prophecy to the world, but he felt tired and thought it best to rest before embarking on a dangerous escape. Sheltering himself within the warm sheet, he closed his eyes.

"Maybe tomorrow."

6 MASTER FEARING

Heaven's realm elevated majestic before Lucifer's eyes. This was the dawn of Creation. It was a place of light and reflection; crystal sands that echoed the brightness of auroras in the sky. On the horizon, watery-like energy flowed aloft, twirling over seven spiral towers erected next to each other. It gave the naked eye an illusion of glowing waterfalls with currents pouring upwards instead of down.

Diamond-shaped churches everywhere lit with fires of rebellion. Heaven bled angelic lives by the thousands; each cut short by blades that siblings raised against each other. Most of the young ones cried confused with no reason as to why they needed to die except that God had called upon them to defend Creation and Lucifer betrayed them all. Choir harmonies distorted into agonizing screams. There was a new song to be learned; a new chanting transformed by holy war.

For seven decades the war raged. Ophanim, cohorts of Lucifer, began to lose faith in their leader. Unwavering, Lucifer rallied his warriors. Golden angelic inscriptions laced the hooded white tunic he wore; his large butterfly wings spread. He scanned his followers with eyes almost entirely black but for his white irises that stood out in a frighteningly penetrating stare.

"Do not be afraid," Lucifer said to them. "I promise you that Heaven will fall soon enough, and a door will open to something new. I am very eager to step through. Who will join me?"

After years of hammering at the seven strongholds said to have been built by God Himself, it was Lucifer who used all of his power to bring them down. One by one the towers fell, and a black tear in reality opened as high and wide as the seven fallen towers once were. Clouds and winds revolved around the abyss in a circling rapid movement that created a powerful suction into the dark rip. Weakened by this feat, the Morning Star staggered. The Seven Archangels saw their opportunity to deliver the final blow to Lucifer's insurrection.

Michael, clad with crimson armor and blade in hand, cut a path through a legion of Ophanim insurgents. The other six Archangels and a battalion of Seraphim militia followed her as they tried to force their way towards Lucifer.

Astaroth, a high priest of the Ophanim, puffed breathless with sweating desperation. He clanked his blade against his armored chest and yelled orders to his army.

"Do not let them reach the Morning Star! Fight on!"

Lucifer remained still, barely able to stand, staring quietly into the abyss.

Michael made her way with her sword, slash after slash, enemy bodies piling behind her, until she finally found herself just a few feet from Lucifer. He kept his back to her, his attention married to the rip in front of him.

Michael turned towards her siblings, all of them occupied in battle against the Ophanim. But they saw their sister as she was about to face the first and most powerful angel of all. Jophiel, Raphael, Gabriel, Zadkiel, Metatron, and even Abaddon, Archangel of death; all of them were silent.

"The armor will hold," Zadkiel finally yelled. "It has to…"

Michael nodded, and gripped her sword tight. She stepped forward.

"Lucifer! Face me!"

Lucifer ignored Michael.

"You will pay for what you did." Michael's voice rang clear and powerful. She advanced and raised her blade.

Lucifer, the Morning Star, turned towards Michael and tilted his head slightly as he studied her eyes.

"I believe I may have left a scar."

Angered, Michael lashed at Lucifer with her sword. He waved his arm and created a shield of solid golden light out of thin air. Michael's sword clanged against the shield. Lucifer's body froze and slowly began to fade. He appeared to her right. Michael swung her sword to strike, but Lucifer's body froze again and again it began to fade. He now appeared on the opposite side next to her, and he touched her back. Her armor flared up. Michael tumbled, coughing and taking off whatever remained of her protection. She quickly jumped back up, grabbed her sword, and pointed it towards Lucifer. But his body froze and faded yet again. Michael swung her sword savagely in all directions, trying to slay these vivid shadows of Lucifer that appeared and disappeared from everywhere.

"Hold still, you coward! I will cast you into the abyss myself!" Michael yelled.

"So it was written…" he whispered to her ear from behind.

Michael turned, but Lucifer was no longer there. Just another fading echo of the Morning Star. As she moved back around, he stood directly in front of her. The scarlet warrior roared, frustrated, and stabbed her sword right through his torso. This time, no fading figure formed. He remained still, staring at the blade forced into his chest. Light beamed from his innards. Michael kept pushing the blade and Lucifer tripped backwards, ever closer to the abyss. Michael swiftly pulled back her sword off from him and kicked him into the rift. As he fell, Lucifer and Michael locked eyes for a brief last second. He smiled and winked at her.

Lucifer's fall roused the angelic horde and they pressed on the battle against the Ophanim. They pushed them back and forced them all into the abyss. The last to fall was Astaroth, who had to be carried and thrown into the black tear by four Seraphim warriors.

The holy war was over. Everyone now looked to Michael with awe; the scarlet warrior that conquered Lucifer had become a legend and tales would be told about her glory among angels and humans through scriptures and paintings and songs for generations to come. Michael held her sword as she stood on top of a large piece of tower rubble and addressed the angels.

"We must seal this rift to darkness. What God made and Lucifer destroyed, let the angels build again."

. . . .

Astaroth fell forever. The friction of the tear clawed at him and his body was ablaze. His wing feathers and all of his hairs went up in smoke. His skin became as black and brittle as burned charcoal. He no longer recognized the raspy voice that screeched in agony from his scorching throat. And he kept falling.

The fallen angel managed to turn his head downwards and see his kindred suffer the same fate as him. They all seemed like fast moving fireballs raining over a new world. This world he started to see as it drew nearer was a wasteland. A desert of pure black ash, with thunderstorms and red skies. There were ruins of ancient temples, all demolished and crumbled. He also saw a lake. It was a red lake so vast that it extended to the horizon.

Astaroth crash-landed on the burned soil of the new world. Most of the bones in his body crushed upon impact. He was not able to stand so he dragged himself, like all of his comrades did. Ash fields were infested with crawling seared fallen angels. Upon touching the ground, all of them felt the anguish of their bones growing out of control. Their finger bones bred claws, their toes bred hooves, their teeth bred fangs. They grew frames and membranes where once their wings were. And their light halos faded, replaced by long sharp horns.

Lucifer was the only angel standing. He was naked, wings spread. He looked strong and healthy with no sign of injuries, including the chest wound inflicted by Michael. He took a deep breath and smiled.

"I am home."

"Master! Look at us! We are damned! What shall we do?" Astaroth pleaded.

Lucifer unhurriedly stepped over the crawling bodies. His eyes fixed on the horizon.

"I am going for a swim in the lake. Then, I shall build a tower of my own, a silver citadel. Right over those hills…"

"You said we would rule! You promised—"

As he kept walking, Lucifer opened his welcoming arms.

"Behold your kingdom, Astaroth."

The Morning Star approached the blood lake. He knelt on one knee at the shore and dipped his hand into the red liquid. He took a moment to feel the red water. Something was wrong. Blood trickled down his arm as he lifted and clenched his wet fist. He stood up, breathing heavier while trying to contain his anger. He stretched his arm and reached into the air next to him. Lucifer pulled a creature from out of nowhere, tightening his hand around its neck.

The being choked and gasped for air. Its body's skin was translucent with luminous veins that changed multiple colors like a lighted prism. A small baby curled up in the creature's torso with its little face cringing in pain. Lucifer pulled it closer to him.

"Where are they?"

The glowing being remained silent, struggling to resist. Its fish tail wagged aimlessly and fast. The Morning Star insisted.

"Where. Are. They?"

"Safe— From you."

Lucifer slammed the being to the ground, knocking its head unconscious. He dragged it by the neck through the desert of black ash, leaving a small trail behind as he headed toward the hills.

"Sooner or later, you will talk."

....

It was a cold morning of February, 1986 in New York City. Lucifer had just left his apartment at the lower east side where he lived in temporary exile. He wore a long black trench coat that mostly hid his white shirt and black tie, pants, and shoes. He stopped in front of *Salem's Electronics*; his wide aviator sunglasses covering his eyes as they stared through the glass display where several TV's were on sale at 50% off. They all showed *Wake Up, Brooklyn!*, a local morning show in which the day's guest spoke to the public about a new book that collected his prophetic writings. Lucifer listened:

"Oh no, there is a God and angels do exist. There's massive proof of that too. What I propose in my new book Satan Has A Rocket Ship is that this is not an either / or type of situation. The undeniable truth, the one masterfully hidden by our government, is the co-existence of aliens and angels, who have kept in contact throughout millennia to plot the course of humankind."

"What a buncha' horseshit! You believe this guy?" another man said to him. He was a local about fifty years of age who wore a blue hoodie, Mets cap, grey sweatpants and sneakers. He barely glanced at the TV screens as his brown Shih Tzu finished peeing on a wall.

"Stealing people's money with cockamamie devil stories. Who falls for this crap, anyway?"

Lucifer did not respond to the man and eyed him strolling away with his dog.

"It's all in my book, available in hard back at your nearest bookstore."

He looked at his watch.

After walking two blocks uphill, Lucifer stepped into a place named The Books Boutique. It was a small bookstore cluttered with old tomes and had a dusty paper smell. It felt like a damp closet. He approached a nineteen-year-old female sporting a gothic leather outfit, thick white makeup with black lipstick color and punk black hair. She sat behind the cash register, her eyes immersed in a vampire novel.

"I'm looking for a book by author Matteo Tsekalo," he said.

The clerk did not lift her eyes from the volume. She pointed towards the center aisle of the store.

Somewhere way in the back of the aisle, the fantasy section was a mess of scattered paperbacks such as A.J. Rowling's *Queen Amy and The Parliament of Talking Trees*, along with Sir Sal R.R. Blue's classic *Jadyn: Boy Bohemyth*, and misplaced copies of the bestselling *I Am Shangri-La, and So Are You* by renowned self-help author Eliot Cantowill. Lucifer found a small table with a disorganized pile of *Satan Has a Rocketship* copies. He picked one and paid for it before leaving the bookstore.

Lucifer entered and sat at a café. He called on a waiter, ordered a cappuccino, and began to read.

That evening, the arcade gallery was a chaotic mess of digital sounds and youthful screams from a crowd of youngsters playing more than thirty video games at the same time. Lucifer made his way through a maze of game consoles and stood next to a particularly shaggy teenager with a beanie hat that wore a dirty t-shirt and pajama pants. He played Ms. Pacman. Lucifer placed his hand on the adolescent's shoulder and spoke to his ear.

"Stop playing around. There is something I need you to do."

Fearful, the teenager lowered his head. The sound of Ms. Pacman's death cry as she was eaten alive by a ghost flustered the boy.

"Hrm…"

. . . .

Alex Kraus drove his jeep through Causeway East highway just outside of Cape Canaveral. When he glanced at the digital clock in his dashboard, he saw it was just a few minutes after midnight. He parked to the side of the road and sat on the hood of his vehicle to contemplate the full moon, the stars, and their beautiful wavy reflection on the calm Banana River. Alex couldn't sleep. Space shuttle Defiant would launch a mere few hours away and as his first time commanding the crew, it was his responsibility to make sure that the mission became a success and that his people returned home safely.

Alex went through launch protocols in his mind, repeating every bit he learned day after day in his simulation exercises. Word by word, again and again. He did not realize that he softly enunciated some of the words in his mind.

"T minus 9 and counting... Starting automatic ground launch sequencer – Roger, tower."

"Wait. Say that again," a voice spoke to Alex's ear.

Lucifer was sitting on the hood right next to Alex Kraus. He placed his open palm at the center of Alex's back and dug his fingers through his flesh, tightening his grip on the astronaut's soul. He lifted Alex a few inches upwards and had him hanging from his hand. Alex weakly twitched and breathed hoarsely. He was unable to move any muscle in his body. His life literally placed in Lucifer's hand. He slowly moved his eyes to the side and was horrified to see a splitting image of himself staring back at him; brown hair, short beard, wide chested. Only his eyes were different, almost entirely black with white irises. Lucifer repeated Alex's last words, playing with his articulation.

"'Tee— Tee minus nine— T minus 9 and counting... Starting automatic ground launch sequencer – Roger, tower' – How am I doing, Alex?"

The Defiant blasted through the atmosphere later that day, and three nights later, it reached the Moon's orbit. While astronauts Malcom and Hannibal made repairs to satellite Emersyn with the help of science teacher Yan, Laura tried to keep herself busy going through the inventory of medical supplies once again. She was used to move around fast in zero gravity and her jumpsuit was light enough to maneuver, so she pushed herself from cabinet to cabinet, up and down with ease. Suddenly, the lights went out and the auxiliary red lamps kicked in.

"Oh, man."

Laura hovered upwards through the shaft and headed to the cockpit.

"Guys, what's wrong with the power?"

What Laura saw made her scream in terror. Both shuttle pilots were dead. Their bodies were strapped to their chairs by safety belts and lacked any skin color as blood flowed out of their eye sockets and floated over them. Alex stood beside them, staring at Laura with dark penetrating eyes. He wore a white shirt under his opened blue jumpsuit.

Laura immediately realized that Alex had gone mad and murdered the pilots. Panic overcame her. She quickly sped down the shaft and moved to the next chamber. She knew there was no escaping Alex, but if she could contact Malcom and Hannibal, maybe they could come and overpower Alex before he killed her. As she moved closer to the communicator, she began to feel weaker. She felt dizzy. Her eyes bothered her, forcing her to wink rapidly. When she touched them with the tips of her fingers, blood dripped from them. Her heart beat slower, and slower, and she found it hard to breathe. Laura was being drained. Just as she was about to touch the communicator control pad, what little she had left of her life had gone.

Lucifer as Alex, stepped around Laura's floating corpse. He was unaffected by the lack of gravity in the ship. As he reached the engine compartment he looked around and studied his surroundings. He took a step closer to the engine and then looked over his shoulder. Yan Fan, the teacher, had made it back to the ship and was staring at him frightened. Lucifer smiled at her and touched the engine with his open palm. He observed the ship's behavior. Several luminous cracks were created on the engine and they quickly extended and multiplied throughout the space craft. He sighed, clearly irritated by the disappointing outcome of his action. The entire space ship shook, and Yan spiraled backwards. A huge burst of fire quickly surged from the cracks and it filled the chamber. Seconds later, the Defiant was destroyed.

. . . .

More than thirty years passed since the explosion of the Defiant. The silver stronghold rose high and majestically to the thunderous red sky of Hell. Astaroth looked up, and grinded his teeth. It would take him days to reach his destination. He was about to step all the way to the top. The fallen angel had accomplished this journey before, a torturous reliving of his fears and failures reflected in the mirrored walls inside the citadel. Surviving this voyage to his master's throne room at the top meant surviving the nightmare of his monstrous self. But if Lucifer called upon him, he would not dare to make him wait. Once again, he entered the fortress, but this time, he had to push.

The Morning Star stood at his balcony, appreciating his empire of ashes and ruins. Hell, to every being that has ever encountered it, was misery made reality. It was a cold cesspool of vampirical hate; the damned cannibalized to survive every moment, minute by minute in an eternity of chastisement and hopelessness. But to Lucifer, every cindered remnant, every crumbled wreck of his kingdom embodied something else; something he could not fathom being separated from far too long. He could see the lake of blood from the balcony of his citadel and his thoughts wandered for an instant until the sound of squeaking wheels caught his attention.

Astaroth had arrived. Soulless, barely alive, and tired of pushing a bed.

"Master," Astaroth said. "Prince Sloth is here."

Lucifer saw the teenager arch-demon sleeping on his medical bed. Astaroth had escorted him all the way from Earth under his master's order, but Lucifer barely acknowledged his lackey's presence. The Morning Star waved his hand.

"Leave."

Humiliated, Astaroth left Sloth to his master's side. Lucifer approached the bed.

"Wake up, Belphegor."

Sloth sluggishly sat up, his drool hung reaching all the way to the floor.

"Hrm…"

"How goes the prophet?"

"Hrm…"

"Speak louder."

"Hrm— 'is prophecy—hrm— last one—hrm"

"Good. Make sure you keep him hidden from the Seven Lights. I do not wish them to discover the truth."

"Hrm—beat'em 'fore— hrm— Zadkiel's muh bitch— hrrrmmm— hung in his ship— hrmmm— gaming fer weeks— hrrrrm…"

Lucifer turned his dark daunting eyes towards Belphegor. "What… ship?"

"Hrm—blue spaceshuh— hrrrrm…" the teenaged arch-demon said.

Lucifer leaned closer to the youngster, placed his hand on his shoulder, and gave him a golden fidget spinner. "Tell me everything."

Sloth played with the spinner as he gave every detail he remembered to his master.

Hours later, Astaroth pushed Sloth's bed through Hell's black ash desert. The arch-demon focused on making his new toy spin after hypnotizing spin. Astaroth was upset, but not surprised at all to see Sloth in a state of bliss. Horror and a wink, this was Lucifer's way with everyone after all, he thought. He briefly turned his head to stare at the silver citadel behind them and silently cursed the day he chose to follow Lucifer's rebellion.

7 SEVEN ANGELS ARE NOW LESS

There were some people still living in Downtown Phoenix, Arizona. Not that many remained in the ghost town, but enough to warrant faint bleeps in its lifeline. The city was full of promises broken by a recent market crash. Its few dispersed residents had no choice but to stay with all their savings spent on properties that lost their entire value overnight. Construction came to a halt where there should have been condos and office buildings and restaurants and malls. Instead, for every few poorly maintained houses, there were three or four empty desolate dirt lots that divided the area in brown square blocks like an empty gameboard.

One of the many deserted buildings was a movie theater. Its two main entrances bookending the ticket stand were boarded with padlocked wooden panels. Unpainted walls displayed barely legible and discolored upcoming movie posters from seven years ago. And the white billboard that roofed the entrance had some scattered black letters that made it impossible to guess the name of the film that the theater featured before closing out.

It was there where seven sundry out-of-towners met. The first one came by bus; a Greyhound that parked right in front of the theater. As the door opened, the driver cried unconsolably and mumbled something about not seeing a child on a bicycle he ran over ten months ago. The only passenger in the bus came out. It was Uriel, the violet angel of emotions. She was a purple haired teenager that hid her pale face under an indigo hoodie and wore a black skirt with lilac rain boots.

"It's okay. Not the end of the world… yet," Uriel said to the driver.

The driver calmed down, wiped his tears, closed the passenger doors, and drove the bus away. Uriel stood on the sidewalk checking messages on her cellphone. She texted *I'm here* and waited. A skull emoji popped.

Just around the corner, two girls rode in on a mangled pink bicycle. One pedaled the bike while the other rode on the handle bar. The rider was blond and sported a dirty and torn blue dress. One side of her head was crushed; her rotted skin was stained with dried blood from top to bottom, and she only wore one shoe.

The black haired pale girl on the handle bar was Azrael, the Black Angel. She wore the same grey tattered dress and black school girl shoes as always. A black halo spun over her head. Azrael had resurrected the girl to travel to Phoenix. As soon as she got off the bicycle, the blond putrefied girl in the blue dress dropped lifeless on the sidewalk. The Black Angel touched the dead girl's forehead and briefly prayed in silence. The dead girl turned to ashes.

Uriel noticed thick tire marks on the dead girl's atrophied face and dress.

"Everything is connected, I guess…" she said, rolling her eyes.

Azrael hugged Uriel.

"I've missed you, Black," the purple clad teen said. "I better call you Azrael, though. I don't want Isophie on my ass."

Azrael smiled and brought her flat hand to her lips, and then moved it forward and a bit down.

"*Thank you?* Was that sign language?"

Azrael nodded and smiled.

"Blue is so going to flip!" Uriel said.

They were interrupted by the sound of gusting winds. Airstreams increased, picking up dirt and merging into a tornado that took form in the middle of the street. The whirlwind moved erratically from side to side, as if it was dancing. Its shape changed, shrinking on itself and developing curves that finally became the body of the green angel of nature, Jophiel. She wore an olive halter top and a ceremonial loincloth that fell just below her knees. Her brown afro sheltered multi-colored flowers that bloomed and withered, and butterflies that coasted around her thick hair like beautiful satellites.

Azrael ran towards Jophiel and threw her arms about her, letting one of the bright butterflies alight upon her hand.

"I want all my insects alive today, Azrael. No demises please," Jophiel said to her sister.

Uriel still hadn't moved; she looked down at her feet, twisting her hands.

"Uriel," Jophiel called. "I won't bite. Come give me a hug."

Uriel hesitated. "Sure," she said, doubt crossing her face as she took a small step towards her sister.

Jophiel warmly held Uriel in her arms, but she noticed the teenager avoided looking at her.

"Stop feeling guilty, sister. My choices were never your doing."

Jophiel released Uriel and turned her gaze upwards. A blinding white light saturated the skies. The harmonic sound of Cherubim angels singing echoed throughout the ghost town, soothing every citizen into a profound sleep. Ricadel, the white angel of life and leader of the Archangels, descended towards her siblings. She wore a long beautiful dress of solid white light with trim laces, and a single diamond on her forehead. Ricadel would have been a vision of perfection except for a bloody hollow cavity in her stomach area. It was a wound that she chose to keep open to remind herself of something missing in her life.

"Sisters! I am so happy you are well! I've missed you all!" Ricadel waved. "Little Azrael, how tall and beautiful you have become!"

Ricadel hugged both Azrael and Uriel at once and then turned to

Jophiel. She grabbed both her hands and held them tight as she pouted and nodded to convey solidarity.

"I have been praying for you every single night."

Jophiel gave an awkward nod.

"Do you guys hear that?" Uriel asked.

The four angels noticed the Cherubim choir melody being drowned by brash guitar noises. Motorhead's *Ace of Spades* blasted from the distance.

"Isophie's here," Jophiel said, shaking her head.

An old grey van riddled with graffiti zig zagged towards the abandoned movie theater. The passenger that rode shotgun sat on the door window and banged the van's roof with his fists. The vehicle screeched to a halt in the middle of the street and the side door rolled open. Three long-haired gangly guys wearing black leather and chains were crammed in the narrow back space along with some electric guitars and amplifiers.

A heavily tattooed punk rocker with a red mohawk stepped out of the van –a few empty beer cans clattering at her feet. The red angel of freedom wore a brick colored leather jacket with many small belts and zipper pockets, ripped jeans, and big worn out combat boots. Isophie whirled around and glared into the van.

"Yo, where's my sword? Gimme my damn sword!"

One of the men in the van handed her a long glittering sword cased in its scarlet scabbard to Isophie. He leaned close to her and tried to kiss her.

"I love you!"

Isophie pushed him back to the van and slammed the door shut.

"Go fuck yourselves!" she said as she flicked the guys in the van. The vehicle sped away.

Isophie turned around to face the four angels on the sidewalk.

"What? Those are my boys!"

The other angels stood silent. All but Azrael had disdainful looks.

"Relax!" Isophie said. "They got a designated driver! We're all good here, okay? Now let's get this shit going. I got places to be. And Uriel, none of that color naming crap. We're Archangels, not Power Rangers. It's Isophie; not red or ruby or scarlet."

"I'd never call you scarlet..." Uriel muttered.

The Black Angel stepped closer to hug Isophie, but the punk angel's cigarette stench made her cough and stay back. Isophie walked pass her straight towards the theater's locked entrance.

"Somebody open up this joint!"

"Yes, ma'am! Right away, ma'am!" A blonde lady in a classic yellow buttoned up usher uniform said from the ticket booth.

"Raphael, where is he?" Jophiel asked.

"Oh, he's already inside," the usher answered. "Three, four, five— Why, all'a us are here now! We're ready to get this show on the road!" the blonde ticket girl fixed her hat. "Let me make my entrance first!"

The usher disappeared from the ticket booth, leaving only falling gold sparkles behind. Fireworks exploded above the angels. They found themselves arrested as they looked up to an impressively bright and colorful light show in the sky. Raphael, golden angel of miracles, appeared from out of the biggest firework explosions. She rode a flying winged pig that released a luminous rainbow trail from its behind. When the flying pig landed on the ground, Raphael no longer wore an usher uniform, but a beautiful golden silk night gown and high heels. Her slick makeup and hairstyle resembled Greta Garbo's on a1930's Hollywood premier gala.

The Archangels were so enthralled by Raphael's visual effects that they missed the movie theater behind them come to life. Its walls were painted, movie posters replaced by new ones, bulb lighted billboard letters read *Now Showing: Alien Life: A Space Heresy*. Both front entrances were open and red carpets extended all the way to the street. Crowds of excited screaming fans, press, and photographers gathered.

"Raphael! Raphael! Who are you wearing tonight?" a paparazzi asked.

"Oh, daaarling, this old thing!" she answered in a sassy voice.

The five angels stepped on the red carpet and followed Raphael to the entrance. Azrael and Ricadel smiled and waved at the crowd. Uriel pulled her hoodie further over her face and kept her head down. Isophie traded insults with the photographers and incited fights like a wrestler. Behind her, Jophiel pushed her to move forward and rolled her eyes. The moment the last of the Archangels entered the building, the red carpets, gleaming lights, photographers, screaming fans, and fireworks were gone. The closed movie theater was silent and deserted once again.

. . . .

They all entered a narrow auditorium with a small cinema screen. Blue sat at the center seat in the middle row as he worked to improve the image quality in a beam that projected from his cobalt tech-suit.

"Hi, everyone. Have a seat. I just installed the projector in my wrist drive."

Uriel slouched in her seat at the back row. Two rows in front of her sat Isophie, who put up her legs and boots on the seat before her. Her long sword rested in its casing on the chair next to her. At a seat all the way to the left there was Raphael, who now wore a golden suit and top hat that made her look like a circus ringmaster. She dirtied her thin white gloves as she stuffed her mouth from a big bucket of popcorn. Jophiel kept to herself at the seat to the right of the room. Ricadel sat in the first row. Azrael, sat next to her and held her hand.

The footage was played in unending loop; alien life form runs into a cave. Over and over and over again. The images were as clear as Blue could provide considering recording interference by the lousy atmosphere on planet Hell Part Two. Still, as short and grainy as the visual was, the Archangels found themselves watching in disbelief as they tried to understand the meaning of this discovery.

"Ha! I knew it!" Raphael broke the silence while munching on popcorn, nodding with pride and vindication. "Youse all thought I was a looney!

That's a Martian right there, see?"

"Turn it off, Zadkiel" Isophie grunted. "So, aliens exist. These transients, as you call them, to me they're just the newest threat to Creation. I say we kill them before they kill us. End of story."

"How can you say that?" Ricadel asked. "These creatures have the same right to live as we do!"

"Not at the cost of humanity's freedom, and definitely not at the cost of our lives," the punk warrior replied. "I really don't see the issue here."

"I agree with Isophie," Jophiel said, thorny weeds grew from her hair. "We cannot risk these beings coming to Earth and affecting the balance of—"

"Nature!" Raphael interrupted. "You were gonna say nature, wen'tcha?"

"The balance of Creation," Jophiel finished her thought.

"Sisters, please think about this," Ricadel argued. "We know very little about these beings. Their intentions could be noble. And we do not even know how many there are."

"They're in the millions, congregated in the caverns below the surface of Hell Part Two," Blue said as he switched his suit's projector off. "When I spoke to Yan Fan yesterday—"

"Man, how could you leave a soul stranded on that planet?" Isophie asked. "That was reckless and against everything we stand for. If something happens to her—"

"Azrael already let me have it, sis. I didn't summon you to scorn me. We know what we know about the transients only because of Yan. According to her, the planet's climatically unstable. The transients won't survive. She's asking for our help to migrate them to another world."

"Absolutely not, bro!" Isophie said. "That's my answer right there."

"It's a no from me as well," Jophiel declared. "It is not our burden to bear."

"I say it is!" Ricadel countered. "We are the Seven Lights, guardians of Creation. Creation entails everything made by God, even if we may not like or understand it. It is not for us to judge but to protect."

"And how do you even know if these creatures were made by God?" Jophiel asked. "How do you know that if by helping these beings, we're not actually endangering the Earth?"

"Jophiel, there is much more to the universe than this Earth," Ricadel replied. "We have now seen that life exists in other worlds. Clearly, we have not begun to comprehend the extent of God's divine plan. Doesn't that excite you?"

Jophiel raised her eyebrow in contempt. Blue held his forehead and shook his head.

"Yan Fan requested to speak to us on behalf of the transients, but I haven't been able to reestablish contact with her. We need to figure out what to do about this discovery by ourselves."

"It's obvious what we do! We introduce ourselves to these folks!" Raphael proposed. "We put on a show, special effects and all, see? *Goldie Presents: The History of Earth*! A twenty-three-part saga starring Dwayne Johnson and Sophia Vergara! We open in total darkness. Suddenly, a flash of light and a loud BANG! God creates the universe— God could be Tilda Swinton—"

"I agree with sister Raphael," Ricadel said. "Not the show part, but the part about introducing ourselves to them. If we let them know that we do not mean them any harm—"

"Nope," Isophie insisted. "We attack them now. We already may have lost the element of surprise if they discover that ghost girl roaming around."

"Guys," Uriel spoke from the back of the room. "Does this feel to you like the beginning of one of those huge messes we can't really fix and that we end up sweeping under a rug after one of us dies in an ultimate sacrifice to save humanity?"

The room fell silent.

"You know? You are such a ray of sunshine, sister..." Isophie said to Uriel. "Maybe you can look at your arm a little more thoroughly and find a vein you haven't cut yet?"

"Whatever! Just saying..." Uriel muttered. "Anyway, you guys know the nightmare we just went through with the demonic invasion in New York. Some of us almost died. And some of us did... For all we know, those things are like them or worse. I just don't want to deal with that right now. Sorry, I'm out."

"Finally, she says something that makes sense!" Isophie said.

"Shut up, you Michael wannabe!"

"Well, I got her sword now. Whose fault is that, Uriel?"

"You're such an asshole!"

"That doesn't make me wrong."

"Both of you be quiet," ordered Jophiel. "We're not here to open wounds of past mistakes."

Blue ignored the squabbling between Isophie and Uriel. He turned to Azrael.

"What do you think, snow face? We go save them or let them die?"

Azrael expressed her thoughts through sign language. Blue translated for those that didn't understand. She gave a compelling and heartwarming argument that moved everyone and brought Ricadel to tears. Even Isophie seemed touched by her sister's words.

"Okay, we get it. The angel of death is pro-life," Isophie said. "But I'm still pro-choice, so it looks like we're tied, bro. Three yeas and three nays. Your vote decides. What's it gonna be?"

Blue hesitated as all of his siblings stared at him.

"I really hoped you guys would've taken this decision out of my hands."

. . . .

Blue left the abandoned theater after the Archangels parted ways and headed towards an empty lot where Matilda waited. As he neared the lot, his thoughts were absorbed in bringing Yan Fan to safety and he was still conflicted over the fate of the transients.

The rocks underneath the ground rose and formed a wall in Blue's path, forcing him to halt. Jophiel touched his shoulder from behind.

"Speak your mind, brother."

He turned to face his sister.

"We're not here to open wounds of past mistakes," he addressed her sarcastically.

"Lucifer made an offer to bring someone very special to me back to life. I accepted."

"Lucifer… You made a deal with Lucifer. Why would you do that?" He shook his head. "You were never a fan of humankind. It's always been you and the birds and the flowers. Why give yourself for this human? People die every single day."

Jophiel did not respond.

"I mean, I get it, you had feelings for this guy. I've loved too. But to sacrifice to Lucifer for him— it just doesn't make sense!"

Jophiel took a moment to find the right words to say.

"…He died because of me. His death was meant to hurt me. And it did. For all the natural wonders of this world, living did not make any sense to me with the guilt of his death. He is alive now, Zadkiel. He will live his life and someday he will die without any influence our kind may bring. And when that day comes, I will belong to Lucifer. I am at peace with that."

Blue fell silent.

"…I'll think of something, Jophiel. If I could just—"

"No one outthinks Lucifer. You know this well."

"Then I'll fight him!"

"Brother, he will kill you."

"Are you expecting me to stand idly when he——"

"Yes, I do. I'm sorry, Zadkiel. There is nothing more to be done."

"Yeah. I guess for the angel who makes the earth turn winter into spring, it's just too hard to make shit happen."

Jophiel shrugged, ignoring his comment, and made the stone wall crumble and open a pathway for Blue. He held his sister's hand briefly and then let go before he walked away.

. . . .

Matilda soared through the skies as orange sunset clouds faded into blackness of the night. Blue crawled underneath the flying lounge's floor, fixing wires and running diagnostics on all programs. Everything seemed fine to him at first glance – rocket boosters, navigation systems, fuel tank, life support; but his scalp prickled, and his stomach felt queasy; something was wrong.

"Hey, how fast are we going?" he asked the ship.

"31,000 miles per hour," Matilda replied.

"What? Who told you to speed up? Slow down!"

"Unable to comply."

"Reduce velocity by twenty-five thousand miles!"

"Unable to comply."

"Well, that's just great! Where do you think you're going in such a hurry?"

"Nebraska, United States of America."

"Nebraska! Matilda, what is wrong with you?"

"Unable to ascertain."

"Land now. Find a safe spot and land."

"Unable to comply."

"Oh, hell no! I'm manually overriding your behind, young lady."

Blue tried to open the floor hatch to climb to the lounge. But as much as he pushed the door, it would not move.

"This is not funny. Let me out!"

"Unable to comply."

Blue felt Matilda land. The hatch opened by itself and the Archangel quickly pulled himself up to the lounge.

"Matilda!"

There was no answer.

He noticed a used empty glass next to an open Don Perignon bottle at the bar counter.

"Who is here?" he asked.

Matilda's door opened. Blue stepped out of the ship and found himself stranded on an endless Midwestern prairie. There was a stream flowing a few yards away. Blue saw a man's figure standing by the riverbank, but he couldn't distinguish who it was. As he walked closer to the stranger, the man turned towards him. Blue froze as he stood face to face with a mirror image of himself smiling back at him: tall and thin, blond hair, futuristic cobalt armor and boots. But his eyes were different. The man in front of Blue had piercing black eyes with white irises. He pointed his finger at the night sky.

"Look. No stars," Lucifer said to Blue. "Let's have a talk."

8 SATAN HAS A ROCKETSHIP

FADE IN:

INT. ALIEN SAUCER CONTROL BRIDGE - NIGHT

The spaceship's control bridge shakes uncontrollably and tilts sideways as five silver uniformed alien crew members hold on to their seats at their work stations. Emergency red lights illuminate the compartment with the sound of alarms stressing the danger that the alien crew is in. LIEUTENANT BARDAKOK (28), a gray-skinned bug-eyed bald alien, makes his way through the chaos and reaches the Captain's chair in the middle of the bridge.

SOUND EFFECTS (SFX): Wheeooo, Wheeooo, Wheeooo

LIEUTENANT BARDAKOK

Captain! We are losing power!

CAPTAIN GARABEK (60), same description as Liutenant Bardakok, but older and sporting a sagacious gray beard, presses a button at his chair's arm and speaks.

CAPTAIN GARABEK

All hands, brace for impact!

EXT. OUTER SPACE – NIGHT.

The damaged alien saucer lights up on fire as it rapidly approaches earth's atmosphere.

INT. ALIEN SAUCER CONTROL BRIDGE – NIGHT

Zoom in to close-up of Captain Garabek.

CAPTAIN GARABEK

May the seven light goddesses of Maska'hli protect us!

EXT. HAWAIIAN SKY OVER VOLCANO – NIGHT.

The damaged alien saucer trailing smoke falls from the sky and crashes into the side of the volcano, causing a grand explosion.

SFX: KA-BOOM!

{Production note: Hey, Rodney. Don't worry about the budget for these scenes. I know a guy that can do very good clay animation for cheap. Trust me, the geeks are going to eat this! – J.P.}

INT. ALIEN SAUCER CONTROL BRIDGE – NIGHT

Pan view of the ship's destroyed bridge. Red lights turn on and off leaving the crew in the dark at times. Some of the control panels explode with electricity sparks. The five aliens help each other up as they recover from the crash landing.

CAPTAIN GARABEK

Status report!

LIEUTENANT BARDAKOK

No casualties, sir. But the ship has suffered substantial damage. We have lost our main engine and it may take some time to find the materials we need to fix it on this planet.

CAPTAIN GARABEK (Stroking his beard)

This planet, Lieutenant, is called Earth! I have studied it closely and its inhabitants are the most remarkable beings I have ever encountered in my space travels. It is a species full of so much potential. We must reach out to them for help if we are to survive!

Lieutenant Bardakok reads one the control panels and flips some switches.

LIEUTENANT BARDAKOK (Alarmed)

Captain! We are being boarded! Intruders!

Flashes of light and a smoke curtain appear at the left side of the bridge, forcing the alien crew to retreat to the right side. SATAN (30), crimson skinned and leather clad horned monster in high heel boots, appears holding his trident. He is accompanied by four DEMON GOBLINS (20), gray skinned little people, point short swords and hiss at the aliens.

SATAN

I am Satan, Prince of Darkness! For centuries I have waited, banished to hell by God and his angels! Hand over your spaceship to me and I will finally travel and exact my revenge on Heaven!

CAPTAIN GARABEK

We will do no such thing! We are a peaceful alien race and we will die before allowing you to tip the cosmic balance towards evil!

Captain Garabek takes out his ray gun and fires a laser at Satan.

SFX: PTEW!

Satan blocks the laser with his bare hand.

SATAN

And die you shall! For I am Satan! You can't match my power! Goblins, attack!

The demon goblins advance against the alien crew. Each one touches an alien crew member and disappear as they do so. The alien's eyes turn red.

LIEUTENANT BARDAKOK (Eyes turning red)

Oh, no! I am being possessed! Aaargh!

{Production note: Guys, is this character really necessary? I feel like we're paying too much for small bullshit speaking roles and we can't cut corners on royalties with S.A.G. on our asses. I hope you fuckers haven't started casting. Let's have a meeting to streamline this god-awful script. - Rodney}

Satan moves towards Captain Garabek. Captain Garabek shoots his lasers, but he's blocked again by Satan.

SFX: PTEW! PTEW! PTEW!

Satan uses his trident to hit the alien's ray gun away. Satan touches Captain Garabek's chest and disappears.

CAPTAIN GARABEK (To the TV audience)

No! We have failed our mission of peace! Our advanced alien technology has fallen to the hands of evil! The only hope this universe has now lies in humanity. Aaaargh!

Extreme close up at Captain Garabek's eyes turning red.

SATAN (As Captain Garabek)

Ha,ha,ha! With this, my mothership, I am invincible now! I will bring the humans to their knees! Heaven and the universe will be mine!

> – *Satan Has a Rocketship* ® (1990) (Excerpt)
> Unproduced teleplay loosely based on the book by
> Matteo Tsekalo.

....

Most likely, it should've been the end of the world. The Seven Archangels united in epic battle against Lucifer; Creation at the brink of destruction and humanity's fate at stake. Something dramatic like that, or maybe a daring rescue mission to Hell, bringing down Lucifer's silver citadel with the hope of making him relinquish his hold on Evergreen. Of all the ways that Blue had imagined facing Lucifer, he never thought it would be like this; alone, staring at his own face in some random plains of the mid-west. Surrealistic and frighteningly personal... Total darkness illuminated only by his ship's lights. A quiet river behind him, and nothing but grassland for miles.

Blue was not prepared for this.

He watched Lucifer take his time in the silence, tearing at it with the crunching sound of his boots stepping on the meadow. Blue felt he was being studied, standing in front of Lucifer; his fear was being studied. He knew the devil was taking pleasure in his confusion. There was no need for violence, Blue thought. Lucifer didn't need to show Blue the things that he could do to him. There was a reason why the angels shuddered at the sound of his name.

"I hope you appreciate all I've done to meet with you," Lucifer said to Blue. "No Archangels around, no technology to control. Just you and me."

Blue's heart raced with fear. He was about to face a being with power second only to God. There was no winning this duel, but maybe, if he could hold off long enough, he could try to escape.

"Matilda! Fire the sonar waves at that other Blue! Full power!" Blue shouted.

The small space craft hovered towards Lucifer. She unloaded two parabolic dishes, one at each of her sides, and pointed them at him.

"Matilda, fire the sonar waves at that other Blue. Full power," Lucifer calmly repeated, in a voice identical to Blue's.

The sphere-shaped ship aimed at Blue, then at Lucifer, then at Blue, then at Lucifer again. She lowered her weapons.

"Unable to comply."

"You took my physical form to confuse Matilda!"

"I did dress up for the occasion," Lucifer replied, tapping on the chest armor protecting the body he copied from Blue. "Though this is a bit cosplay for my tastes."

"Shoot us both! Now!" Blue ordered Matilda.

Matilda complied. She unleashed her sonic power on both. Blue leapt to the side, evading the incoming shock waves. The brunt of the attack hit Lucifer. His body faded and appeared a few meters away. Matilda shot at Lucifer again. His body faded and reappeared closer to Blue.

"Matilda, stop," Lucifer ordered. The spaceship halted her firing. He turned to Blue, "Why do you waste my time?"

Blue pressed the controls on his wrist and a small screen displayed the words *Battle Mode*. His chest armor released a layer of thick metallic plates that expanded and engulfed his entire body. Blue's suit was now a mechanical beast; a heavy walking tank. As the cobalt mecha-armor advanced towards Lucifer, several laser riffles and plasma canons came out of Blue's arms, shoulders, and chest, all aimed at the devil.

Lucifer held his forehead, trying to contain his laughter.

"Zadkiel…"

Desperate, Blue fired everything he had at Lucifer. It was a video game massacre; huge blasts of luminous blue and white energy mercilessly showered the Morning Star. The Archangel knew this was not remotely enough to beat him, but maybe it would slow him down.

When the rapid fire ended, Lucifer's scorched body froze and slowly began to fade. Only smoke and dirt were left in his place. Lucifer appeared next to Blue. He tore open Blue's mecha-armor all the way from his neck to the crutch area and pulled the angel out of it, throwing him several feet away. Blue landed head first, eating a bit of dirt and grass.

"Let's not play this game," Lucifer said.

The angel dragged himself away from Lucifer. He tried to control his nervously shaking hands, so he could tap on his wrist controls again.

"Come on, babies. Don't fail me now…" Blue whispered, staring at his wrist screen. Out in space, nine satellites from different nations orbited the Earth. They aligned themselves and interacted, regardless of their different technologies and languages. They no longer obeyed the governments that controlled them, but the divine being that shaped them.

Lucifer followed Blue's eyes. The angel was staring over the devil's shoulder and towards the sky.

"I took away your armor, and there are no cars or tablets here you can throw at me." Lucifer said. "What other little movie toys are you going to play with now?"

The black clouds above the angels burst into illumination. A huge white beam burst and seared from the skies and struck Lucifer. The singed ground around his position became a small black crater. Blue saw that the Morning Star resisted the light ray attack, which lasted for half a minute. He had unleashed his most powerful weapon on Lucifer, but he was practically unscathed; he barely rubbed the back of his neck. Blue knew Lucifer's patience was at an end when he saw his smile disappear and his attention turned solely on him.

"Satellite pulse canon blast. Like in the movies," said Blue, still crawling away from the devil. "Matilda—"

"Enough, Zadkiel!" Lucifer yelled.

He caught up to Blue and grabbed his leg. He lifted him, dangling him like a struggling fish, and slammed him against the ground. Blue's entire body began to fail him. He found it hard to breathe and felt a sharp pain in his chest. He was almost certain the leg that Lucifer yanked was broken, too. Blue wanted to just break down and cry, but quitting was not going to serve him at all. He pressed on.

He tried to reach for his wrist control, but Lucifer clasped his arm and squeezed hard. Electric sparks and blood shot out of the angel's broken arm. With wrist panel pieces encrusted in his flesh, Blue bellowed and trembled from the pain. He tried running scenarios in his mind, but he couldn't think of options as panic overcame him.

Lucifer backhanded Blue hard and fast several times. Each thunderous hit bruised and bloodied the angel's face. Blue fought to keep awake.

"Why do you try my patience?" Lucifer asked. "You know well you cannot beat me."

"Unh...Michael did."

"Ah, well. Hasn't anyone told you?"

Lucifer wrapped his hand around Blue's neck, choking and pulling him closer. Blue could not breathe. Lucifer smiled with contempt.

"Michael. Is. Dead."

He let go of Blue's neck and stepped back. Blue laid face down on the ground, coughing. He held his injured arm and tried to slow down his breathing.

"What... do you want?" Blue asked.

"Like I said, I just want to talk."

"We have... huh—nothing to talk about. Unless you're here... to free Evergreen from your pact."

"Jophiel will be treated well when her time comes to join me."

"You tricked her into bowing to you!"

"I do not 'trick' anyone."

"Liar!"

"The devil is a liar! Oh, Lordy!" Lucifer sighted. "It seems we will not be able to move on with this conversation until you air your grievances with me. Tell me something, Zadkiel. How much do you love your sister?"

"Y-You know the answer to that."

"Then you would consider taking her place when I come for her. Am I correct?"

Blue felt his heart about to burst from his chest. Here was his opportunity to save Evergreen. She was right in saying there was no outthinking the Morning Star. Submit to Lucifer. Better him than Evergreen, whatever the consequences may be. Blue struggled to get off the ground. He knelt in front of Lucifer, head down on the grass. His arms dropped.

"...Yes."

Lucifer grinned and stepped away.

"Well, that's too bad, Zadkiel, because that offer was never on the table for you. I don't need to concern myself with you and your superfluous little trinkets... I can see why Sloth has a thing for you, you keep the masses stupid with your devices. But I honestly couldn't think of anything useful to do with you."

Lucifer stooped next to Blue and scooped some dirt and grass with his bare hand. He showed it to Blue.

"You see, someone like Jophiel, what she can do..." he continued. "She has the soul of the Earth in the palm of her hand. That is true power. Hers is one of the most dangerous ministries of Creation. When she comes to serve me, I am confident there will be quite a few secrets she will reveal to me about this world."

"That will never happen!" Blue cried. We will stop you!"

Lucifer laughed and shrugged. He scattered the dirt and wiped his hand before standing up in front of Blue; the glint of the sun on his blond hair, the command in his eyes. Blue was daunted by Lucifer.

"Who will stop me, you? Are you going to hit me with a selfie stick? How about the angry drunk with Michael's sword? Oh, surely not the depressed teen or that adorable little mute girl. Maybe the miracle nut with A.D.D. She's got some power there. Too bad she only wants to use it to sparkle her next Broadway musical... I don't think so."

Blue breathed heavily, his mouth tasted blood. Lucifer placed his hands behind his back and stared into the dark horizon.

"There are very few beings in the universe that could have hindered my plans. Michael, Gabriel, Abaddon; those were real Archangels. True warriors, all of them. And look how they have fallen by my hidden hand, Zadkiel; one after the other. Jophiel was the last of them, and soon she will walk willingly into my arms."

"Then why are we here? What do you want with me?"

Lucifer turned his black eyes to Blue as he pointed at his ship.

"The only good thing you ever made..."

"Matilda?"

Lucifer leaned closer to Zadkiel and they locked eyes.

"You have seen them, haven't you?" Lucifer asked.

"What— What are you talking about?"

"Stop wasting my time, Zadkiel."

"The transients? Is this all because of them?"

"I am going to use your ship. But I will need to be able to use a corporeal form different than yours. Give me control of your ship."

101

"No!"

Lucifer placed his hand on Blue's face, squeezing. Blue felt the pressure of his fingers digging into his jaw.

"Do you know how you are able to speak? Because I let you. Because it pleases me. Do not waste this gift I've granted you and state your next words carefully."

"I will… not…give you what you want." Blue managed to say.

"Then I will take it."

Blue screamed in agony as he felt his jaw and part of his throat tear; flesh and ligaments ripping away from him. Blood gushed, his inner bright angelic azure light leaked out. He watched horrified at his own jawbone held by Lucifer's hand. Blue almost fell face down, but Lucifer pulled his head by the hair and pointed his jaw towards Matilda.

Blue was entranced. Lucifer invaded his thoughts as they became an eerie voice channeled through the bloodied torn jaw.

"Matilda, override code sigma-4975-RyanGoslin-001, transfer all access controls to Lucifer," the jaw voiced.

"Acknowledged," the ship replied.

Lucifer threw the jawbone to the side like trash and let go of Blue, who dropped almost lifeless to the ground. He walked towards the ship and changed his physical form to his true self: naked first, four wings spread, long gold hair over the back of his shoulders; then he changed again: no wings, short buzz cut, and wearing a red tuxedo. Lucifer fixed his cuff links as Matilda opened her door to him.

"Hello, Lucifer. How may I serve you today?" Matilda spoke.

"Take me to the aliens."

Blue, shivering and devastated, tried to call Matilda, but his throat only gurgled with blood. In his last moment awake, the Archangel made an unfinished and unspoken prayer to his siblings.

"Sisters…"

Matilda flew up to the night sky as everything around Blue went black.

…………

The dark starless night belonged to Lucifer. He stood at the lounge's bar, pouring himself a drink. He took a sip.

"How is your drink?" Matilda asked.

"Fine."

"Is the room temperature satisfactory?"

"Yes."

"You still have several messages saved. Would you like me to play them?"

"No. How long until we arrive."

"E.T.A. to Andromeda: three weeks, five days, seven hours, and forty minutes."

"Very well."

"Today is nineties karaoke night. Would you like me to display the catalogue of available dance tunes?"

Lucifer rolled his eyes.

"No. Show me everything you have on the aliens."

Matilda presented a looped visual of the transient running to the cave while playing Yan Fan's audio recordings. Lucifer listened carefully to her findings.

"*Ah, that sounds tragically poetic. But you know, we need a better way to refer to them than faceless. I bet you can come up with a better name for our biped friends, can't you?*

I have. I named them transients."

"Transients…" Lucifer said. "He never bothered to name them…"

"End final recording. Would you like me to replay?"

"Tell me about Yan Fan."

Matilda displayed images of Yan on several holographic screens. Lucifer read her biography, newspaper articles, and viewed her video interviews. Lucifer was transported back to 1986, seconds before he destroyed the Defiant. Hers was the face of the last human he saw then. The last video he saw was of Yan as a ghost, still wearing her space suit. Yan waived goodbye at the ship as she descended to the surface of the planet designated Hell Part Two. Lucifer waived back.

"Hello again, Yan."

Suddenly, a preppy cartoon of a smiling sun appeared on all holo-screens along with a cock-a-doodle-doo sound.

"It is six-thirty am. Good morning!" Matilda said. "Are you ready for today's morning trivia question? How many number one hits did Lady Gaga—"

"Quiet."

Lucifer stood at the exact center of the lounge. He went down on one knee and placed his palm firmly on the floor.

"Lucifer, you are accessing the mainframe databanks. Is there anything I could do to assist—"

"Be quiet."

"Warning: Altering memory files from the mainframe may result in irreversible damage to—"

"I said… Be. Quiet."

Matilda fell silent.

Lucifer applied his power to connect with the machine's mind. He proceeded to rearrange his new transport as he saw fit. Matilda's metal carapace shrieked as it contorted and expanded. Walls clanking, wires melting, memories erasing. The ship grew exponentially and painfully altered from its small glowing blue spherical form into a menacing golden cylindric behemoth. Whatever unique spark made Matilda once was now dead. A new thing was born, and it cried its birth pains with the bass sound of loud horns.

As the new monstrous carriage soared through space, Lucifer remembered Matteo's divinations, the misconstrued visions in his book and the absurdity of it all. Alien armies invading Earth, the devil traveling on the mothership and reveling in the glory of humankind's demise, while the angels ablaze fell from the skies like shooting stars.

"Satan has a rocket ship," Lucifer said. "Another prophecy fulfilled."

"Vessel systems online. Please enter vessel's designated name," a hoarse, moribund robotic voice spoke to its master.

Lucifer smiled. "I will call you Mother."

9 STOWAWAY

Day 134

I never thought I'd ever felt like this after I died. Dizzy, foggy... like I've done circles around myself and I just pinned the donkey's tail on my own butt...

There is nothing here – Why am I even whispering? — This is... never ending. So golden; smooth, shiny, golden nothing. Gold under my floating boots, gold above my head. Gold extending to the horizon. Except there's no horizon. I mean, by logic there should be, but... I've been moving in all directions for days. In between and right through frozen still transients, this place just won't end. If I didn't know we boarded an intergalactic spaceship, I'd swear I just discovered purgatory, Blue.

Feeling a bit better now. I just stayed put for a while and my head is getting clearer...

The transients are quiet. They've been like that since we entered this ship— about... what, a week ago? God, it's only been a week! — As soon as we boarded back on Dog Shit Mesa, they marched one behind the other, led through a narrow black labyrinth of corridors. It must have been the horns that guided them; that lurid, vibrating bass that hasn't stopped since we were in those caves. Whatever it was, the transients have forgotten that I exist. It made it easier to blend in with the herd, but I lost any minimal control my presence had over them. And that worries me.

Moving along with the transients through the dark maze for hours, the proverbial light at the end of the tunnel finally appeared, and it was golden. I kept searching for that long-tailed winged transient I saw coming out of the ship, but I lost sight of him – or her, when we came into the corridors. This was an advanced transient; it had to be. If so, then how did this synergetic relationship work? Was she some kind of queen controlling the worker bees? Or maybe just some sort of golden shepherd within a more complexly constructed hierarchy of transients? And how advanced were they? Were they aware of our existence? Humans, I mean. The mere thought that somewhere out in the universe there's a civilization of see-through-skinned beings capable of creating this massive vessel is daunting. It started to make sense to me how poorly the transients were able to adapt to their natural environment in planet Hell Part Two. That must have never been their home planet. They were brought there for a reason. To colonize it, maybe? Lousy job they did of that...

Somehow, we all ended up in this place, this endless and empty golden vault. The loud hooting noise that lured the transients to the ship seemed to bring them perfectly into line; hundreds of thousands stood two feet from each other like an obsessive action figure collection in display. The only thing the transients did apart from standing erect was to reproduce. Bodies divided into more bodies and then those bodies birthed more and so on. They extended beyond my purview as they kept multiplying by the thousands each day; it's like the ship was a transient incubator.

I'll keep trying to find an escape, but no matter which way I go, I'm stuck in an infinite reflection of myself looking at myself in a mirror. But there has to be a way out...

....

Day 140

The other day I flashed out, the first time it happened since I boarded this ship. I couldn't tell how long I was out because everything was exactly the same when I came back. This is a fancy transient mannequin warehouse, that's where I'm at. Everything here is driving me mad and I--- Ah, fuck it! I told you all of this already...

Did I ever tell you of the dreams I had in the days before I flew on the Defiant? Oh, they were these ludicrously interplanetary epic follies of me. I think it was my subconscious manifesting hidden fears in expectation of launching into space or some Freudian nonsense like that. Some of these dreams ended with the ship stranded in the void of space and me without air to breathe or crash-landing on a planet shaped like my uncle Chen's head. Man, one night I dreamt the Defiant was alive and it was chasing me until it caught me and ate me. "Feed me, Yanhua!" – Hahaha! Stupid…

But other dreams were quite wonderful. I remember dreaming of myself standing naked on a red star. I'm sure it was a star; it wasn't Earth. That one was vivid. I think you were in that dream, too…

. . . .

In your honor, I sing to the transients. I stand facing the legion of frozen faceless fans and I hear their cheering in my mind. They're my captive audience. Sometimes I flash out in the middle of a tune, but I don't care, man. I perform a whole concert.

I get knocked down, but I get up again! You are never gonna keep me down!

Chumbawamba's Tubthumping! That's my favorite nineties tune. You showed it to me. I sing the song and then I throw myself backwards and roll over several of them. I lift my arms and pretend they carry me in a wave. *Woaaaaaah!*

I spend my days remembering karaoke space nights at Matilda's lounge with you. Two-drink minimum! I never did that when I was alive… I never got the courage to get up on a stage and sing in front of people. You gave that to me…even if I was singing only to you.

I hope you haven't forgotten about me wherever you are. And I hope you think of me the way I think of you…

God, you're so handsome… I fucking love you, Blue. Have you ever been with a ghost? Do you think ghosts are capable of doing it? First thing we'll do when I see you again— If I ever see you again, I'm gonna rip that sexy space suit off of you and I'm gonna… I…

Ow... Why do I have a throbbing headache? I'm dead. I'm not supposed to have headaches...

....

Bored... So Booooooorreeed... Buh-Buh... Bluuuuuue! –

....

Day 146

I woke up here from a random flash out. And by here, I mean at least 300 feet above the transient storage field. I remember in little chunks of time. As a drunk spirit, I kept elevating, maybe to see how far up I could fly. The flash out must have happened to me as I wandered aimlessly.

I think I was high... All the headaches and the fogginess; there had to be something in the air at that golden transient incubator area. Some kind of chemical that affected me even as a spirit. I know it's not that obnoxious horn sound. I can still hear it from here, but I'm feeling better now. I don't know what it was, but it almost drove me mad. If I hadn't found this place...

From what I can tell, I'm inside a wall, a thick huge one. I've never traversed such a long distance. I'm phasing through solid metal. It's taken me a while to cross through this wall. I sense it pushing me back. It feels like walking against savage hurricane winds. But I press on because I need to know what's going on with the transients. I need to find that golden transient and figure out a way to communicate with it.

As soon as I cross to the other side of the wall, I stand on a passage, but this one's different from the others. The floor and outer wall are made of some strong polymer-based glass. I'm standing on space. I am looking at the stars with nothing in between me and them. I'm immediately reminded of that first time I stepped out of the Defiant and the universe seemed so close that I instinctively reached out to it and wished I could shed a tear. I find myself second guessing my existence. I think of who I am as a ghost. Is it as an obstacle to being a part of the cycle of life? I'm afraid that whatever I became after I died will forever set me apart from everything and everyone. Ashes not to ashes, dust not to dust. That's me, just a speck of dust asking to return to the cosmos.

Yan, get a hold of myself! I continue to move through the corridor. I hear buzzing— no, the fluttering of wings. I fight my first instinct to run back and hide. I keep moving forward and I turn a corner before I reach the end of the hall. That's where I see the golden transient staring out through the glass, at a yellow star rising from behind a small planet covered in ice.

The golden faceless transient with its slow waggling tail, with its four butterfly wings, with the child inside its translucent torso wearing a crown of fire...or a halo. An ancient thing of power. It pulls away from admiring the melting sunrise and it places its attention on me. We face each other now, and with the light of that yellow star rising behind it, I can't help but think that I'm in the presence of some sort of deity.

A speck of dust in the presence of the morning star...

. . . .

Day 147

Blue, I'm falling and I— I can't even...I can't focus...

I remember standing in front of the golden transient. But in a blink, the transient was no longer in front of me. Confused, I thought for a second that I had flashed out, but I didn't. Not this time. It was the golden transient that disappeared before my eyes. I grappled with my fright and said hello— At least I think I said hello.

A male voice whispered softly to my ear. But not from his face; from inside my head.

"Hello."

I turned around and the golden transient hovered right behind me!

He grabbed me by the neck as if I had a solid body! I tried to phase away through his hand, but I just— I couldn't. I was trapped. He tightened his grip and I actually felt that my head would be torn away from my body! His blank faceless head pointed directly at me as he pulled me closer to him. Then I heard... there was that voice again speaking inside my head. The voice invaded my thoughts and it felt like I was pushed out of myself. I became so... exposed. His deep voice resonated briefly, and he only uttered two words; two startling words...

"Yan Fan."

He— He knew my name...

For the first time, ever since I died, I became afraid for myself, for the idea that I could die again. Suddenly, this faceless transient opened his eyes, breathed through its nose, and smiled wide at me. There was a face staring back at me. I've had horrible nightmares as a kid of someone standing close to me. No one particularly, just someone gazing at me with unreal penetrating eyes. Eyes nailed in my mind even after I woke up from the dream. That's what it felt looking face to face at this nightmarish golden god with black eyes and small white irises focused on me. And just like I did so many times as a child when I had those dreams, I screamed...

And then— Then I flashed out of existence. I must have been out a few seconds because when I came back, the winged transient gave his back to me, still staring at his empty hand. He quickly turned to face me and I panicked. I fled away from him as fast as I could, heading back to the wall. But I felt him coming after me. The fast fluttering of his wings was right behind my back. For a moment I feared I wasn't going to make it. But even if I did, would he be able to follow me all the way through?

Extending my arms, the tip of my stretched fingers reached and traversed the wall. I already sensed myself slowing down, pushing through a high tide of tightened molecules. I was making matter become part of me and then rejected it when I advanced inch by inch. But the winged transient broke through the metallic barrier. He tore through it. I kept forcing the laws of physics to get out of my way, but the golden transient followed me, ever closer, until he clawed through me, tearing the back of my ghost body open. Being a ghost, I thought I couldn't be hurt, Blue. I was wrong. I came to discover the hard way that a rip of my spirit felt like an abrupt void of the soul. Much like when you've lost someone close to you or when some horribly traumatic act was forced upon you. Every second he slashed through my back, I wailed, but I kept moving, even when I almost lost my balance. I wasn't thinking straight. *Faster! Go faster!* My thoughts were pure pulsating aching terror.

I finally crossed through the other side of the wall. I let myself fall on to the transients bathing in the golden bright of the infinite chamber. I slithered aimlessly through the immobile bodies as the golden winged transient entered through the wall. He hovered over the transients searching for me. I saw him pass by me a few times. Afraid that I wouldn't be lucky to avoid him forever, I decided to inhabit one of the transient bodies. Possession is still something that I haven't learned to control completely, but I was in pain after he attacked me, and I needed to hide. I didn't want to face him again. I picked a transient, closed my eyes and pictured its hands as my hands, its body as mine. When I opened my eyes, I was the transient. I remained motionless, as the winged transient got closer, a mere few feet away from me. I could tell he moved his eyes side to side looking for me.

The winged transient stopped cold when he heard a change in the sound of the loud horns. The noise became intermittent; it sounded like a very slow and sick alarm clock. This caught the golden transient's attention and prompted him to stop his search. He flew upwards until I lost sight of him. He must've crossed through the wall, but I didn't see him leave because I was distracted by the transients moving around me.

They were organizing in groups, gathering into perfect circles. I followed their lead in my transient body, afraid that the golden one would return and see me. I joined a group and ended up surrounded right in the middle with no way through. I felt lightheaded from whatever chemical it was that affected me last time. My vision was becoming blurry and it was hard to concentrate.

I felt the ground vibrate under my feet. The golden chamber began to break around us. Thin metal cylindric barriers rose from the ground and encased the transients, forming circled cages around each group. Once we were completely enclosed, we were in the dark. I felt rumblings and heard grinding noises, until we all shook. Then, there was a strong push, and the floor inclined slightly. The movement of our circled cage led me to think we were being ejected from the golden chamber. I was right.

The floor underneath us opened and all the transients fell through it into the nothingness. I found myself falling with them. I managed to turn my head and see the vast spaceship hover over us, getting farther away. Other circle cages were being released. Only, they were not cages, but small luminous oval crafts heading in every direction. But none of that changed anything for me or the transients. I'm still plummeting to this planet's surface.

I can't focus…I'm trapped inside this transient and I can't bring myself to leave it. I'm still groggy from whatever phantom drug I'm on. I can't… There's no way I can avoid this fall. I can't hear myself scream with the wind swooshing and dominating my world. I'm dropping head first through thick dark gray clouds among thousands of transients dropping with me. The clouds begin to dissipate, and I see my destination, I notice so many small lights coming fast towards me, but I'm falling towards dark territory.

As I get closer to my destination, I can already hear loud bangs of transients dropping on land like bombs. If I had a jaw in this transient body, it would've dropped. I'm confused and frozen scared while this dark planet gets closer and closer, eclipsing my peripheral view. It is the only thing I see. The dark and the lights. The small lights that begin to take shape. And they… Oh, no. Oh, my God. Oh, shit…

Blue, if you are hearing this, you need to answer me now! I know where I am!

This is Earth! I'm falling towards Earth!

10 ANGELS INVADED

Violet ran for her life. That night, the Archangel of emotions, one of the most powerful beings in God's known universe, couldn't defend herself against her adversaries. She ran because she couldn't fly away. Her attackers rained from above. They were coming at her from all directions, hundreds of them. Still, as she made her way towards the city alleyways, her eyes couldn't help but look up if only for a moment.

In her short stint as an angel, Violet had seen bloody wars in Heaven between rebelling Seraphim and other angelic factions; she had witnessed a time when a human somehow managed to defeat Lucifer and became the Queen of Hell; she had even experienced a brief disentangling of the universe into a maddening asphyxiation of live colors and dazzling mathematics. But the purple angel never imagined seeing an alien starship shadowing the skies of New Orleans.

And yet, there it was; casting a golden shadow over the city, expanding to all horizons, impossible for her to measure. Earth was being visited – no, conquered by a golden fortress dragging through the clouds, moving by the inches to the naked eye. To Violet, it appeared like the mother of all skate ramps, only upside down opposite to the world; it had an inclination that widened at its lateral plate. *Is that the front or the back of the ship?* she wondered. Rows of multicolored lights moved horizontally on the smooth metallic surface. After a while, they departed the ship and became a fleet of luminescent saucers that traveled in infinite directions.

Transients, the translucent beings that Violet's brother Blue had previously described, poured from the small crafts, and landed hard on the ground, crashing through buildings, vehicles, roads. Upon impact, these walking bombs stood up from the rubble and filed together in destructive humanoid waves. Contrary to all the information the angels received from the astronaut ghost, these violent presences never remained still as they savagely jostled to seize the humans. Military planes and ground vehicles fired their artillery on the faceless invaders, but the transients quickly overran them. Violet saw all of this and wondered why was there not a single prophet that could have predicted the events of this apocalyptic night. Suddenly, 1950's campy sci-fi became foretelling.

Violet kept running through the alleys from the transients closing in while struggling to keep her sanity in check. News had spread in the few minutes it took cellphones to capture and livestream the starship's arrival. Humankind became aware that they were no longer alone in the universe and there was no accord among Earth's nations on what to do about it. Fear manifested in prayers and the Archangels answered as fast they could. They heard their pleas, but it was Violet that felt every one of their emotions. Panic, confusion, uncertainty. Seven billion, six hundred and twenty-seven million astounded men and women of all ages, races, and creeds, looked up to the skies, realizing that the world as they had known it was at an end. It was the burden of Violet's ministry to process these feelings, overwhelming and devastating as they were, and it was her duty to try to shepherd them to harmony in times of chaos. Even though her heart was about to explode in terror, she needed to be strong for her siblings and for the world.

The Archangels made their first stand at the city bay of New Orleans where the golden ship hovered. The town by the Mississippi water had already lost several street blocks demolished by plummeting transients. The invasion was being combated by five of the Seven Lights: Violet, Isophie, Black Angel, Goldie, and Evergreen. Ricadel remained behind attending their fallen brother Blue, but she reminded them to keep themselves unrevealed to the humans. Isophie took the lead as she swung her fiery sword and singlehandedly slashed through dozens of the translucent beings. Evergreen created a hailstorm with thousands of sharp ice pellets propelled directly at the transients. Goldie flew low on her winged pig, swerving to avoid the alien beings falling from the skies. She was followed on the streets below her by a legion of giant plastic toy robots with oversized fists that she ordered to charge against the alien invaders after yelling a paraphrased speech from one of her favorite alien invasion movies.

"We ain't going quietly into the night! We won't vanish without a fight! Today we celebrate Canadian Civic Day!"

Black Angel walked through a transient horde and took the life of many as fast and painless as she could. Violet felt her sister's heart break as each transient she gently touched with her fingers dropped to the ground, and the babies inside them became pale white little corpses. But Black was the only one from whom Violet sensed any compassion, compassion that she would maybe share if she wasn't utterly frightened by the transients.

The purple teen angel assisted as much as she could in calming people down as a city-wide evacuation of the area took place. But after fighting to influence a large crowd of humans around her to flee for safety, she found herself surrounded by a legion of transients. The angel withdrew into an alley, but realized too late that its other end was walled up. She gasped for air as she stooped behind a large metal trash bin and prayed for help. The transients entered the alleyway reaching out their arms to grab her and emitting loud shrieks. One of them lifted the trash bin over its head as the others moved in to take Violet. The young angel saw Isophie's fire sword cut right through all the transients' abdomens, burning the infants inside. Isophie killed the entire transient group easily. She grabbed Violet's arm and pulled her up from the ground. Embarrassed, Violet looked away from Isophie.

"Thank y—"

"Why is the Archangel of emotions hiding behind a fucking trash bin?"

Violet shrugged. "Dude, I tried scanning for emotions, but I only found fear in them; just sheer terror. I couldn't alter their feelings. It's like they're only capable of being afraid. I-I'm powerless against them."

"Oh, for the love of—"

Isophie placed her index and thumb between her lips and blew a loud whistle.

The other Archangels gathered around Violet and Isophie at the alley. The sword wielding punk warrior stepped forward.

"Hey! Hey guys, what the hell are you doing? We got thousands of these fuckers to kill! Why are you holding back? Raphael, you can do better than rock and sock 'em toys!"

Goldie adjusted her black top hat. "I ain't messing up reality, toots! You have me pulling too many big tricks, the universe unravels like a noodle on a lindy hop!" she replied.

Isophie turned to the Black Angel.

"And are you going to keep playing tag with those things? Can't you summon your army of the dead? Come on! There's a cemetery full of bodies a few blocks from here! We could use the manpower!"

Black Angel shook her head in negative. She signed her response.

"What? What are you—"

Violet stepped between Isophie and Black Angel. The little pale girl held the teen angel's hand and hid behind her.

"She says the undead will rise only to fight evil. We're not even sure transients are truly evil and stuff."

Isophie raised both her arms to the air. "People are dying left and right! What other reason do you guys need? I thought we were here to protect humanity!"

"She's being merciful! Just leave her alone, okay?"

Isophie rolled her eyes and turned her attention to Evergreen.

"I suppose you're not calling your predator animals to fight because you don't want to risk them against those transients, right?"

"I don't need to," Evergreen replied.

The sound of loud thunder prompted the angels to look up. Clouds clustered in the sky under the golden ship and became dark gray. Multi-colored lightning showered over thousands of transients. They instantly fell to the ground and convulsed before bursting in flames.

"Now we're talking!" Isophie exclaimed.

Evergreen sauntered by Isophie, bumping her shoulder against hers. She briefly placed her hand on Violet's shoulder.

"Uriel, you do not need to face the transients. Help by evacuating the humans. Keep moving ahead of us to the east and compel them to move to safety. Raphael and Azrael, try to find a way to get into that big spaceship and stop it from releasing more transients. Leave the rest to me."

Evergreen created a wind torrent that lifted her above the ground and transported her away. Only as an afterthought she acknowledged Isophie.

"Do not get in my way."

After the other angels left the alley, Goldie waved Violet goodbye and grabbed Black Angel's hand.

"Come on, toots! Say, we got a mothership to catch! Ever flown on a pig before?"

Violet watched her sisters walk away. The Black Angel stopped and turned to face Violet, her eyes showed immense sadness. Violet gave her a gloomy smile.

"I know…"

. . . .

Yan Fan's consciousness slowly returned as she tried to make sense of her surroundings. She was still inside the transient's body, and she landed in a hole; or rather she made that hole when she impacted the ground. She used the transient's arms to pull herself up from the small crater and stepped up to the edge. Wooden panels, hay stacks, farming tools; Yan was inside a barn. A puncture on the ceiling right over her head confirmed she had fallen through the roof.

"Oh, boy…"

Her voice made a sucking noise, startling her; like she was talking through a breathing mask. The transients didn't speak, but if they could, this was how Yan figured they would sound.

Yan stared at her four-fingered transient hands and tried to picture her own in her mind. She was still unable to depart from the transient body she was trapped in. Frustrated, she walked towards the barn doors and pushed them open. Both doors broke in half as they were hurled several feet away, landing close to an armed farmer and his scared young daughter.

"I'm so sorry, I didn't mean to—"

"Get inside the house! Run!" The farmer yelled at his daughter. He aimed his shotgun at Yan.

The girl screamed and ran into their home, slamming the door behind her. The farmer fired twice. One shot hit Yan in the shoulder. She didn't feel pain, but was shocked to see the shell floating in the plasma of her transient shoulder. The farmer jerked the shaft of his weapon to reload it and Yan found her opening to sprint for the nearby hills.

When Yan reached the other side of the mounds, she had a clear view of a small town teeming with transients. She was stunned to see the destruction left in their wake. Buildings burned as people scattered for their lives. The transients seemed bent on hounding humans just like they did with her back at Dog Shit Mesa's caverns, only more desperately. Anything that stood between them and their target, like a car or a light post, didn't seem to matter to them; they just rammed right through like it didn't exist. But to what purpose? She knew they were not predators. She knew they were not killers. Or were they? If she had been alive back at Hell Part Two and they caught her, what would've happened then? The fact was that her insight on these beings could have been dangerously biased. She also observed that many of the faceless jumped at very high altitudes in and out of the town. The only theory that came to her mind was that this was caused by a difference in gravity from planet Hell Part Two having twelve times mass and density compared to Earth. But studying transients was not a priority at that moment.

Yan Fan entered the town through its main road and saw one of the transients chasing after a bus full of people. She saw the horrified faces of the passengers as it clutched the rear of the moving vehicle and lifted the back a few inches from the ground. The back wheels screeched in unison with screams from the passengers. Some of them in the back seats fell on top of others in the front. A woman held on to her crying boy and shielded him with her body. A man desperately broke a window frame open and tried to escape through it, but he couldn't fit his body through. Yan ran towards the transient and elbowed its head. She held onto it as hard as she could until it released the bus. The bus slammed loud against the street concrete with its back wheels already spinning. As soon as the tires touched pavement the vehicle was off leaving behind tendrils of white smoke.

"I'm not letting you go!" she yelled, keeping her grip tight on the transient. It struggled wildly to get lose and produced an unnatural howl that almost intimidated Yan. She waited until the bus was at a safe distance before releasing the transient. Yan noticed the creature remained quiet and still. It wasn't until a military armored car drove close by, that it renewed its wailing and slipped through Yan's grasp to follow pursuit of the vehicle.

Yan Fan looked around. She scanned the area two blocks over. She didn't recognize any of the street names, but there was an abandoned US postal truck a few feet away from her. She gently opened the rear doors, still getting a handle on her transient strength. She picked up a few packages and read the receiver addresses.

"La Costita, CA…"

She rubbed her transient chin. "Huh! Well, I guess I'm in California."

As Yan stepped away from the truck, she heard several gunshots. Then she noticed several punctures in her right arm and left leg. The sound of gunfire caught her attention. She was being shot at again. Two state policemen emptied their rifles on her, bent on taking their alien enemy down. But again, her transient body did not seem to be hurt by bullets. And she barely acknowledged the ones that lodged into her plasma-based body. She raised her arms and cautiously stepped closer to the law men. Yan could see the horror in their faces.

"Guys, I give up! Stop! I'm here to help!"

The cops stepped back and continued to fire. Several bullets hit Yan's transient body, but only one went through her lower chest and faintly grazed a finger of the dormant infant inside Yan's torso. Yan fell on her back and gripped her chest in pain.

"Gah! That-that hurt! What the—Oh, God! Stop shooting at me! Stop! Stop!"

The policemen kept firing at the possessed transient. They moved in for the kill. One of the cops waived the other to stop and pointed at Yan's lower chest.

"Hold it! Hold it! Look at that! Is that a baby? Is that thing pregnant?"

Yan, took advantage of the ceasefire and scrambled away from the cops. She fell on her back to the ground and panicked as she turned her head to face the policemen. Both cops stared at her frozen with disbelief. She continued crawling until she could stand up and run for safety.

Yan staggered for a few blocks until she reached a narrow bridge that arched over a cove. Once there, she hid underneath it to rest. The pain was unbearable, but even more so was the impossible realization that she was a ghost feeling pain.

"Hello? Miss Fan? Is that you?"

Yan jerked, astonished to realize that someone was calling her on her helmet receiver. It was nice to know that even trapped inside a transient body, the communicator worked. But this wasn't a voice she recognized.

"You're not Blue. Who is this?"

"You sound—"

"I know my voice sounds weird, but trust me, I'm Yan Fan."

"Very well...My name is Ricadel. Zadkiel... Blue; he is my brother."

"I don't understand. Where's Blue?"

"I— You should come to Nebraska. I will send you the address."

"Nebraska? Look lady, if you haven't turned on your TV, we're in the middle of a worldwide crisis here and I can't—"

"Blue is... not well. He needs you."

"I'm in freaking Cali— Just put him on the line, please. I need to talk to him now."

"I'm sorry. I'm so sorry. I can't..."

"I don't understand. What's going on?"

"I'm so sorry. I think— I can feel that Blue is dying. Please, Yan, come fast."

Yan needed a moment. Her mind went blank.

"Dying?"

She did not wait for a reply. Fighting through her physical agony, Yan Fan stood up and resumed her walk.

"Tell Blue to please hold on. Tell him I'm coming."

. . . .

When she arrived at the central district area of New Orleans, Isophie saw thousands of transients filling out the streets in a paralyzed march. Their bodies crammed next to each other and were corralled by skyscrapers. Some of them remained still, others shoved each other while very few jumped high and away from the horde.

"They're moshing…" Isophie said.

The red angel put on her earbuds and closed her eyes as her entire body synchronized to the fast and heavy beats of Metallica's *Battery*. Opening her eyes, she spread her fiery wings wide and allowed the flames to disperse wildly through the streets. She hovered over the transients, flaming sword in hand, followed closely by the engulfing blazes she created. The angelic fires melted through the thick gelatinous skins of hundreds of howling beings. The red angel imparted hardcore judgement over the enemy. Those transients that briefly noticed her, reached out and wailed at her. But that meant nothing to her. To Isophie, they were just roaches and she was the pesticide. She zoned out as her lips unconsciously trailed the lyrics of the song.

"Lashing out the action, returning the reaction. Weak are ripped and torn away…"

Rumbling noises caught Isophie's attention. She saw her sister Evergreen at a distance, also soaring over the transients. Evergreen created contained quakes that cracked open the ground, swallowing transients by large clusters.

"We keep this up, we won't need those other losers to finish the job," Isophie yelled to her.

She followed Evergreen as the Archangel of nature descended on the roof top of a deserted hotel. Isophie stepped close to a corner to watch the transient masses below. She could tell her sister was about to get judgmental.

"Why do you belittle our siblings?" Evergreen asked.

Isophie took off her earbuds and stood closer to Evergreen.

"What?"

"Why do you deride them?"

"Because they're stupid and I've got no patience for stupid. Their minds are still playing harps and eating fruits in the aerial gardens of Heaven while evildoers shit on us here on Earth. For thousands of years, we fight to keep these fucking days of end at bay. If we fail only once, just once, Lucifer wins and the world gets fucked sideways to hell."

Isophie gestured mockingly. "But, noooo! they only see the best in humanity, the best in the universe, the best in God. And wouldn't you fucking know, we get betrayed by all three at every fucking opportunity. They choose to live blindly to that fact, living in la la fucking land…"

Evergreen shook her head.

"Then let them. Encourage them. They cannot lose hope, Isophie. We need them to keep the faith. We are constantly forced to make impossible decisions that forever mark us. You can make those hard decisions because you see the world differently from them. But I know that, like me, you also believe in the idea of the Seven Lights, in the hope we represent. It is that hope that you and I sometimes forget, and the others remind us of. Be ready. If you are to lead the Archangels, be ready to save them."

Isophie hung her head and scratched the back of her neck. "Look, sis, I got a band. I don't have time to babysit the catechism club."

"You must protect them when I am gone, Isophie, from everything and everyone," Evergreen said. "And when the time comes for me to join Lucifer… I fear you may also have to protect them from me."

Isophie scratched the concrete with her sword. "Well, then why don't I just kill you now and save everyone the hassle?"

Evergreen glanced at her. Isophie held her forehead and made some distance between them.

"Fuck me! Sorry, babe, okay? I didn't mean —"

She knew Evergreen was still staring at her. She stopped and turned to face her.

"Look, I hear what you're saying. Fine. Fine! Let's just table this fun conversation for now and get back to kicking alien ass."

"Fine," Evergreen replied.

Isophie put hear earbuds back on and lit up her sword and wings. She jumped from the ledge and glided down to attack the transients.

"Fine."

. . . .

The angel of death rode on the back of a flying pig that left a rainbow trail coming out of its anus. Her sister Goldie was riding shotgun. The Black Angel stared at her sister's long blonde locks and could not remember a time she was ever sad in her presence, the miracle maker. The angels of the Pax Dei, and even some of her Archangel siblings regarded Goldie as a liability. The ability to weave the threads of reality— that is to say, the laws of physics, was a highly volatile ministry to be guarded by an angel that behaved like an A.D.D. riddled artist. They were afraid that she could become as dangerous as the first Archangel that held the ministry of miracles before her. But the Black Angel saw something different in Goldie. She saw someone in love with Creation and not afraid to make a spectacle of it. She wrapped her arms around Goldie's stomach and held on to her tight, trusting that her older sister would take her on another fun adventure. This was her show now.

Goldie turned her head to speak.

"We just need to find the cockpit, see?" She winked proudly and tapped her long black top hat with her index finger. "Every ship has to have a cockpit. That's how we crash the party. Trust me, kid. These wise guys ain't gonna see what hit'em!"

The winged swine carrying the two angels flew upwards and zigzagged to avoid falling transients from the sky. One incoming faceless grabbed on to the pig and began to pull it down with its weight. The hog squealed and instinctively tilted to its side, trying to get lose from the transient's grip.

"Whoa, Nelly!" Goldie exclaimed.

The Archangel of miracles took off her hat and aimed its hole at the faceless being. A boxing glove popped out from the hat and hit the transient on its head, forcing the translucent being to lose its grip on the pig and fall. The flying pig veered just in time to avoid being dragged down and rose even higher into the clouds. Both Archangels were awed to finally see the enormous size of the golden starship as it hummed quietly in the air. The angels on the winged hog swept its endless surface, trying to find a way in.

"This is nuts!" Goldie complained. "How's ya get ta fly a plane without lookin' where ya goin'? Gotta be a cockpit somewhere!"

Black Angel tapped her sister's back to get her attention and pointed at a section they had missed. It was a glass covered viewpoint at the west side of the ship.

"Aha! Hold on, sistah!"

The winged pig dived straight towards the glass walled platform and crashed through it. Both angels were propelled forward and landed on a corridor.

Goldie stood up from the floor, wiped imaginary dust from her shoulder and fixed her hat straight.

"Easy peasy! Say, that was a juicy piece o' lemon merengue, wasn't it?"

She turned to realize she was speaking to the wind. The Black Angel was nowhere to be found. There were only broken pieces of glass on a rather plain and empty corridor.

"Hey, toots! Where'd ya go?"

Goldie tiptoed further into the hallway faking a scared look on her face, like a classic Scooby-Doo haunted house scene.

"Well, Alice, into the hole ya go! One of these days… Pow! Right in the kisser! Wait. Think I got my Alices confused…"

The angel was blinded by a bright flash of golden light coming from the hallway doors. When she opened her eyes again, she was at a park. There were many cafés with outside tables. The Eiffel Tower loomed in the distance. She saw a crowd of people running towards her in panic. They were followed by a horde of transients that destroyed kiosks and tables and everything in their paths to get them. One of the transients caught a little girl with one hand. Her mother screamed terrified. She picked up a fallen tree branch and hit it repeatedly. The transient released a loud static shriek at her. Goldie ran towards the transient, pulling up her sleeves and thinking of the right trick to pull out of her hat.

"Never fear! Goldie's—"

The golden angel was now in India. The streets of New Delhi were overrun by transients. People were being trampled as they fled to escape the invasion. Buildings crumbled, impacted by transients falling from the sky.

"Here?"

Goldie saw a transient at the top of the Gurudwara Bangla Sahib Temple. It tore off and lifted one of its golden cupulas.

"Hey! You put that down!"

The Archangel of miracles reacted to a scream she heard from behind. She spun and realized she was at a large city plaza in Beijing. The sound of gunfire and unearthly wails mixed as the Chinese army battled waves of incoming transients.

Goldie had enough. "Look here! This ain't the time to play Guess Where! Fun as that game is you better make up your mind, see! Whoever you are!"

A male voice spoke inside Goldie's head.

"You're one to appreciate a good show. Italy, Japan, Zimbawe, New Zealand, Irak, Chile… Live. The world. Invaded."

Goldie was back at the corridor of the starship. She saw Lucifer in mid transformation. Below his chest, he was a golden butterfly-winged fish-tailed transient. His face, shoulders, and arms looked human. Lucifer held up an unconscious Black Angel from the back of her shirt. She hung like a flaccid puppet from his hand. The angel of miracles posed her legs one in front of the other and waived her fists at Lucifer like a vintage boxer.

"You! Why I oughta…Why don'tcha pick on someone your own size? Put'em up!"

"Right," Lucifer smiled. "You're too much of a wild card, Raphael. I can't have you running around playing at your little miracles."

The Morning Star's body froze and then appeared behind Goldie. He tapped the back of her head once with his index finger. Goldie's mind became bleary. She felt like a cloud overpowered her thoughts.

"Whuh-Whatchu do to my head?"

"A touch of Ritalin..." Lucifer whispered to her before returning to his body that stood still a few feet away. He threw the Black Angel's body at Goldie's feet and turned his back to her as he fluttered his wings and slowly moved away.

"You've already lost. Get out of my sight. –Mother..."

The walls around Goldie wrapped around her and the Black Angel, trapping them in a circular shaped jail. A hoarse robotic voice spoke. "Initiating saucer launch in T-minus 10."

Goldie knelt and gently lifted the back of the Black Angel's head. She fought her confusion while she touched the Black Angel's face with her gloved fingers.

"Hey, darling... wake up. Time to... time to skedaddle."

The Black Angel remained limp in her arms.

"Toots, you okay? Wake up... There-there ain't no death angel coming for ya... That's your job..."

Goldie felt groggy, but she could still discern that the pod she and the Black Angel were in was moving.

"Saaay...Where are we going?"

"Destination: 238,900 miles from Earth's atmosphere. The Moon," the robotic voice replied.

"Whoa, mama... Turn back. Turn back!"

"Unable to comply."

"I can fix this... I can..."

Tired, Goldie sat on the floor. She rested the Black Angel's head on her lap and played with her hair.

"Bang... Zoom... You're going to da moon... Heh. Looks like... got my Alices right after all..."

. . . .

It was almost midnight when Yan Fan left the bridge after feeling somewhat better from her injury. She walked across a highway that led to the desert. There were a few abandoned cars on the side of the road with several craters and downed light posts left by passing transients long gone. She kept her pace as fast as she could. Even though it was only the child's finger that got nicked, the pain made it hard for Yan to concentrate on the task at hand.

"I'll never get to him on time..." she lamented.

Yan found a green jeep with its engine running and emergency brake on. She decided to try her luck. To fit in, she needed to tear off both the driver and passenger's seat. She got in the car and sat on the backseat. Yan felt ridiculously big for the car, like a clown driving a tricycle, but her arms easily reached the dash which is all that she needed. Gently, she took the break off and turned the steering wheel towards the middle of the high way. The jeep moved forward a few feet on its own decelerating almost to a halt. Yan slowly stepped on the accelerator, but her foot broke through the pedal and the floor. The jeep accelerated to 69 miles in seconds. Yan couldn't pull up her foot, and her other leg didn't fit, making it impossible to press the brake. She tried to get a hold of the steering wheel, but her fingers were too big. Yan yanked the emergency brake, but it broke, and the jeep kept speeding up directionless. The vehicle veered out of the road and sped towards a canyon cliff. It dove, dragging Yan with it. She screamed all the way down the high drop as the sharp rock-fill at the bottom quickly moved closer to her.

"Shit! Shit! Shit!"

The vehicle exploded upon impact. Yan's body was fired from the blast and landed several feet away from the fire. Her torso felt like it was about to burst open. She lay on her back and rested on the desert dirt, trying to think of other ways to get faster to Blue. As she watched the stars directly on top of her, hundreds of transients rained down in the horizon. At that moment, another transient flew over her in an arched trajectory. Yan sat up and saw the transient farther away in the distance. She stood up. The pain reminded her that she may not recover if the crazy idea she was about to try failed.

"I hear you, baby. But if he jumped, why can't I?" she said to the infant inside her.

Yan jogged slowly first, but then she accelerated her speed. She ran straight towards the canyon hill and hopped a few times before she sprung high. Shot upwards, she felt the same thrill and trepidation as riding a roller coaster. Gravity pulled her back down and she impacted the ground hard, chest down. She felt a jolt of pain from the injured child inside her, but it wasn't as agonizing as what she thought it would be. The rest of her body was fine.

"This is fine… We can take it. Right, champ?"

She looked behind her and saw the canyon hill she jumped about a mile back.

"Oh, damn! That-that wasn't bad at all. Okay, gotta stick those landings better…"

Yan stood up and ran to jump again. The second time, she landed even farther, but on her butt, instead of her feet.

"Haha! Hurt even less this time. Only my dignity. Progress…"

Yan went for a third jump. She wanted to time her leap and subsequent fall better, aiming to land on her feet. She focused on keeping her legs bent, knees close to her chest. Only when she felt her body being pulled, she extended her legs and opened them a bit to get some balance. When she impacted the desert ground many miles away, her legs stabbed the dirt and got buried up to her knees.

"Hoo! Good. Good."

Yan dug her limbs out of the hole and continued to jump-travel at great speeds. At one point, she managed to do it without having to run to get momentum. She stopped at the top of a hill and stared at the horizon.

"I'm pretty sure east is this way…"

11 CATCHING ICARUS

Leo woke up among bedsheets warmed by the mid-day sun rays. He stretched his arms and realized he was alone in bed. The young black-bearded Italian looked around his studio. It was a mess of browns and creams between unfinished canvases, scattered tomes, and rolled up scrolls. As he shifted his sight towards the room's window frame, a naked blonde male smiled back at him.

"Those are for you," said the blonde male, pointing at a dark grey leathery mask with thick golden goggles. "They will help you with your work."

Leo grabbed the mask and put it on. He noticed that everything he looked at through the lenses appeared closer than it really was, like looking through a telescope. He rotated the lenses clockwise and things got bigger and blurry. He rotated counter-clockwise and things looked farther away. He also tried other settings on the lenses, including one that absorbed the light in the room and made it dark as night.

"Angelo, it is not my birthday today," Leo said.

"I know. I wanted to give you something to remember me by. We've had quite a time you and I, but I'm getting busy and won't be able to see you as often. Things are moving faster now because of people like you. And I for one am glad that we are finally getting some progress."

"You give me too much credit, sir," Leo replied, smiling back at his blonde companion. "It was bound to happen eventually."

"Not without people like you… This was fun, Leo. I will miss you."

Leo jumped out of bed, put on a burgundy robe, and pulled Angelo by the arm. "Wait. Before you leave. Let me show you something I've been working on."

He dragged a stool next to his work table and sat the Angelo there. Scrambling through his scrolls, he spread one open across the table. Angelo leaned forward eye-wide at penciled designs of mechanical wings. The bottom sections of the wings were curved between pointy edges giving them a bat-shaped aspect. The designs were riddled with ruler traced lines and scribbled notes.

"I've been praying on the idea. It is one of those things that come to me in a feverish dream," said Leo. "I'm very sure I could make them work."

"Oh, those look ghastly!" Angelo said with admiration. "But please don't tell me you are planning to give yourself wings."

"Me and everyone in the world who ever dreamed to be closer to the sun."

Angelo smiled. "That is an amazing thought… Ancient Greece is new again… But, too close to the sun— those are too many people for me to catch when their wings sear."

"Who says we'll need you to catch us? My wings will resist anything the devil throws at them. Besides, I am sure you have already traveled a thousand times to the sun. So, who catches you when you fall?"

Angelo stood behind Leo and wrapped his arms around him. "I do not need catching, Leo."

Leo stood up, releasing himself from Angelo's embrace and quickly rolling up his scroll.

"But men do. Is that it? We are just bumbling babies to you. Sometimes I wonder why I even bother…"

"No, no, no. You don't get to judge, signore! We are merely coming out of 1,000 years of pure repressive and superstitious darkness! Yes, I am angry at humanity, but don't think for a second that I don't see what you are doing and how important it is. Here, let me look at it again."

Leo unrolled the scroll again. He picked up another scroll from a pile and opened it. An illustration of a human male with his limbs stretched out was revealed. The masculine image had a harness wrapping his chest like an X, and the same bat-shaped wings from the other scroll spread behind his back. Leo pointed at the figure's harness.

"The way eludes me to make the wings incline for course alteration without having to pull a damn chord like a sail. If I could somehow use the harness... That would leave the flyer's hands free..."

"Well, that's easy. Just install a po—"

Leo raised his index finger. "Hush! Not another word. I will figure it out myself. You will see. I will finish my wings and when you least expect it, I will catch up to you," Leo paused. "It is not good for you to spend an eternity alone in the stars. Someday you and I will fly side by side."

Angelo nodded and hugged Leo tightly. "I have no doubt that we will, my friend. Godspeed, Leo."

"Angelo, as a last request from one that will miss you immensely for the rest of his bumbling existence... May I see them?"

As the room ignited before a squinting Leo, the black-bearded inventor quickly put his goggle mask back on and adjusted the settings. Angelo stood in front of him, his two long luminous wings spreading and flapping. Leo stepped closer and tried to touch them, but he felt nothing as his fingers went right through the wings.

"I have never seen light flutter. I hope to do it justice when I paint it."

"Why do you enjoy calling me Angelo? Would you care for me calling you Umano? You know my name."

"I know your name." Leo smiled. "We will speak again in my prayers..."

The light of the blonde angel's wings shone increasingly brighter, making his silhouette fade into an encompassing blinding flash. Leo woke up among bedsheets warmed by the mid-day sun rays. He stretched his arms and realized he was alone in bed.

"Blu."

This was Florence, Italy. April of 1476.

. . . .

A few days before the transient invasion began, the Black Angel barely caught an echo of Blue's faint prayer calling for help. After sending for all of her sisters, they all came to his aid as he lied almost dead on the ground by the creek in the middle of nowhere. The grasslands of Nebraska were deserted for miles. Not many transients fell from the skies in that area as their attacks seemed focused at the more populated cities. That was one of the reasons why the Archangel Ricadel decided not to move her fatally injured brother from where he was found.

To make Blue comfortable, Goldie reached into her top hat and pulled out a big cloth bag full of toys she kept from one of her previous crazy Christmas capers. She browsed through the toys and took out a small Fisher Price hospital set that she blew up to a life-size structure. It was a two-storied square-shaped plastic building painted in solid bright colors and a red cross displayed over the front door. A small inscription on the lower right side of the wall read: *Ages 3-8*. There were two large hinges that divided the lateral wall and if opened, they could divide the hospital in half. Its roof had a chimney from which giant soap bubbles floated high in the air before bursting. Once inside, Goldie made some of the fake medical furniture and equipment real, including the bed where they laid Blue.

As the other Archangels departed to protect the world from the alien invasion, Ricadel stayed and attended to her sibling. She was frustrated at herself for not being able to do more; healing angels seemed to be one of the most difficult sacred disciplines to master. The glowing white angel sat beside her brother tending to fevers and wrapping him up with anything she had in hand to keep his angelic essence from ebbing away from his body. She scanned his bandaged face and neck, double checking there were no remnants of dried blood that may have been left unwiped. Feeling helpless to do more, she held his hand and rested her forehead close to his belly.

"Brother, what am I not doing? Why will you not wake up?"

At sunrise, Ricadel heard a loud thump noise that came from outside the hospital. She stepped outside and was astounded to see a transient digging its half-buried body out of a hole in the ground. The transient turned and froze when it saw Ricadel. It reached out its four-fingered hand and emitted a loud sucking sound.

"I do not wish to hurt you. There can be peace between us," Ricadel said.

The transient produced its echoing roar again, but this time Ricadel realized that she could discern most of its words.

"That's nice to hear," the transient said. "But I said, can you give me a hand here, please?"

"Are you Yan Fan?"

"Hi. You must be Ricadel. I like your dress. Just grab my hand and pull. I can do the rest."

Ricadel moved closer to Yan and cautiously tugged her arm. Yan heaved her transient body and freed her lower body from the hole she was in. She stood up straight and looked down at an amazed Ricadel. The angel was stunned and a bit intimidated at Yan's size. She studied the transient's physique, focusing her attention at the crying infant inside Yan's torso.

"The infant you carry... It's hurting."

"Yeah, we got shot by cops. Long story."

"We?"

"Well, it's me here sharing this body with Boy George. I'm kind of possessing him? I just can't manage to get out. But I can feel him upset and afraid."

"Boy George?"

"I like Boy George. Karma Chameleon is such a great song."

Ricadel looked confused.

Yan sighed. "Listen, everybody needs a name."

Ricadel nodded and smiled. She turned her attention to the suffering infant and stepped closer to it as she briefly scratched her chin.

"If you allow it, I would like to try to heal... Boy George."

"Really? Uh, sure. Can you do that?"

Ricadel touched Yan's lower chest, concentrating her white glow on the infant's nicked finger.

"I am the Archangel of life, the divine healer," she said. "I don't know if I'll succeed, but I owe this poor creature to at least try."

Ricadel's light beamed from her hand and sheltered the baby. Its finger wound quickly disappeared. The Archangel of life noticed that even though the infant was still frightened, it became less agitated.

"How was that?" Ricadel asked.

"Wow... The pain is gone! Thanks."

Ricadel stepped back and smiled. "I am so glad that I could help! It is such a blessing to know that my ministry extends to beings from other galaxies!"

Yan glanced at the hospital in front of her with curiosity.

"Um, why am I seeing giant bubbles coming out of the roof?"

"My sister Goldie grew the hospital out of a Fisher Price toy set."

Yan shook her head.

"Sure. That makes sense, I think? Anyway, Ricadel, what happened to Blue? Is he inside?"

"He-he was attacked. We think it was Lucifer."

"Lucifer? Like, the devil, Lucifer?"

"Yes. We think he stole my brother's spaceship."

"What? Why would the devil steal Matilda? How could he even—"

135

Ricadel's voice lowered. "He— he tore off my brother's jawbone."

"Oh, my God! I need to see him!"

Yan stepped fast towards the hospital entrance.

"Please, wait," Ricadel pleaded. "I do not think it wise for him to see you as a transient."

Yan glanced down at her body.

"You're right. You're right. Can't you— I don't know– exorcise me?"

"I have only been an Archangel for a little more than a year. I still have much to learn. I'm afraid there is not much I've been able to do for my brother or my other siblings."

"What about the other Archangels? Could they help me?"

"They are trying to stop the invasion as we speak. But we are all out of our element here. I do not think we can succeed without Zadkiel's unique insight. I was hoping that if he heard your voice, the voice of a friend…"

"I get it…Okay, we need to try to get me out of Boy George. Maybe you can try that light thing you did again. I have an idea…"

"It is the sacramental heal… I am not sure how that would help."

"The problem I have is that in sharing this body with another consciousness, I can't focus to separate myself from him. But maybe if you use your light on the baby, that will calm him long enough for me to hear my thoughts."

"I see," Ricadel said as she began to kindle her hand with white light.

"Hold on," Yan said. "If this works, we need to figure out how to contain him. We don't want him to destroy this place…"

"Do not worry about the hospital. I will try to keep Boy George calm after you leave. If it doesn't work, I will lead him away from here. I am more concerned with his wellbeing. Will leaving his body cause pain to Boy George?"

"I honestly don't know. I've only possessed another body before and it was a dead baby."

Ricadel covered her mouth. "Oh, dear!"

"It was an accident. I didn't even know I could do that when it happened. But, I agree with you. I don't want Boy George to suffer on my account. If this affects him, we'll definitely need to find another way to do it."

Ricadel held Yan's huge transient hand and inhaled deeply.

"You are a brave soul, Yan Fan. As soon as you are released, head straight to the second floor. My brother is there."

"Sounds like a plan," Yan said before looking at the infant inside her torso. "Ready, Boy? Don't be scared. We'll be with you all the way. Here we go…"

Ricadel lit up both her hands in bright white light and touched the transient's torso. Yan concentrated and pictured her human hands instead of transient. The thought became clearer in her mind until she felt it was real. She heard distant murmurs that quickly became louder and discernible. The transient was wailing and Ricadel was shouting at her.

"Boy George is in agony! You cannot stop now! Push through!"

Yan was being shaken in all directions and her vision blurred. It was hard for her to assess her situation. She looked at her hands and they were human, gloved by her space suit. The process was working. But as she lowered her eyes, she realized her ghost body was only halfway out and everything below her hips was still inside Boy George. She assumed the transient was moving erratically from side to side to shake her off.

"Jesus!" Yan exclaimed.

She saw that Ricadel tried to reach and touch Boy George with her healing light, but the transient moved too fast for her. It was up to Yan to finish releasing herself. She closed her eyes and focused, struggling to block Boy George's loud inhuman cries.

Little by little, she felt Boy George's shifting slow down. She opened her eyes and saw that her entire body was free, hovering above the transient. Yan observed him as he staggered aimlessly for a moment and then stopped. He remained still underneath her, reaching out to her. But instead of emitting loud noises, Yan caught new soft honking sounds she'd never heard before from any transient. She turned to face Ricadel.

"I think it —"

Yan flashed out of existence.

. . . .

Spending time with Leo was the dream that Blue didn't want to wake up from. He didn't know why, but it was the memory replaying in his mind that he came back to with looping ease. He felt safe in that bed with that genius man bombarding him with brilliant visions of a technological future in a time when the old world had yet to officially meet the new.

I don't know where I am.

I don't know if we'll ever see each other again...

Blue was somewhat aware, because angels don't really sleep. He could hear Yan Fan calling to him from across the universe. She needed him. But he didn't dare to open his eyes. That meant he'd have to acknowledge that Lucifer had taken his most precious creation, Matilda; and the devil would most likely use his ship to harm his friend Yan Fan. She was in grave danger, and so were an entire species of transients. Whatever it was that Lucifer truly wanted, it would only end in the deaths of millions. There was nothing Blue could do in time to stop it.

In the briefness between the dream repeating in his mind, Blue felt his essence fading. Maybe it was better if he let it. Maybe someone else could take over his ministry; someone with a fresh perspective. Maybe Lucifer was right. After all, what had Blue really accomplished? Garbage to keep the masses stupid, as Lucifer put it. Earth was not a world where technology and science were used by people to help each other. It was a planet of lazy addicts connected 24/7 to digital rocks that fed constant pornography and social hatred; advanced weaponry easily accessible in the streets while healing medication was denied to the needful ill; a place that chose convenient misinformation even in the face of environmental collapse. No matter how many timetables Blue kept or how many steps ahead he planned... Did he ever truly make a single difference to humanity?

Maybe Lucifer was right...

I begged the universe to help me. I asked to be granted just a few more seconds. Just a few more seconds...

...I saw someone. I yelled your name. But the closer I got, the better I was able to see this luminous being. It became clear to me that it was not you.

This was the world that Blue was leaving behind by just dreaming of the past and of what could have been. It was the dream of Leo, the man who flew by Blue's side, beyond the farthest stars; remaking the universe, out in the utmost reaches of his mind. Blue opted to anchor himself in that memory, as the alternative would drag him down to his nightmarish reality. Lucifer's hand on his jaw; pulling, tearing away. Why wake up to that? Why wake up to a permanent reminder of how easily he was broken?

Prayer was not an option to Blue, not anymore. Why try to ask God for enlightenment when he couldn't even trust what God wanted for Creation? At the moment when Blue was at his lowest, he did pray, but not to God. When he was left for dead by Lucifer, he uttered a weak and incomplete plea to his sisters before losing consciousness. Now, his only wish in that second between replaying dreams was for that prayer to go unheard. He could keep his eyes closed and continue pretending that he had already died.

I'm at a loss here. I don't know what to do. I'm praying to you, Blue... Where are you?

Maybe Lucifer was right...But what about Yan?

. . . .

Yan Fan was relieved to once again move freely in her spectral form. No gravity, no lack of depth perception, no physical pain; it was a silence of senses that she welcomed after more than thirty years of taking it for granted. But as she entered the hospital's cheerfully primary colored painted recovery room, the sight of Blue devastated her. He lay face up on his bed. His face above the upper lip was dead pale white, and two deep black holes replaced his eyes. Bandages covered from below his teeth to his upper chest. Yan could see small fragments of bright blue energy slowly slipping from the angel through his bindings and dissipating in the air like fading flames.

The astronaut ghost approached the dying Archangel. She remained quiet for a while, trying to find the right words to say to her friend. But those words never came, and she felt her time to brainstorm was up.

"Hey. I'm here. And here is… We're inside a Fisher Price set. Ha! I used to have the boat. It was a yacht with the little lifeboat on the side. I had a captain and a mariner and the girl with the blonde ponytail. Oh, and the dog. Well, they always included the dog in most of those sets…"

Yan paused. She still struggled to see Blue's current state. "You know, the transients are here, too. Not getting along with humans. They're acting strange. I swear this is not like them. I can feel it. We need to find a way to talk with them. Figure out why they've changed. I think that golden transient from the ship is controlling them. I don't know, he's— Sorry. Yeah, there's a golden transient, too. He's different. He speaks and, man, he knew my name… He scared the shit out of me. We need to do something, Blue. I get that your family has to protect the world, but they're killing them. We have to help them. We need to get Matilda back; get them off the planet…"

Yan swallowed hard. "Blue, please wake up. I need you."

She felt Ricadel's warm light as the white angel stood behind her.

"He looks…" Yan couldn't bring herself to finish the thought.

"We must keep the faith," Ricadel said. "Are you alright? You disappeared momentarily when you left the transient's body."

"I'm fine," Yan replied unconvincingly. "I don't have time to deal with that now. Is Boy George okay?"

"He is standing immobile outside. I concealed myself from him, so I do not think he saw us."

"Hmm. We need to make sure he doesn't go off after an airplane or whatever. I feel we're going to need him to figure out this transient invasion."

"I will watch him. Please stay with my brother," Ricadel said. "I will return soon."

The room became a bit darker after Ricadel left.

. . . .

Yan could swear she noticed Blue's index finger pulsating. Or maybe she was mistaken. A few hours had passed since she arrived and stayed with Blue. The sun was setting.

"I'm sorry. I have to go now and try to stop this insanity. I'll be back for you. Just promise you'll pull through. I'll find a way to—"

Yan caught Blue's finger moving faster.

"Wait. Is that just a reflex or are you awake?" Yan took a closer look at his twitching hand and then moved away. "Hold on! Stay right there! I'll be right back!"

The astronaut ghost phased down through the floor of the room and into the first level of the plastic building. She searched everywhere until found Blue's armor inside a big blue chest. When she saw the wrecked wrist panel, she realized a new control pad was needed. Yan opened the bag of toys left by Goldie and, after scanning through them, she took a small red farm animal themed laptop. She phased the objects back to the room. Yan opened a small plate at the back of the suit and was taken aback by all the ports and screens that were way ahead of her time.

"Okay, okay... This is definitely not like installing cable. How do I do this?"

Yan picked up the laptop and held it close to the ports to see if one of them matched the output. A blue laser beamed from Blue's armor and scanned the laptop. Two thin wires came out of the back plate and latched onto the toy computer. The armor immediately projected a holo-screen

141

above Yan and Blue. Yan pressed the letter A and the screen displayed an A.

"Oh! Well, there's that way…"

Yan opened the red laptop and placed it on Blue's belly, making sure it was in his view. Then, she gently put his hand over the keyboard.

"Here. Use this. Not the big square keys, those are farm animal sounds. Use the letters."

Yan waited. After a while, she heard three faint sounds. Tap, tap, tap. Three letters appeared on the holo-screen.

yan

She quickly turned to lock eyes with Blue. His light cobalt eyes were open and teary, almost lost in the blackness under his temple as they fixed on his ghostly astronaut friend. Her soul raced. Ashamed, Blue turned his look away from Yan. His fingers tapped the keys.

you prayed to me

heard you

too afraid

couldnt save you

couldnt

Yan hovered closer to get Blue's attention.

"Blue. Blue, it's okay. Yes, I was scared shitless and there were times I ached for you to come for me, but… turns out I did okay by myself. I mean, for a while there, everything was a whole mess of crazy planetary-scale geological destruction and horrific alien abduction with a side of body snatching and mob lynching— God, so many people with guns! — but somehow I made it. I'm here."

cant save transients

142

cant fight lucifer

he will win

"No, he won't. You want to know how I'm sure? Because Ricadel said he stole Matilda from you. This guy needed a ship and he couldn't build one for himself. That tells me he's not that smart. We're going to win this, Blue, because you got science on your side. And me!"

Blue's eyes widened. Yan imagined that if he had a mouth, he'd be laughing.

"What do you say, Blue? You and me." Yan said, pointing at the side of her forehead. "All the answers in the universe are right here in our noggins. We just need to find them. Together."

Yan heard Blue's key strokes.

we fly side by side

She smiled for both of them.

"I like that... Now, let's get you up from that bed, my friend. We got work to do."

Blue pressed a key. Yan heard a sound.

"Moo!"

12 SOUNDS OF SCIENCE

just a bandaid

need to work on something permanent

dont burn the rotor mast

need that

"Brother, please stay still and be quiet. You are distracting me," Ricadel said.

Yan Fan observed as Ricadel, following Blue's instructions, replaced his bandages with an improvised prosthetic for his missing throat and jaw. She soldered plastic parts of a melted toy helicopter to a thin aluminum panel they took from the back of Blue's armor leg. The smooth metal sheet covered the injury, but allowed for very little lateral mobility. The toy copter's landing skids were placed at the sides of his neck to serve as support, like a brace. After Blue had Ricadel tinker with the small propeller, adding some wiring they took from his suit, he had it placed on the metal plate over his throat area. He switched it on and it rotated, making a weak sucking sound. He turned it off.

"What's that for?" Yan asked.

Blue typed on his toy laptop using two, sometimes three of his fingers. The words augmented in projected holo-screens.

crazy idea

for later

Using her sacramental heal, Ricadel sealed the implant to his skin to stop his angelic essence from leaking. This allowed him to recover faster in the last couple of days, although Yan knew he was still far from being his old self again.

how do i look?

Yan tilted her head.

"I'd say you look quite handsome," she replied. "I bet there's a few super models that would kill for a long neck like yours."

"I agree," Ricadel spoke. "You remind me of an ostrich, or the letter 'P'."

Yan shook her head. Blue stared at Ricadel.

"What? I very much enjoy ostriches and the letter 'P'!"

The ghost and the glowing white angel waited for Blue at the level below while he finished putting on his space armor, which he insisted on doing alone. Yan's attention shifted to Ricadel, who sat on a yellow toy chair across the room. The angel stared through the small square window from time to time, keeping an eye on Boy George outside. Yan approached Ricadel and peeked through the window.

"If you stare at him from far away, he kind of looks like a doll, doesn't he? Our adorable ten-feet-tall doll."

"Oh, he is bigger than that," Ricadel replied. "He is at least twelve feet tall."

Yan took a closer look.

"That can't be. I measured a bunch of them back at Hell Part Two. They were all exactly ten feet tall. Unless…"

Ricadel stared at her attentive. Yan felt a bit pressured to come up with a scientific explanation.

"Maybe the atmosphere or the lighter gravity on this planet is making them grow? No, that can't be right."

Yan kept ruminating, but anticipated that her train of thought wouldn't lead her anywhere productive. It was a feeling she abhorred and there was no effective way to fight it except to file her query for another time.

She was also distracted by Ricadel's belly area. The Archangel's radiant white garment looked as beautiful and regal as a wedding gown from a fantasy tale. She would've been a perfect vision if not for a huge uneven hole in the middle of her stomach. It appeared to be an old wound judging by the scabs and dried blood stains on the dress. A fist could easily fit in there, maybe two. How weird would it be ramming both fists into her belly, she thought.

"You can ask, Yan Fan," Ricadel said. "I can see that you want to."

"I'm sorry. I shouldn't have stared."

"You are wondering how I am still alive with such a lethal gap in my body. It is not an injury. At least not anymore. It is a marking, a reminder I have deliberately kept."

Yan moved closer to Ricadel as the angel continued.

"Many years ago, before I was an angel, I had a different purpose to fulfill. I was in love and dedicated to a man, my husband, and a woman, my sister. They betrayed me. She made sure to let me know how much better they were for each other and how irrelevant I was to their lives and to God's divine plan... before she tried to kill me."

"Oh, no! I'm so sorry!"

Ricadel gave Yan a sympathetic smile.

"I managed to hide from them both, and in my seclusion, I realized I was not alone. I felt life's miracle inside of me. I was scared at first, but then, at least for a brief time, I was truly happy. That was until Lucifer appeared to me and tried to tempt me. In exchange for my baby, he offered me revenge and power. I did not accept, of course. Lucifer could not understand that the only thing I truly wanted was to be my child's mother. There was nothing in the universe I would have ever traded for that. But as you already have seen with Zadkiel, what Lucifer cannot get, he takes..."

Ricadel's breathing increased slightly.

"He—he ripped my child from the womb and left me to die...To this day, I do not know what became of my baby. I do not even know if it was a boy or a girl."

"Wait, Lucifer took your baby? Jesus, Mary, and Joseph! What is wrong with this guy? But why would he—"

"I do not know. In the short time I have been an angel of the Seven Lights, I have grown to love all my siblings. They are my family. And to see all that Lucifer has done to hurt us... What he did to Evergreen, to Blue... to me..."

Ricadel clenched her fist, her eyes were absorbed, but they no longer stared at Yan.

"As our days of end go by, we angels may forget ourselves in battle. This wound is a reminder that until I learn the fate that befell my child, I will never be complete."

The angel stared again through the window. Yan knew she was looking directly at the baby inside Boy George. She noticed Ricadel's hands were trembling and concentrated to make her ghostly hand touch Ricadel's if only for a moment. Ricadel lowered her eyes.

"I am the Archangel of life. My ministry is the merciful essence of Creation itself. I take so much joy in caring for all living things. But Yan, I sometimes think of him and I just... All I want is to murder him."

Yan Fan didn't know how to respond. She touched Ricadel's hand until hers slowly became intangible again. Yan supposed that a tattoo would've probably made a healthier choice for a physical reminder than keeping an open stomach wound the size of a grapefruit. She also didn't quite understand what Ricadel meant by the phrase 'days of end', but she thought it best not to ask her and just be there for her. It pained Yan to see so much sorrow coming from a being that optimistic and cheerful. She stayed with her for a while. The irony of a ghost watching over an angel didn't escape her.

After some time passed, Yan floated upwards towards the ceiling, to cross through it.

"I should check up on Blue."

. . . .

As Yan reared her head through the second floor, she heard a jumbling of voices. Blue sat on his plastic bed, cushioned with large soft pillows and stuffed animals. He watched dozens of news channels broadcasting the coming of the alien starship and transient attacks all over the world.

"Blue, are you okay?"

Blue muted the volume on all channels.

thats matilda

he frankesteined matilda

"What are you talking about?

know her design

built her

thats her

or was

"But she looks so big! And the golden transient—"

you said he had black eyes and white iris

lucifer

"Hold on. Lucifer is a transient?"

no

one of many faces

when he beat me

said he needed to change forms

maybe to control transients

"Okay, he attacked you specifically to steal Matilda and bring the transients to Earth; part of his evil masterplan to kill us all or whatever. But how did he even know that transients existed in the first place? Not even the Archangels knew before you and I discovered them, right?"

dont know

"Right. I guess we'll have to ask him ourselves when we get Matilda back."

you dont understand

a change that significant

mustve altered main frame

no way to fix her

matilda is dead

Yan hovered closer to Blue. He kept watching the muted holo-screen streaming of the invasion.

"Do you need some time to grieve?"

Blue turned off the screens and stood up, adjusting levels on his cobalt armor.

my boot on his face

all the grieving i need

Lucifer is quite popular among angels, Yan thought. She changed the subject.

"How's the suit working out?"

took a beating

48% efficiency

need to fix wrist control

manual still works

also serves as angelic cast

allows movement while healing broken leg and ribs

"That's good. Let's get started, then... We know that's Lucifer up there on that ship controlling the transients. Could his plan be as simple as just staging a world invasion?"

why use transients

has army of demons

"He knows something about the transients that we don't. That's for sure. For the moment, though, we need to figure out how to isolate them from people. That's when they become violent, when they get in contact with humans."

highly difficult to isolate

too many to corral

but

"Yes?"

Blue circled around the room. Yan hovered in the opposite direction, sometimes crossing right through Blue.

been thinking about what you said to me

talking to transients

"Well, we know they're smart. I told you in one of my recorded studies, the way they keep in clusters, their nomadic demeanor, even how they stack their dead in burial mounds; it's a very similar behavior to that of an ant colony. There has to be a way for them to communicate between themselves."

agreed

nonverbal or telepathy maybe

test for sound patterns

Yan halted her pace.

"Now that I think of it, I never recorded their sounds. Too busy running away from them when they screamed at me. Should I tape Boy George?"

Blue shook his head and tapped a lighted panel on his chest.

no need

live streams and video footage

hundreds of samples

collecting and analyzing now

"Oh. That's great! Anything else we're missing? Maybe we could review—

inconclusive

"Huh?"

no pattern detected

"From hundreds of sound samples? That's odd."

Blue sat back on the bed, frustrated.

need another way to decode

"Yeah. Did you try checking hi and low pitch undulations? Maybe—"

Yan was interrupted by Ricadel, who stormed up through the pink plastic stairs and into the room.

"Brother Zadkiel! Yan Fan! Please come quickly! Something terrible is happening to Boy George!"

. . . .

"How long has he been like this?" Yan asked Ricadel as she stared out the small window.

"About half an hour, I think."

"He's at an advanced stage already in just half an hour! This is not good at all, Blue."

Blue remained silent and immersed in his calculations, running an analysis from his suit tech and also using the mini-calculator from his toy laptop.

Ricadel turned to Yan gravely concerned.

"Is Boy George dying?"

"Ah, no. No, he's not dying. Boy George is about to become a mommy."

A wide-eyed Ricadel watched Boy George carefully. He was outside on the grass several feet away from the Fisher Price hospital. The transient had four legs instead of two, and three arms instead of two. Another faceless head came out of his chest. A different transient body pushed itself out of Boy George. Once it separated completely from its progenitor, it stood still next to him in an identical pose. Feet close together, arms straight down, head erected, chest spread.

"Wow…"

Yan took another peek through the window.

"It's a girl!"

"How do you know?" Ricadel asked.

"I mean, she's not really a she. I just thought to give her some personality. I don't know, it helps to connect, right?"

The white angel smiled, but she was still confused.

"I do not understand. Why is this not a good thing?"

"See, I've studied quite a bunch of these transient births. This is a process that usually takes at least three to five days to complete. We just witnessed a new transient be born in less than an hour."

any guesses

Yan's face lit up and she bit her lower lip.

"Actually, I think I have one! There's a proven correlation between gathered food and population growth in animals. Simply put, the more food is available to a species, the more their reproductive output increases. I mean, come on, transients have been living on planet diarrhea for only God knows how long, barely surviving acid super storms. What sort of nutrients were they getting from that place? But this is Earth now. They're absorbing yummy microbes and minerals or whatever through their membrane skins like crazy. And of course, they're growing in size, too. As long as they're here, they're going to keep multiplying exponentially and they're going to keep getting bigger and stronger."

could have billions of transients roaming earth in just weeks

theoretically

"I see…" Ricadel said as she flopped on the plastic yellow chair. "So many new lives…"

"Okay, so now the clock is ticking for us to get the transients the hell outta dodge and find them a juicy uninhabited planet with lots of food for them."

ill work on that

will take some time with tools i have

matilda wouldve pinpointed a planet in minutes

"Spilled milk, Blue. No use crying over it."

true

have a project for you

something id like to try

"Now we're talking. What's on your mind?"

Ricadel's concern was still elsewhere as she pointed at the window.

"This new transient, it is our responsibility to nourish her, just like Boy George. We should name her, Yan."

"Sure. You get the honors. Bonus points if you make it an 80's reference!"

Ricadel shook her head.

"I'm afraid I was… indisposed in the 80's. I am not familiar with your times"

The white angel leaned closer to the window. She held her chin and pondered.

"She is female, begat by Boy George, which makes her of the George lineage. She shall be named… Girl George."

Ricadel scanned Yan and Blue for approval.

ha

"Love it! And we finally get an answer to that age-old Madonna question: 'Who's that girl?' It's Girl George, of the George lineage!"

80s reference right there

Ricadel beamed proud.

. . . .

Blue and Yan Fan stepped outside to the grass, but stayed at a safe distance from the Georges' reach and purview. Ricadel remained vigilant by the hospital's door. Blue revealed a small square metallic green box with a decibel measuring screen, an attached speaker, and some wire lining.

Ricadel helped build this

couldnt find pattern from transients sounds

cant translate their speak

but we use this to convey new language

combines most of their sounds in a continuum of equally distributed frequencies

masking voices enough to deliver simple messages to transients

"A white noise machine?"

exactly

layer transient sounds

reflect their voices back at them for familiarity

insert a message for them

its mathematically coded

basic language of the universe

"Quoting Galileo to me now, huh! Okay, so— what, instead of 'hello', we say 'one plus one is two'?"

yes

use gestures to compensate

"Interesting… This could work. What do you need me to do?"

need your space helmet

Yan Fan positioned her hands at a short space from each other. Her helmet appeared between them and she gave it to Blue. He made some quick adjustments to the communicator he had previously installed before he handed it back to her.

test on the georges

turn on speaker

talk to them

will route to me

collect and decode responses we receive

Yan walked straight to Boy George. She turned on her helmet speaker and transmitted Blue's looped message to him. It was a sucking sound, very similar to the clatter transients produced, but weaker.

one plus one is two

Boy George honked softly at Yan. Girl George soon imitated her father and honked softly too as they both extended their arms to Yan. Blue began to receive a numerical translation of Boy George's hooting. He tapped his machine to fix it.

this isnt working

"What is he saying?"

nonsense

one plus one is one

over and over

increasing decibels

Yan's helmet transmission became louder. Boy and Girl George increased their honking, but soon became irritated and emitted a terrifying howling that reminded Yan of her time in the caves of Dog Shit Mesa. Both transients ran towards Yan, waving their arms to catch her, but swinging right through her. She hovered away from them and floated to Ricadel. Blue signaled his sister.

your light

do it now

dont let them reach the hospital

The white Archangel raised her arms and her hands released an intense light beam that spotlighted the toy hospital and surrounding terrain. Even blinded by the light, Yan drifted in a straight line heading toward Ricadel. Blue stumbled after, hindered by his improvised limbs. The transients stayed behind, not knowing where Yan was. After the angels and the ghost were safe behind doors, Ricadel ended her light, and the transients remained outside.

. . . .

There was not a sound heard in the room. Yan Fan stared quietly at Blue. She could feel his defeat. Ricadel peeked through the window to check on the Georges.

waste of time

"No. It was a good idea." Yan replied.

only good ideas are ones that work

"You of all people… Do you really think that? Let's not lose our heads. We'll come up with a new plan."

The room fell silent again.

science is not enough

we are missing something

"We have no prophets," Ricadel spoke. "We have no prophecy."

precisely

"What are you guys talking about?"

"This is a world ending scenario, Yan Fan. An apocalypse," Ricadel noted. "Thousands of years ago, one of our own, an Archangel named Metatron, foresaw that the angels would forever battle to prevent Creation from being destroyed. He had visions of every single disaster, an infinity of doomsdays, days after days of terrible extinction events. Metatron wanted to share his visions with the angels, so we could prepare for each coming threat. But many angels thought him to be a heretic. His mere existence divided Heaven in a war between its angels. Disheartened, Metatron exiled himself to Earth. He met a man named Abinadi who was able to see him, even though our brother had concealed himself from everyone. Abinadi suggested for Metatron to share his visions with humanity. But it needed to be only one vision for each prophet chosen, as a single human heart could not resist all of Metatron's predictions. Our brother planted the seed of the sacred third eye in Abinadi. The first prophecy came to him and the Archangels listened. And the third eye passed on to Abinadi's children, generations that spread to all corners of the Earth and still continue spiraling reveals to this day. That was Metatron's gift to us and to the world. Since then, we Archangels have never stopped fighting to keep humanity from its demise. We refer to it as our days of end."

"Wow. That's… amazing. And you're saying that someone was supposed to predict this crisis for you guys to have clues to better prepare for all of this?"

yes

no prophet

no prophecy of a transient invasion

Yan was astounded. She imagined a secret history of prophets foreseeing many catastrophes. How many tried to warn humanity and were ridiculed as phonies? How many of these unsung heroes died without the world knowing that because of them humanity got to live one more day? Her mind flew. Memories buried for decades came back to her. Days before she stepped into the Defiant, a bouquet of flowers on the train…

"The man in the subway…"

Yan spun in the air.

"Guys, there was a man I met when I was alive— God, what was his name? — He knew I was going to die, that Lucifer would be on the Defiant! He said he saw it! He— he even said something about Lucifer conspiring with an alien race. And he wrote a book about it, yes! The Satanic Rocket, or something like that. I thought he was a nut job! What was his freaking name? Blue, can you search for books published in 1986? Any titles related to Satan and aliens in space or rockets?"

googling

found one entry

satan has a rocketship

by author matteo tsekalo

"That's the guy! That's your prophet!"

Blue and Ricadel stared at each other wide-eyed. He projected a holo-screen that displayed documents, news, or articles related to Matteo. There were not many.

after he published his book

committed to an institution

tompkins county mental health

ithaca new york

most likely hes dead by now

but no death certificate

"We don't know if he's dead." Yan said. "We need to find this guy! Ricadel, you can fly, right?"

"Yes! I have wings. They are made of holy feathers and pearls…"

"Great! Let's get cracking!"

Blue closed his eyes.

wait

sister

can you hear?

Ricadel fell on her knees and joined hands.

"I do. Our sister Azrael prays to us. She is frightened."

black angel and goldie

trapped in space

"Yan, if we do not help them, they could die. As Zadkiel's is science and mine is life, their sacred ministries are death and miracles. If they perish, reality itself will be at stake."

they are our priority now

Yan paused.

"I get it. Yes. You guys need to do this. I'll find a way to find Matteo Tsekalo."

he can wait

"No, he can't. He's more than thirty years late already to share his prophecy with you. I just need to find a way to get…"

Yan looked out the window.

"There."

She looked back at Blue and Ricadel.

"I'm about to do something very interesting or really stupid."

Yan phased through the plastic wall and floated over the grassland.

Ricadel and Blue left through the door.

"Yan, what are you doing?"

Yan Fan hovered cautiously towards Boy George. She extended her hand to Boy George. The transient reached out to Yan and responded with soft honks.

"Hi, baby boy. I think I understand. Is this what you want?"

Girl George went wild. She emitted loud howls at Yan and moved to grab her. Yan stepped back instinctively to protect herself. To Yan's astonishment, Boy George gently placed his hand on Girl George's chest and shoved her to the side. She immediately halted her aggressive movement and fell silent. Boy George extended his hand to Yan and resumed his soft honking at her. Yan turned her head and smiled at Blue.

"Do you hear that? One plus one…"

Blue nodded.

is one :)

"I do not understand." Ricadel said.

when you helped yan leave from boy george

did not fight to push her out

Ricadel gasped.

"Oh! He wanted her to stay inside him!"

Yan Fan faced Boy George again. She struggled to control her fear.

"Okay. This is it. One plus one is one. One plus one is one. One plus one is one…"

Yan extended her ghost arm to reach his as she slowly stepped forward to enter the transient's body. She closed her eyes.

Ricadel cried out and lurched towards Yan. Blue grasped her arm to stop her.

"Brother, I cannot explain it, but…"

feel it too

astronaut meets alien

perfect union between human and unknown

a unique moment

"Yes. This could even be a crucial piece of God's plan."

dont get ahead of yourself

Awed by the marvel they were witnessing, the Archagels held hands. Yan Fan stared at her familiar four-fingered transient limbs. She was part of Boy George once again. Yan walked towards Ricadel and towered over her. She raised her arms and flaunted her transient muscles.

"Look how strong I am! If he's still alive, I'll find Mr. Tsekalo," she said, moving her arms to the sides and lifting her knees to stretch. "I'm heading to Ithaca now. Ricadel, please look after Blue and tell the other angels to take it easy on the transients. We're on the brink of a breakthrough here."

"I shall." Ricadel answered.

"Rescue your family. When you come back, find a way to amplify the white noise machine. It's gotta work on all transients if we're going to save them."

Blue paused, then nodded.

keep your

Yan rolled her eyes.

"Keep my communicator open. Yes?"

Yan approached Ricadel and bent down to hold her hands.

"Hey, Ricadel. I wanted you to know, your ex was an asshole that didn't deserve you and your sister was a total bitch. Lucifer needs to die a disgusting and painful death, but not by your hand. He's not worth the dirt you walk on."

Ricadel lowered her head.

"And you are not irrelevant," Yan continued, "You mean a lot to us, to humanity and now to the transients. I hope that you find out what happened to your baby. You deserve to know."

Ricadel gripped Yan's big transient hands tighter. Her voice cracked. "Thank you."

The angel closed her eyes and whispered a short prayer.

Yan lifted Blue from the ground and held him in a tight hug.

put me down yanhua

"Come here, you! Who's a grumpy little angel? You are!"

ow

break my ribs

Yan let Blue go and wiggled her fingers goodbye. The moment was interrupted by Girl George, who let out a loud groan as she charged towards Ricadel. Yan grabbed the transient from behind the shoulder and pulled her back.

"Ah, ah! Don't even think about it, girl. You're coming with us. Time to go! New York's that way, right? My sense of direction is pathetic."

She ran fast towards the stream and Girl George followed close behind. Just before they reached it, both transients jumped high and away from the angels at the Fisher Price hospital. Ricadel noticed Blue's worried eyes.

"Stop it. Yan Fan will return. She is resourceful and quick on her feet. She will do what needs to be done."

Blue hesitated.

not worried about her

bravest person i know

"Yan is such a brilliant soul... How did you two meet?"

only way you meet someone like her

on a trip to the moon

— From the secret journal of Father Anselmo Duarte.
September 18. Ortega, Santa Cristal

In this world of angels and demons, of werewolves and vampires, of witches and immortals, I never thought that aliens could exist. Yet there was one outside my window. And I knew right then and there what the sight of it meant for me. It was going to be a long night, and I needed more whiskey if I was to write all of this down.

God dammit.

But let me recapitulate. At the time of these events I'd relocated to Santa Cristal, a small God forsaken island in the Caribbean. Stricken by an Olympic-level record crime wave, blatant political corruption, a crass absence of basic services, and half a dozen hurricanes each year, this hellhole of a place also hosts the largest rate of demonic possessions, supernatural apparitions, and undead attacks per capita on the face of this Earth. The cause of this phenomenon needs to be revealed in its own tale, for another time. Suffice to say I won't be able to return to my chalet in Salamanca any time soon. There is so much work for me to do here, but I am a tired old fart. And I'm getting more exhausted and gassier with every waking moment.

The world was about to end again. This time, aliens invaded Earth. As with all my previous accountings of these apocalyptic days of end, I've enjoyed christening them for posterity and this occurrence with the aliens wouldn't be the exception. Just indulge me. I call this incident:

13 THE CASE OF THE MISSING THIRD EYE

You've already seen the videos online, you've probably been part of large city-wide evacuations, or maybe you've experienced the terror of the attacks first hand. Aside from the possibility that before you read this the Archangels may have once again reset reality to make you all forget that these events even happened, you are most likely better aware of the details of this alien invasion than I will ever be. Or at the very least you didn't spend your time drinking, vomiting, and sleeping through most of the incursion.

In any case, I've collected and attached several news articles as supplementary reading to my following testimony. I won't get too much into the UFO sighting angle of it all. Essentially, these faceless giants came to Earth in a massive spaceship that launched smaller crafts to all corners of our planet, destroying everything in their path. Widespread panic, nowhere to hide, lives lost, humanity at peril; you get the gist of it.

My interest lies in the divine aspects of this phenomenon. Where were the Archangels while all of this was going on? And what were they doing to protect us? The answers to these questions wouldn't be known to me until later on, but apparently at the time they were attempting a daring rescue in space, or some of them were anyway. But we'll get to that.

Whenever I am able, that is to say, whenever I'm sober enough to remember to keep my pants on, I serve mass at San Felipito's church, an old, yet still rather strong building, notwithstanding its neglected façade. Located in the middle of the town of Ortega, its walls are in desperate need of paint coating, and a few broken mosaic windows and angelic statues here and there; but other than that, not a bad joint for a priest to hang the collar. I happened to have kept the church keys while the other minister in my house went missing, presumably fleeing from the alien invaders. This made me one of the few lucky clergy members on the island ordered by the Archbishop to stay and open the parish for any who'd lost their homes in these attacks.

I was to coordinate receiving food and first need supplies, make sure the refugees didn't steal any valuables, establish communication with organizations like the Red Cross and the National Guard while following their often contradicting instructions, and also smile on behalf of Pope Matthew and the Catholic Church if we were visited by the press.

This was going to be a problem. Not because I was intoxicated while performing my duties, I can hold my booze rather well if I put my mind to it, but because it conflicted with my other job. It was just a matter of time before the angels would have me go on a world spanning caper. And as predicted, I stood in front of the closed doors of San Felipito holding the keys in one hand while reading text messages from Archangel Zadkiel in the other, and a long line of hungry homeless families waiting behind me.

Zadkiel asked me to meet with the spirit of one Yan Fan, the science teacher that died back in the 80's in the explosion of the space shuttle Defiant. She was heading to New York to find a prophet named Matteo Tsekalo, hoping he could give some light into the invasion. Quite frankly, with the prophecy already realized, I thought the Archangels were grasping at straws, but if it meant getting this alien nonsense behind us, I was willing to roll up my sleeves.

Before I continue, it is necessary for me to apprise you of a few particulars about myself as they will come into effect during this tale. Even though I have not been canonized by the Catholic Church, and pretty much doubt I ever will, I was made a saint by the Archangels themselves. Notionally, I am San Anselmo Duarte; patron saint of go-get-my-latte. A genuine ecclesiastical intern of the Seven Lights; "Anselmo, please exorcise the Archdemon Envy from a possessed Uriel. Anselmo, go find half a billion missing newborn souls and bring the thief to us. Anselmo, can you hide Metatron's destiny staff somewhere safe from the legion of bloodthirsty Satanists looking for it? Anselmo, it would be so great if you helped the Black Angel close the gates of Tartarus before the four horsemen of the Apocalypse escape." Like that.

The true concept of sainthood as demarcated by the Archangels is not a mere title given post-mortem by the Pope after reviewing a life of selfless deeds, but an authentic connection with the entity that grants said status through a sharing of his or her angelic essence. When it happens, it is sometimes physically manifested by conceding unique "blessings" or abilities to the saint. Therefore, said saint becomes an extension of the Archangel's ministry with the means to perform specific tasks related to it.

However, for reasons unknown to me, I'm the only saint ever to be connected to all seven Archangels instead of just one. Instigated by a gross miscommunication between them, I suppose? I don't know. And why was I chosen specifically? Your guess is as good as mine. But because of this I have become the proverbial lone worker with too many bosses, and I also came to possess seven extraordinary gifts, one from each angelic ministry. The first of these blessings you should already be familiar with; the *lifting of the veil*, granted by Archangel Raphael and termed as such because it allows me to see through new certainty threads woven into Creation. In other words, it is why I can remember erased events after the resetting of reality. I'll let you know of my other six gifts as we go along in this narrative when using them became necessary during my dealings.

My church keys and the fate of Ortega's displaced community were delegated to Julito, an 11-year-old altar boy with a permanently confused look, and Sor Juana, a 94-year-old mumbling nun that haunts the halls of San Felipito, dragging a broom that I've never actually seen her sweep the floors with. I saw many incredulous faces and heard quite a few cursing protests when I walked through the long line of people to get to my '77 olive green Datsun. Some clown even threw an empty can of Red Bull that hit the back of my head.

"I'm on my way to save all of you ungrateful pricks!" I yelled at them as I got into my car. "¡Joder!"

No doubt that was going on my record.

The first obstacle in my holy quest was to figure out how I was supposed to travel to New York when all flights and boat trips were cancelled during the alien invasion. A few dozen calls to friends of friends led me to Don Ramirez, a retired vet pilot and devoted catholic who lived by the northern coastline. Ramirez was happy to escort me, but his only means of flying was *La Chiringa*, or 'The Kite' in Spanish, a rusty two-seater jalopy that had remained moribund in his backyard since 1992.

In the early hours of the day, La Chiringa flew us over the Atlantic. Doing justice to its name, I had to get used to the plane's wobbling and frequent plummets. One or two of the alien saucers passed somewhat close to us, but apart from that, the trip was quite uneventful. Once we reached the states, we raced over New York City with no time for sightseeing. Ramirez proved to be very adept in avoiding falling giants from the sky. We zig zagged through a shower of them, barely grazed only one at a certain point. We landed safely over some construction fields further north at a place called Ithaca in the upstate region. I thanked God and promised the man a Dos Equis six pack. Ramirez immediately began prepping the plane for our return trip while I tried getting directions in my cellphone to the Tompkins County Mental hospital. I found myself walking eight blocks uphill through a ghost town. Everyone was gone even though the buildings seemed to be fine with no sign of alien presence anywhere. I could hear my footsteps and the occasional rustling of trees urging me not to reach my destination.

And I'm not saying this just to write with dramatic flair. I was literally advised by the trees not to enter the clinic as it was haunted by a very dangerous spectral presence. This is the *Whispering Earth*, a blessing by Archangel Jophiel, which is a special understanding of impending warnings conveyed by animals and plants. Now, before you assume that this could be an amusing boon to have in a Dr. Dolittle sort of way, you wake up at 5 in the morning with birds singing a cheery tune about Satan's demonic horde feeding on our souls and setting the world on fire and then tell me if it's fun.

In any case, I ignored nature's warnings and arrived at the psych establishment. There was nothing particularly compelling about the structure. There were no eerie Victorian gates leading to expansive gardens left untreated by time or anything of the such. It was just a bland-looking six-storied brick-red corner edifice, very much like most of the neighboring buildings. And its glass doors were open, so I let myself into the lobby.

With no one at the front desk, I perused through some of the files, looking for any reference to Mr. Tsekalo, but didn't find anything. I didn't bother with the computer either; I'm just bad at those. I did see a small table next to the side of the room with a coffee maker, Splenda packets, creams, and plastic cups. A small handwritten sign on the wall read *Please serve yourself.* Who was I to disobey? Black, no sugar. They even had a packet of fresh buttermilk cookies from which I took a couple. I have to say, I had never felt more welcome at an insane asylum haunted by some sort of supernatural threat.

"Are you happy just staring at me taking my coffee or are you going to say hi?" I said to the spirit of a smiling tall man in blue scrubs hovering behind me.

"I'm so sorry, Father. That was very impolite of me. But you can never be too careful when it comes to the safety of the patients here."

"Oh, you don't need to worry about me. I was called in to give last rites to one of your interned sick, you may have him listed as Matteo Tsekalo. Anselmo. Nice to meet you."

"Likewise! I'm Hiran. I'm one of the nurses here. Unfortunately, due to HIPAA regulations, I cannot divulge any information that may expose the privacy of our patients here at Tompkins. I can't even confirm if the man you're asking for is here."

"That's understandable."

"Though I can confirm that as a faithful servant of the deadly seven arch-demon princes of Hell, I have to kill you now."

I took a sip from the cup and placed it on the table.

"Of course you do."

. . . .

Her fingers were the first to wake up. They wiggled even before she opened her eyes. Black Angel sensed movement. Was she being transported somewhere? The last thing she remembered was crashing into Lucifer's spaceship. But now she was seeing her sister Goldie sitting against a metal wall, legs spread and head hanging like a Raggedy Ann doll. She stood up, intending to get closer to her, and staggered briefly until vertigo overcame and dropped her head first.

Black Angel looked at the emptiness of space through a small window to her left. She realized they were protected only by the craft's confinement. Her heart beat out of control. The resulting panic attack made her hyperventilate. As terrifyingly powerful and old as the angel of death was, she shared many common virtues and flaws with humanity, such as her fear of open spaces. This was a secret not even her siblings knew.

A heavily sedated Goldie rambled just a few feet away from her. Black Angel could discern from her sister's gibberish that they were on a collision course to the moon. If she crawled to Goldie and stirred her out of her funk, she'd be able to save them with just a snap of her fingers. But the young death angel was immobile. Her hands wouldn't stop shaking and she couldn't contain her fright. Dozens of dreadful thoughts paralyzed her.

It was a nightmare that she feared was about to become an imminent reality, like a passenger in a car about to crash, and there was nothing she could do to stop it. She saw in her mind the walls and floor of the ship exploding into infinite directions. She felt her freezing body floating in dark nothing. She wanted to scream, but the only sounds she made were short gasps of asphyxiation. Her vision doubled and blurred and as she struggled to hold on to anything near, her hands felt wet on the floor, touching her own sweat, drool, and tears.

Her sister, she fought hard to remember her. Salvation was so close, yet out of her reach. Black Angel dragged herself with one strong thrust, her hands manically trying to get a hold of Goldie's shoe. She stopped to breathe again. She needed to get a hold of her feelings. It took her another couple of minutes, but she dragged herself again. Her right hand clutched the sole of Goldie's shoe. Black Angel shook it as hard and fast as she could, but the angel of miracles didn't respond. She pulled her shoe off and scratched her foot deep enough to make her bleed. Still, Goldie remained dopey and slurring senseless babble.

Black Angel heard loud banging noises from the space craft's walls. The metal clanking echoed louder. She desperately wanted it to stop, but it just wouldn't. She pulled her own hair as her entire body tensed up with anger and fright. Convinced the ship was about to crack open, she coiled up in fetal position, and cried unconsolably. Time lost its meaning for her. Everything around her seemed to slow down, or maybe she was the one moving too fast. Even the lighting shifted slightly. There was nothing to anchor herself to. She made fists from her shaking hands and rhythmically punched the side of her thighs.

A male hand twice as big as hers seized her fist and stopped her from self-hitting again. Black Angel turned and saw a monster reaching to get her. It had no face like the transients she had seen before on Earth. Her first reaction was to curl back and pull her arm away from its hold. But it didn't attack her. It just stared at her patiently... stared, with blue eyes. Blue eyes... It wasn't faceless, she realized. It was her brother. She recognized his eyes and she remembered finding him almost dead on that grassland. Black Angel hopped forward and fiercely hugged Blue. She hung on to him relentless. Ricadel stood behind them with a worried look.

"She's not well. What ails her?"

Blue's hovering holo-screen displayed his words.

never seen her like this

trembling

panicky

sweating cold

maybe our angel of death is agoraphobic

Ricadel combed the girl's hair with her fingers.

"I don't follow."

severe anxiety disorder

perceives expansive environment around her unsafe

"How dreadful. Thank the Lord we made it in time to help."

Ricadel kneeled next to Goldie and softly patted her face.

"Sister. Can you hear me?"

Goldie continued her gibbering. Ricadel touched her sister's pupil to open her eye wider.

"I think she is drugged."

not much time

almost reaching the moon

cant alter course

bring them to our saucer

Black Angel was being carried in Blue's arms. She was still tense, but his armored chest was the only safe place she wanted to be and it eased her breathing. She distinguished Ricadel's glow through her blurred vision as she had Goldie's arm around her neck, helping her stand up and step forward. Blue reached up at a gap in the ceiling where he intended to lift Black Angel through. However, as soon as she saw the hole, she shook, trying to get lose from his arms. Blue held her tighter and stared at her eyes in a way that let her know to trust him. She allowed to be carried up the opening and then Blue came back down to help carry Goldie up.

The four angels had entered another identical saucer, but it was messier than the previous one; riddled with cables, hack-opened panels, nuts and bolts lying about, and four installed screens. Blue stood by the screens and gripped a control stick.

everyone hold on

detaching moon routed ship

He pressed a button. Black Angel heard the same loud clanking sound as before and her heart raced momentarily. She felt Ricadel's hand gripping her shoulder. It comforted her.

"It's okay," Ricadel said to Black Angel. "We are safe here. We managed to capture one of the flying saucers and our brother took control of it. He had me carry cables and some tools across an entire state, but it was worth it in the end."

Black Angel didn't care for explanations. She was just glad to hold tight to Ricadel's arm and be able to breathe better with her embrace.

Blue pointed to one of the screens.

look

The spacecraft they'd departed from exploded upon impact at the moon's surface. They journeyed at full speed back to Earth, but it would take two full days to return. Two days of transient attacks. Two days of Lucifer with no one to stop him. Blue did everything he could to boost the engines. Black Angel stared at him rewiring and changing program settings at the control panel. She felt vibrations surge from the ship's floor through her feet. They were going a lot faster.

"What are you doing?" Ricadel asked him.

routed all reserve power to engines

extra jolt of adrenaline

save us half a day

Just as Blue's typed words appeared on his floating holo-screen, the space craft's rear side exploded in flames and the ship shook heavily. It went so fast, all four passengers were thrown to the floor. Ricadel held the Black Angel close to her chest and used her free arm to protect Goldie. Blue reached for the controls and tried to regain maneuverability. The controls burst into current sparks.

not good

controls are dead

going too fast

we may overshoot Earth

Blue pointed at an incoherent Goldie.

you need to fix her now

"I— I cannot do this," Ricadel replied. "I don't know how. Humans are easy to heal, but angels are different. Nothing I try works. I failed with you and –"

sister

if you dont wake her

we will die

As Blue took the Black Angel in his arms, Ricadel turned her gaze to Goldie. She took a deep breath and bit her lip. She placed both hands on the angel's cheeks. Her palms lit up in bright white. She used prayer to try to get through to her sister. The bright light intensified.

But Goldie just stuck her tongue out and trumpeted a mocking noise.

Ricadel shook her head. Her light dimmed out.

The small ship trembled again. The angels held on as Ricadel looked at Blue. He gazed back at her and nodded. Ricadel held Goldie's hand and prayed again.

"Sister, if I cannot cure you, at least let me share your burden."

Her hands brightened once more. Both angels tilted back as an invisible force pushed them apart and their hands no longer joined.

Goldie caught Ricadel as she fainted.

"Ah, Houston, we have a problem…"

"Boy or girl. Girl or boy. Boy or girl. Girl or boy." Ricadel mumbled.

"This gal's buzzed off her puffy socks!"

we have bigger problems

lost control of this ship

"Hey, how'd you pulled that off with the words on that shiny floaty screen? I feel I'm in a silent movie! Then again, I can hear myself talk, which I guess would make the movie a half talkie? Boy, that's just rude!"

goldie please

"Aye, aye, mon Capitan!"

She stood straight and saluted him before taking over the flaming controls. The electric sparks coming from the panel immediately turned into small colorful fireworks that popped harmlessly around her hands.

The ship entered Earth's atmosphere at creating loud sonic booms.

"Be right back!" Goldie exclaimed before vanishing.

Blue ran over to the controls and saw a lighted sign that read *ludicrous speed*. The small flying saucer seemed to be driving itself. Blue calculated their trajectory and determined they were headed somewhere towards the Pacific Ocean. They were about to impact a tall dormant volcano, but the spacecraft stopped in mid-air. A small sign came out of the ship that read *Yikes!* The space craft immediately dropped straight down. It made a sound similar to Goofy's classic holler.

"Aaah hoo hoo hooey!"

At the precise moment the ship was about to impact the ground, it stopped again and then landed gently in a rocking movement, like a bird sitting on a nest. Blue still carried the Black Angel and held a recuperating Ricadel's hand as they stepped outside the space saucer. The angel of death shyly released herself from her brother and stepped both feet firmly on the green ground. She held her chest and knelt to pray in silence.

The angels were greeted by several Hawaiian luau dancers that gifted them with colorful flower leis they hung around their necks. There was a clear soil path for them to stroll, marked by tiki torches lighted along at both sides.

Goldie waited for them at the end of the short path. There were actually two of her, both dressed in white suits. A smaller sized Goldie yelled "The plane! The plane!" And the taller Goldie did her best Ricardo Montalban impression.

"Welcome, my friends, to Fantasy Island!"

Ricadel applauded, still tipsy, but more aware than before.

"Again!"

and we arrived in less than a day

best crash landing ever

Goldie winked.

"Cha, cha, cha!"

. . . .

"Please let me out!"

"Are you going to behave?"

"Yes! I'll take you to him! I'll take you to Matteo! Just let me out!"

"Good."

I have gained a bit of a reputation among low level demons and poltergeists. We have an unspoken agreement, if you will. They steer clear of me and I don't imprison them inside my soul. That's blessing number 3 on my ridiculous angelic skills list: *Sin Catcher.* I can trap demons and evil spirits in eternally looping memories of my wrong doings, which I believe I have many of. The more traumatic or contrite, the better. And what am I but an old bag of drunken regrets? It was granted by the late Archangel Michael herself after I assisted with some nasty voodoo golem business in Haiti. Never had a better drinking partner. And the stories she would tell… God, I miss that woman.

For more than thirty years now I've been fighting and caging these evil things inside my heart. It takes its toll, I won't lie. But just for the look on their faces the moment they realize they are being sucked into a spectral vacuum makes it all worth it for me. Poor Hiran must have been new at being a ghost. Clearly, he hadn't heard of me or he wouldn't have tried to possess me. Being crammed with hundreds of other demonic presences inside the dark recesses of my soul must not feel comfortable at all.

I let him out. It was just a matter of replaying the sinful memory in my mind. I gave him an empty threat that now that he'd been trapped inside my heart, he was a marked spirit and I could track him anywhere and capture him again if he tried to escape. Of course, that's bullshit, but I thought it'd keep him in line.

"You sick perverted monster!" Hiran cried. "How could you do that to a nun?"

"Hey, it was the seventies and it was her idea. And really. You were just about to murder me and you're judging me?"

I couldn't walk through walls or ceilings like Hiran was used to. We took an elevator to the twelfth floor, where he assured me Mr. Tsekalo was staying. The elevator doors opened to a long white hallway with many empty rooms to both sides. All the patients had been evacuated already along with the staff. Except for poor Mr. Tsekalo, left to the care of a ghost. It definitely made me suspect that more was going on.

"Matteo is in that last room over there, on the other side of the hall."

"He's lying, Father" a female voice spoke from behind me. "I've already checked all the floors of this building twice and there's no one here."

I turned to see a young woman of Asian features wearing a bulky astronaut suit.

"You must be Yan Fan," I said to her. "Zadkiel sent me to help you with—"

"Yes, I know. He texted me too. So, who's this guy and why is he giving you bad information? Wait a minute…"

Yan approached Hiran and looked at him from top to bottom. She phased her hand through his stomach and he did the same with her. As they crossed each other, they both gleamed for only a second. It looked like a change in their spectral coloring that came and went as a wave, from see-through bluish to brighter see-through bluish, and then back to their regular see-through bluish.

"You're a ghost! I've never seen one before. I mean, apart from myself."

"How exciting! I've never seen another ghost either! And talk about work hazards! Did we both die while on the job? Look at you! An astronaut! That is ah—mazing!"

"Hey, man, listen you're a nurse. That's the Lord's work right there."

And that was my cue to interrupt the weird ethereal career fair they were having.

"Well, this guy's actually working for the department downstairs, but I have him on a short leash."

"You're working for Lucifer? You asshole!" she said to Hiran. "Do you know how many transients are dying out there because of him?"

"How many what now?"

"Ms. Fan—" I called.

I shook my hand and let her know with my eyes that it was better not to say anything about the aliens. She changed the subject.

"I haven't checked the basement."

"Then that's where we're going. Lead the way, nurse Hiran. And if you try anything, there's an interesting sin I committed involving three school lunch ladies and Taco Tuesday leftovers…"

When we reached the basement level, the elevator doors remained closed.

"I need to get the security key to open up for you," Hiran said. "They're on the other side."

"We'll go get them, Father. I'll keep an eye on him."

"Fine."

Hiran crossed the closed doors first.

"I'll be right back!" Yan said.

Yan left me alone inside the narrow elevator. I waited in silence for five minutes. Five minutes became ten. Ten became twenty, and I was angrily cursing and pulling from the middle to separate the doors. If Hiran had pulled a fast one on Yan, our pal Zadkiel would never let me hear the end of it. Luckily, the doors opened automatically. Yan waited on the other side, holding the key.

"That asshole got the keys and threw them inside the incinerator. I chased after him, but he got away from me. Sorry."

"That's okay. I'm betting he can't leave this building. He's likely tethered to it."

I followed Yan Fan as she hovered through the murky basement. There was a flickering neon white lamp illuminating the whole level, but it wasn't enough. I kept bumping into scattered old medical equipment, chairs, boxes, and discarded office supplies.

"Then why am I not "tethered" to a particular place like him?"

"There's different kinds of ghosts, Ms. Fan. You're all manifestations defined by your purpose; your motivation for your soul not moving beyond. Question is, what is your purpose, Yan Fan?

"I think I'm here to save the transients."

"Well, you sure can't do that by lingering around in a haunted house."

Yan smiled. She had a beautiful smile, that one.

"Father, you need to know. Blue and I are figuring out a way to communicate with the transients. Not only that, I'm able to possess transients. It's more like we join and we work together, really. I got two on the roof this very moment."

"Wow. Can you get them to leave Earth?"

"We want to find a home for them, but we're still missing a piece of the puzzle. Sometimes it's impossible to explain their behavior. I'd say that Lucifer is somehow controlling them, but then they do something that totally contradicts that thought. We're hoping Matteo can help with that."

"Lucifer is behind the invasion?" I asked.

"Yes, he is! He's in the big golden spaceship. I've met him."

"I've met him, too."

This was not the moment for me to talk about my encounter with the devil. Moving on.

At the far side of the basement, we reached a small panel-walled room, but the door was locked. Yan Fan crossed through it and opened it for me from inside.

"It's him," she said.

I entered the small room and saw an empty medical bed with used sheets. A small table next to it with a glass of water and a dirty bowl that stunk of raw sewage. Ms. Fan pointed down to the floor at the other side of the bed. He looked feeble wearing only an adult diaper. He must have weighed less than a hundred pounds. I could see all his bones as his skin was just a thin layer of veins and paleness. His hands trembled cold. I carefully lifted him from the floor and laid him on the bed. I was afraid to break the man. Then I wrapped him up in bedsheets.

He opened his eyes.

"Close the door. We don't have much time." Matteo said. "He's gone, but he'll be back."

"Who, Hiran?" I asked.

"No."

Yan approached Matteo. I wondered if he could see her in her spectral form. He did. He followed her with his eyes.

"Do you know who I am?" she asked.

"Hello, Yan. It's not every day you get to say I told you so to someone that died."

Yan nodded and gave him a sad smile.

"I deserve that."

I leaned closer to Mr. Tsekalo and held his hands to make them warm.

"Matteo. My name is Father Anselmo Duarte."

"I know who you are. I've seen you many times."

"Then you know why I'm here. We'll get you to safety."

"I know why you're here. That's not it."

"Then why am I here?"

"You and her. You're here to listen."

"Listen to what?"

"The last reveal of my dying third eye... I know what the transients are."

14 ORIGIN OF THE SPECIES

"I saw it. It was the end of the world…but it was not this world."

Mr. Tsekalo's eyes were closed. He was entranced. His frail body rested on the medical bed with his head tilted to the side on a deflated pillow. Watching him in such a state, I couldn't help but feel sorry for the guy. I've met a handful of prophets in my time and I'm sorry to say it never ends well for them.

These people that possess the far-seeing third eye live a life of isolation from the rest of humanity. They're stuck in a haze of the here and now and what will yet come to pass. Their souls become more warning beacons than human as they get morbidly obsessed with sharing their vision again and again. True prophets will talk to anyone who'll listen because all it takes is the right listener to change the outcome of things. And when you think about it, after a lifetime of constantly seeing unwanted spoilers of humanity's gruesome demise, well I can see why the only thing they truly want is the opportunity to make it all go away.

As they get closer to the actual realization of their prophecies, their minds gradually give out. It becomes hard for them to reconcile that they're talking to a person they just saw get their brains slurped by a demon in a vision or the such. A disconnect with their physical health follows as their muscles atrophy, losing motor skills and body mass in response to the lack of interest in anything else but conveying the prophecy. It's just a sad thing to watch. And that's what I was looking at with Mr. Tsekalo.

"Are you writing this down? Write this down," he said.

Yan Fan placed her ghost space helmet on the night table close to Matteo's bed.

"Don't worry. I'm recording this in my communicator. Blue—uh, Zadkiel and the rest of the Archangels will be made aware of your visions."

"I was there. I was as one of them. I looked how they looked, felt what they felt. And what they felt, what they always felt, was fear. We ran in horror from angels falling in tongues of fire under black clouds and red skies. Each burning angel shattered the world around us upon impact. The grounds extending to the horizon were turned into a wasteland of charred black ashes. They—we were confused and despairing. We knew God was angry at us, and we were going to die for it, but we didn't know why. I ran for my life. We all did. With nowhere to hide, I jumped into a lake of red along with thousands of others. Lucifer looked down on us from above. He promised he would save us, he promised... We reached our hands upwards to him, and we howled loud inhuman cries at him. It was the same plea over and over again, made by myself and all those with me in that lake of blood waters..."

"Hold on," Yan Fan interrupted. "We know Lucifer had to steal Matilda to collect the transients from planet Hell Part Two. How could he have reached the transient's home world to destroy it without any transport?"

Matteo opened his eyes and jerked his body.

"No, no, no!" he yelled. "You don't understand! This is not about where! This is about when! Listen! Remember your Bible? In the beginning, God created the universe. He made light out of darkness, the earth, the stars. He made flora and fauna, and he made man and woman to rule over them. And God saw that it was good. Well, before all that, before the beginning, God created the former place. A place of incomplete. And He bore Lucifer from light to make— No, Lucifer was the light that started the universe. Living golden light out of darkness. And by birthing Lucifer, God made his world real. Because Lucifer was the only Archangel; the only everything. But God saw that the incomplete was static. A reality of one; motionless, predictable, a perpetual simultaneity that Lucifer ruled. God wanted to make more. From Lucifer's limbs two more limbs came out. From his head came another, his wings multiplied. Until he was no longer one but two."

"Mitosis…" Yan Fan mused.

"Lucifer was enraged. He felt betrayed by God. The universe had been taken from his hands. It was no longer only his or of him. Creation was shared between Lucifer and his Other. He was reality. She was time. She, in her inner multi-color lightness, turned that simultaneity into continuity and from that, the incomplete could grow. And God saw that Lucifer's Other was good and He craved more.

God mused on creating beings in His image that He could see become much more than their limitations. They were to be humanity. Guided and protected by servant angels, humanity could learn to lead the universe instead of Lucifer. From the Other's skin, the lesser angels were born; I saw them in my visions as winged fish-tailed faceless. And from Lucifer, God began to make something different, something imperfect and fearful, devoted to him."

"The transients came from Lucifer?" Yan Fan cringed. I don't blame her.

"Not intentionally," Mr. Tsekalo continued. "God intended to create his new children from Lucifer's flesh. But in his fury, Lucifer expelled the first still forming being from his body before it was ready to be born. That first transient was not developed to its full potential. It was an unfinished human in every possible way; physically, rationally, emotionally. Unable to make choices for itself, it was only capable of feeling constant utter fear. The infant inside it… its unfulfilled humanity. The first transient reached its hand out to Lucifer and began to divide within itself. And the divided transients multiplied into thousands, then millions, all calling for their messiah; all of them waiting for Lucifer's command."

Yan Fan drifted closer to Mr. Tsekalo. I could tell that her quick mind was putting pieces of the puzzle together.

"Matteo, when you had the vision of yourself as a transient. Do you know what you and the other transients howled at Lucifer?"

"Each howling was distinct between transients. I couldn't tell for sure if they spoke the same as me, but it did feel that way. I do remember what I cried. My own desperate longing that only Lucifer could soothe: You speak. I act."

"You speak. I act," Yan repeated. "Tell me what to do…"

"That's it?" I asked. "You're telling me these creatures just want someone to tell them what to do?"

"Boy George wanted me to possess him. With me calling the shots, he's less afraid. I think that's his goal. It's the only emotional solace he can get."

"Boy George?"

"One of the transients on the roof. Long story. But how do we get from Lucifer, undisputed king of the transients, to him destroying their world?"

"That was not Lucifer," Matteo said. "To the transients, Lucifer was the Word, not God. Lucifer regained his control over the incomplete because of the sheer power of an ever-growing multitude of transients. He reigned over them, easing out their terror in exchange for complete obedience. By his order, they built temples to him. And he told his subjects to kill his Other and the lesser angels. She did the best she could to protect her angels from the savage transient attacks. But every encounter became a massacre that decimated both the transients and the lesser ang—"

Matteo coughed, and I gave him some water from the glass on the table. He took a few sips and continued.

"That's when God decided to end it all and start again. He scorched the surviving lesser angels and showered the world with their fiery corpses. Transients were incinerated in seconds along with the rest of the incomplete. The few thousands that made it to the blood lake were ordered by Lucifer to hide underwater. He said he would come back when the destruction was over. They—we obeyed and waited in that lake for his return. The world became engulfed in darkness. I felt several millennia pass in my mind. Finally, I remember seeing light over the water. Instinctively, we all ascended to the surface towards the light."

"Don't tell me. It was a golden light, right?"

"No. It was multi-colored prism. Lucifer's Other arrived at the lake and she... My visions... they're becoming blurred..."

"The other Archangel got to the transients first! She was the one that took them to Hell Part Two!" Yan Fan said. "Has Lucifer been searching for them all these years? Oh, man! Wait till Blue hears this!"

Matteo Tsekalo coughed heavily. I helped him shift his position and adjusted the bed settings.

"Mr. Tsekalo, are you okay?"

"Yes, I... I remember ripples forming in the air above the lake. She ordered the transients to cross through them, but once I traversed the ripples I stopped being a transient and became... I'm someone else, somewhere else."

"Where did you go?" Yan Fan asked.

Matteo's demeanor changed completely. He breathed slower. His eyes glittered with contempt.

"I think I was in Heaven... I was Lucifer. And I started a war."

"Oh my God!"

"I felt what he felt. Deeply rooted hatred towards Creation. The truth was revealed to me. Heaven was the starting point where God created this new universe using his—my light as the match to lit everything into being. This false paradise beamed right at the heart of the rip from which darkness broke into space.

This was never my world. This was a universe that God made sure I didn't rule alone, but by seven. Seven... Archangels. The only way for me to return to my reality was to bring down seven towers that sealed the chasm to the incomplete, what you and I call Hell.

I rebelled. It took me centuries, but I succeeded. And when I eventually fell through that chasm that returned me to Hell, the first thing I did was to look for my servants in the lake of blood. I stooped on one knee at the shore and dipped my hand into the red liquid. I took a moment to feel the red water. Something was wrong. Blood trickled down my arm as I lifted and clenched my wet fist. I stood up, breathing heavier while trying to contain my anger. I stretched my arm and reached into the nothingness next to me. And I pulled my Other from out of nowhere, tightening my hand around her neck. I was tempted to squeeze...

'Where are they?'

My Other remained silent, struggling to resist me. I insisted.

'Where. Are. They?'

'Safe— From you.'

I wanted to squeeze..."

Matteo Tsekalo sat up on the bed with a sudden gasp. He struggled to breathe as blood dripped from his eyes and nose. It took me a moment to snap out of my shock to assist him. I took a handkerchief from my pocket and gently lifted his head up as I wiped his face clean.

"You need to rest."

"No. You need to run! He's here! He's here…"

"Who's here?"

And as if my question queued them, two of those giant transient aliens came bursting through the wall of the small room. One crouched in order to fit under the basement roof, while the other struggled to pull it by the stomach from behind. When the first transient stretched up the second transient away, it punched its head hard through a wall. The second transient landed on its butt and its head hung momentarily unconscious from the neck. I could clearly see Hiran's luminous ghost essence inside the first wild transient. He was controlling it; wearing it like a bad Halloween costume to be more precise.

"Hey guys! Check out this banging new alien body I have!" he bragged. "So, listen, I hope you don't mind, but I need to kill you guys now and take Matteo away, okay? Thank you so much for your cooperation. I hope your time at Tompkins Mental Health has been rewarding and like my grandmother used to say: *Ave Satanus, demonicus eterno!*"

I was ready to punch his smug face, transient or not.

Any other pair of eyes would miss that inner glow, but not me. What angelic gift was this, three or four? I lost count. *Seer of Dark Truth* granted to me by Archangel Azrael, it allows me to see the supernatural world around me as it truly is. To quote The Sixth Sense: I see dead people, and live possessed ones, too. I see ghosts and vampires and demons and angels and the sort. Nothing and no one is concealed from me. And I don't even know what some of these things that I see actually are. There's this woman of the night I've been frequenting. And I'm not sure that she really is… well, I'll just leave that for another story.

"Father, get him to safety! We'll take care of this!" Yan Fan said as she picked up her helmet from the night table and moved fast towards the downed transient.

"We?"

"Dammit! He took over Girl George!"

"Girl— How on Earth can you discern the girl from the boy?"

"Oh, Father, if I need to explain that then what's the point?" she smiled and winked.

"Very funny." I rolled my eyes.

Yan reached Boy George and inspected his body.

"Hey boy, you okay? Did he hurt you? Let's fight that son of a bitch and get your girl back!"

She extended her hand and touched the transient's chest.

"Here's my hand, give me yours… One plus one is one!"

The most amazing thing happened. As the creature reached out to Yan, I could see her become one with the creature. I have never seen such a beautifully executed possession. No. Possession is the wrong word for it. This was something else. Her spectral form glowed inside the massive body. As if she rested in its embrace. And just like that, the transient stood up and ran towards Hiran. She pushed him through the wall of the room and the crumbling noise echoed in the entire basement. I froze at the sight of it.

"Father, go!"

I broke out of my trance and collected Mr. Tsekalo from the medical bed. I carried him towards the elevator and pressed the star labeled button to the lobby.

"You're too late. He's here." Matteo said.

"It's okay, Mr. Tsekalo, I trust Yan Fan will be able to defeat Hiran. If not, she'll definitely buy us some time."

The elevator doors opened, and I raced towards the entrance glass doors with Matteo in my arms.

"No! Not him!" he insisted.

"Then who is it? Stop wiggling! You know, you are driving me—"

"It's too late…"

I heard a faint mumbling behind me and I turned. I barely made the shape of a shaggy teenager standing by the corner wall behind me as my mind began to shut down. I felt so tired, I immediately dropped Matteo to the ground. My view of this teen getting closer to Matteo tilted slowly and my body gave in to stupid hard heavy gravity and my eyes felt heavy too, and the only thing I could think of was getting a good deserved sleep and…"

"Hrmm"

"Lord Sloth…" Matteo said as he took the youngster's hand. At least I think he did. Maybe I dreamed about it. Maybe all of this nonsense was just a dream. If it was, I'm sure I could have easily slept it all off. Just needed to close my eyes and get… a good needed fucking sleep…

15 JESUS CHRIST WAS A TIME TRAVELER

Matteo's distant moaning woke me up. I stood up from the floor at the hospital lobby and I swear I saw him in his feeble state carrying that long-haired pajama-wearing teenager on his back into the elevator. I staggered lightheaded towards the doors and got there just in time to see them shut on my face as the small round lighted numbers went back down to the basement. The farther away from me they went the more awake I felt.

Loud banging sounds from below ground confirmed to me that Yan Fan was still fighting Hiran inside those transients, so it was up to me to save Mr. Tsekalo away from Sloth. If this was really Lord Belphegor, one of the arch-demons of Hell, nothing in my celestial bag of tricks would be enough to even slow him down. But I'd be damned if I let Matteo die at the hands of that monster. I burst through the stairway doors and raced down the steps. As I entered the poorly lit basement I noticed a disquieting silence. The transients were nowhere in sight. I hoped that Ms. Fan was okay as I crept through a damp hallway. There was a small fire ax inside a break-in-case-of-emergency glass box against the wall. I broke into the glass and took.

Another moan from Mr. Tsekalo led me to the other side of the basement where the small room was located. Not only was there no sign of the transients as I noticed before, but there wasn't any structure damage caused by their fight. That worried me. The door to the room creaked open and I went through it, ax raised. Sloth snored softly on the medical bed. Mr. Tsekalo stood trembling beside him, fanning him with a yellow feather bouquet. Matteo looked at me as a tear rolled on his cheek.

"Help … me," he murmured.

I shushed him with my finger and I carefully approached the demon. Haziness slowly overcame me again. I began to lose myself to the demon prince, but I pressed on. I swung the ax and struck him right through his hairy forehead. Sloth boomeranged up with a ghoulish scream. He fell from the bed and slipped on his own brick-red blood that oozed from his wound and made a mess of the floor.

"Matteo, get behind me quickly!" I yelled.

Mr. Tsekalo acquiesced and headed towards the door. We both knew an ax wouldn't stop Sloth. There was only one play that I prayed would work against him in his weakened state. I searched my heart and remembered a time when I was 12 and pushed my younger brother down a quarry. God bless his soul.

No, I didn't kill my brother, if that's what you think. He died happily in a brothel orgy somewhere in Cordoba 8 years ago. So don't cry for him, Argentina.

Anyway, my sin was chosen, and I uttered angelic chanting. Sloth knew what was going on. He held on to one of the legs of the night table, but his body began to fade out of this world and into its new prison in my soul.

"Hrrrm!...nuh let youh trap muh… Nuhrrrm!"

Having slurred those words, Sloth vanished. I heard faint echoes of his voice inside me, but I ignored them. I turned to Mr. Tsekalo.

"Huh. That actually worked. Can you walk?"

He could barely stand. I wrapped his arm on my neck and helped him out of the room. The moment we reached the elevator, the little light in the basement went out. But a golden light came from the opening elevator doors. I figured we wouldn't be fortunate enough to be welcoming Archangel Raphael. We were about to face someone else. Fixing the cufflinks on his black suit and ruby red tie, Lucifer stepped out through the doors.

"Anselmo. You had to make me come to this rathole, didn't you? That prophet belongs to me."

No matter the shape he takes, when he's around, I always know it's him. His presence feels unnervingly primal. Matteo and I stepped back. I felt him shaking behind me.

"I'm not letting you near him!"

"Letting—? What do you think this is? Do you want me to hurt you again? Or are you stalling until you find the perfect little sin to try to trap me in? It's useless. I know them all."

"Oh, shut the hell up! If you're going to kill me, kill me. If not, get out of my damned way!"

"What are you doing?" Matteo asked. I understood his fright. I panicked, too. Hell, I was a dead man anyway. Might as well go out in a blaze of glory. I kicked the devil's crotch, and as he bent forward in pain, I punched his face. Lucifer fell. I punched him again. And again. I wasn't hurting him; how could I? But he was crouched on his fours, head down for some reason. I kicked his face. Maybe it was the sheer fear I felt, or my rage. Maybe it was because I felt truly done with this asshole. But I just went for it.

"Stay the hell down!"

I pulled Mr. Tsekalo by the arm and we stepped around Lucifer before we got into the elevator. He slowly rose from the ground and turned towards us. I dowsed him with holy water from a small flask I took out of my pocket just as the steel doors closed. Lucifer stepped back and held his face.

"Aargh! I'm melting! Melting! Oh, what a world! What a world!"

I expected Lucifer to burst through the doors and finished us off, but instead I was surprised to hear the elevator humming as we were lifted to the next floor level.

"Soon as that door opens, you and I need to run for it. Don't let go of me. I'll help you."

"Thank you."

"Don't mention it. Everything's going to be alright now."

"Yes." Matteo handed me a cold Guinness bottle.

I gulped a mouthful. Really hit the spot. The elevator doors opened, and the lobby was full of people clapping and cheering.

"Anselmo! Anselmo! Anselmo!"

The seven Archangels waited for me along with the crowd. Archangel Michael was there, too; red armor and all.

"You saved us all, Anselmo," she said to me and winked.

I took a sip from my bottle and turned to Matteo.

"This is all a dream, isn't it?"

"Yes."

"Fuck. Can I at least finish my beer before waking up?"

. . . .

The basement rumbled. Yan Fan had inhabited Boy George to fight Hiran after he possessed Girl George. A slab from the ceiling fell on Yan's transient head. She was trying to drive Boy George out of the basement, hoping that Hiran would follow her out into the open. Many walls were already demolished as both transients pushed each other through them, and she was afraid the fragile building structure would collapse. But Hiran kept hammering at her, blow after blow. Yan managed to pin Girl George to the ground. She tried reasoning with Hiran.

"Dude, stop it! Stop! You're going to bring this place down on us!"

"I have a promotion in the ranks of Hell's army coming up! Feeding you to Lord Belphegor will look good on my resume. Nothing personal."

"Fine, then."

Boy George lifted Girl George over his head and threw her to the ground. A loud rumbling was heard as Girl George's body cracked the ground and found herself half buried in the cracked concrete.

"You want me, come get me."

Yan ran towards the back end of the basement, where the cargo steel doors were located. She tore open one of the doors and exited the building through it. As she got out she saw a line of small vans parked next to each other. She lifted one up and carried it towards the building's back entrance.

Hiran rushed out through the same back opening Yan made. She surprised him by hurling the van at him. Hiran fell backwards, with the van on top of his transient chest. He pushed the van off him and ran towards Yan.

"I'm registering a formal complaint against you!" Hiran said. "You're not pinning all this property damage on me!"

Girl George jumped on Boy George using all her weight to drop him to the ground. They both rolled and kept hitting each other like roughhousing children. Yan was tempted to dig her fingers into the infant in Hiran's torso, which would guarantee excruciating pain for him. But she hesitated, not wanting Girl George to suffer for an evil that she really had no control of. That hesitation cost Yan as Hiran punched her in the torso, harming Boy George's infant. She screamed and rolled on the floor. Hiran took the upper hand and threw Boy George through a glass wall that led to the back of the lobby. The glass broke in thousands of pieces as Boy George landed head first on the floor. Yan had had enough. Dealing with the pain, Boy George slowly got back up.

"Boy, I have an idea, but I'm going to need you to let me go. Come on, help me out. What's the opposite of one plus one is one?"

Girl George ran towards Boy George and he ran towards her. As they met outside the lobby, their bodies grappled each other to a standstill.

"Here goes nothing," Yan whispered. "One minus one is two!"

Yan Fan's spirit separated from Boy George, she floated right between both fighting transients. The astronaut ghost immediately moved closer to Girl George and her spirit was absorbed by her. Hiran and Yan found themselves facing each other with only Girl George's baby between them.

"What do you think you're doing?" he asked.

"Kicking you the hell out!"

Both Yan Fan and Hiran were expelled from Girl George's body. The transients reunited and kept their distance from the ghosts. Hiran was confused.

"How did you do that?"

"Yeah, like I'm going to tell you."

"You think these two creatures are the only ones here? I'll find another one. Better yet, I'll find twenty! I'll take over all of them and you be sure we're going to escort you out of these premises!"

"That's just not gonna happen. Just own it. You're beat."

"I'm sorry, but I'm not going to fall again for that priest and those kinky sin traps of his. How are you going to stop me? You can't!"

Yan Fan shrugged. Hiran felt a soft tap on the back of his spectral body. He turned. Black Angel stood behind him, waving her hand. Hiran let out a high pitch squeal, knowing the angel of death had come for him.

. . . .

And of course, it was all a ridiculous dream. I was still on that lobby floor where the demon left me. In my slow journey back to consciousness, I made shapes out of lines on the white ceiling above. I felt a gentle touch on my shoulder and Zadkiel's face loomed over me; part of it anyway. He was missing his jaw and part of his throat, and somehow his head was still attached to what was left of his neck with what looked like parts of one of those toy helicopters. This guy had definitely seen better days. Next to the Archangel there was a glowing blue hologram floating and shifting in accord with Zadkiel's movements. Words appeared on it one letter at a time.

father are you okay

"I'm peachy. Nothing like smooth hard flooring to handle an old man's bad back. Help me up. What the hell happened to you?"

lucifer

A look outside the glass doors at the entrance revealed that it was night already.

"How long have I been out?"

dont know

found you babbling something about kicking the devil in the balls

sloth did this to you

calls it blueprints of procrastination

when you need to do something and in your mind you paint a detailed picture of

"Yeah, yeah I get it. Listen, he's got Matteo. We should check the basement. Yan is also fighting—"

The angel nodded and pointed at the floating screen.

i know

trust she can handle it

need to take down sloth

fought him before

"Good. How'd you beat him?"

did not

"Well, that's heartening."

The elevator ride with Zadkiel was short, but awkward. He was different. His usual carefree swagger was gone. He seemed more in the moment, but not in a good way. Whatever Lucifer had done to him scarred him beyond his physique.

"So, what's your plan, genius? Soon as we get close to Sloth, he'll lazy us to another nap."

i will face him

you stay behind away from his reach

be ready to put it back on

"Put what back on?"

The elevator opened and Zadkiel marched straight into the dark. I clenched my fist and followed. The basement was silent and again I thought of Yan, but with a twist of deja vu. This time, there was no lighting at all in that basement maze. Only his hovering blue screens and some little tubes from his futuristic suit barely lit the way. That lethargic piece of shit demon could've watched us from any corner somewhere, but Zadkiel didn't seem to care. He kept moving through the corridor. My muscles began to weight down again. Zadkiel shoved me and I stayed back. His floating screen turned bright red.

watch out

I retreated and as soon as I felt like myself again I saw that Sloth stood several feet away from us, his head down slightly wobbling and snoring like a narcoleptic.

"Hrrm… uhlmost kuhlled you buhfore… finish you now…hrrm"

Zadkiel kept moving towards him, but his pace slackened off. He was dragging his feet. He planted his palm against the wall to support himself. His Archangel status didn't protect him from the vapory appeals to laziness from the demon prince. When he got close enough to Sloth, Zadkiel dropped to his knees, his shoulders and arms dropped.

"Zadkiel!" I yelled.

He looked back at me. His floating screen got in my way.

stay back

"What are you—?"

I didn't understand what he was doing initially until I saw him place his hands on his mouth. I heard his low moans. Zadkiel was tearing the toy helicopter off. Blood dripped from his throat, and tears dropped from his eyes. I could see his bright blue angelic essence flow away from his body. He was in immense pain. I realized he was using that pain to stay awake through Sloth's spell.

With effort, he stood up and threw a punch at Sloth. The demon prince leaned wearily backwards, and his hairy feet followed as he took a step back. Zadkiel was unable to land his punches whenever he tried, because Sloth moved erratically, like an inflatable figure at the side walk of a car dealer lot. He would appear to fall at any moment, staggering to the right, but then sloped to the left, he took three fast tumbling steps towards Zadkiel, but then fell on his ass. It reminded me of those Jackie Chan Drunken Master movies. But the Archangel was having none of it. He managed to grab Sloth's right arm and then held on to both his arms tight. Sloth's limbs slumped, his body held up only by Zadkiel like a parent dealing with a child that doesn't want to be at the mall.

The glowing screen turned blue again and moved towards Sloth, but the demon wasn't paying attention.

too lazy to read my words

then listen

I heard a radio feedback coming from the walls. The P.A. system activated in the entire building. A recorded announcement came on.

"Attention. This is not a drill. Please leave the building in an orderly—zkkzzk—Where is Matteo Tsekalo?"

Sloth's head hung to the side and snored loudly. Zadkiel slapped his face hard. This time he didn't miss. The demon's head hung backwards.

"Wake up. Tell me where he is."

The demon prince smiled and pointed to his side.

"Hrrmm…late hrrm…"

Zadkiel shed light to the far side of the dark hallway and we all saw Mr. Tsekalo sitting on a pool of his own blood sweating and breathing heavily; an old crusty mop stuck across his stomach and through his back. The P.A. system spoke.

"Father, please tend to Matteo. Just give me a moment."

"A moment for what?"

The angel punched Sloth out cold and threw his flaccid body into a big square-shaped metal trash bin. I could see the demon's hairy feet hanging out of the bin's edges. Zadkiel turned to look at me for an instant but didn't say anything. He fell on his face, or what was left of it. I ran to him and turned him over. He was still alive, but unconscious. I needed to stop his essence from leaking. Frantically looking around, I picked up the toy copter and pressed it on under his face and on his throat.

Fearing we were defenseless, I glanced at the trash bin, but Sloth's legs no longer stood out from it. I took a closer look. The bin was empty.

I raced over to Matteo Tsekalo and carefully leaned him to the side. I broke the mop stick on both sides and gently pulled off the part that was still inside him. Blood gushed from his wounds, and I pressed on them with my bare hands. With a recited prayer, I invoked a blessing granted to me by Archangel Gabriel, the *Sacramental Heal*. It's how the blind will see and the lame will walk and all that jazz. I can only use it on other people, but not myself; and it won't change the outcome for those who are meant to die.

My hands glowed briefly, and Matteo's injuries closed. But he was still weak and cold. His breathing was shallow. I elevated his head and made him as comfortable as I could. There was nothing more for me to do but keep him company in the dark. I checked on Zadkiel from time to time, making sure he was breathing.

"Father," Matteo said. "I… told you everything I saw…"

"I know. Take it easy. The other angels will be here soon."

"You don't know that."

"Yes, I do. It's going to be fine. They're coming for us. You'll be fine."

Matteo coughed hard, but he kept pushing his words out.

"I won't make it."

"If you'd shut up and tried to relax, you'd at least have a shot at—"

"Listen, please. There are things I need to say… I see the end. I see how this ends. But I… I don't see her."

"Who?"

"Yan Fan… I don't see her anymore."

"She's a ghost. I'm sure after this transient business is done she'll be ready to move on to the afterlife."

"No," said Matteo. "She won't."

I had nothing to say to that remark. I've learned that ignoring prophecies will always end up biting you in the ass. But I also know that prophets work with visions as they can interpret them. And I couldn't afford to worry about Ms. Fan's fate when I had a dying man in my arms and a critically injured angel close by.

"Father…"

"I'm here."

"Jesus… Jesus Christ was a time traveler."

"Oh… Did you— You've seen Christ in a vision?"

"No. Not exactly... But I just know it. There's solid evidence of this. There've been so many... accounts of time travel technology existing right now. And there's a group that's secretly developing it for their own agenda... some of these people... I tell you, Jesus is part of this. I know that if he hasn't... made the jump yet, he's about to. And I'd bet my left arm that the Vatican's keeping everything quiet. They have... recorded proof and they're sitting on this conspiracy."

"Conspiracy? Fuck's sake, man..."

"You don't believe me."

"Look, I've seen my share of shit in my life, but I'm telling you I know the Vatican, and I know the Pope. They're just a bunch of conformist idiots that don't know or care about half the shit that goes under their noses."

"See, that's what the Church wants you to think! That's how they get you!"

"Alright, hey. Don't work yourself up. Why don't you—"

"People think I'm crazy, Father... They think... They think I've wasted my life following hoaxes and... crazy urban legends. But they're not. These are hidden truths they don't want us to know!"

"Who's 'they'?"

Matteo's eyed widened. That's never a good sign...

"The secret society. The ones that hide the truth from the world. They never approached me, but...They're on to you. They know who you are and what you do. Sooner or later... they're going to come for you."

I burst into laughter.

"I got people after me all the time. It's part of being in this business. Look, I really don't want to hear it."

"I'm sorry, Father— I'm so sorry..."

"Are you crying? You don't need to cry. I just don't need to hear—"

"I didn't mean to upset you, Father... I just can't stop myself... I connect these dots... that people don't see. What I see... It's never good. I know... It's never good."

See, now I felt like shit. This poor guy, who knew he was about to die, just tried to share his feelings with me. He spent the last few decades alone in captivity because Lucifer didn't want the angels to hear what he had to say. But he held on, even when his body had already given in. He waited all these years for the good guys to come so he could share this astounding revelation about the transients and their connection to humanity and the devil. I can be such an ass sometimes…

"So, uh, so Jesus was a time traveler, huh? Honestly, I kind of suspected that myself, but I wasn't sure…"

"It's all in the New Testament, Father! Walking on water, healing the sick, turning water to wine. That's… that's technology that we've already achieved or we're likely to in the next five to ten years… I know Christ is out there… He is. And he's read the Gospels and… he's preparing himself to go back in time and fulfill his destiny."

"Makes so much sense."

"It's all a time loop, Father."

"Ah, yes."

I was looking over at Zadkiel. Still with us.

"Do you know… what a time loop is?" Matteo continued. "It's a temporal glitch. A cyclical repetition of events that lead to the unfolding of… those same events. Jesus reads about his exploits in Nazareth in the present and he travels back to make sure it all happens—"

Matteo coughed again. I could see drops of blood on his lips.

"Easy, man. Don't get too excited."

"Thought about it for so long… since I was a kid. Back in the day… I read books, articles, anything I could get on mainstream and… fringe theories that married science and religion. I wanted… to explain my visions."

"How old were you when your visions began?"

"Seven. I was seven."

"I see."

There was silence for a while, which I hated. I needed to say something to break the void.

"You know, back in the early sixties I wrote an article for a science magazine; *Our Galaxy Weekly*. The piece was basically my answer to the concept of the multiverse, very in vogue at the time. I proposed that all these countless parallel universes established by either different gravitational fields, shifting vibrational frequencies, or even causal changes in a person's choices, in the vein of Frost's *Road Not Taken*; they're not really out there in their own realms, but right here in this one universe. My thinking was that the universe is supposed to be infinite, with no beginning and no end. By conceiving the existence of other planes of existence, you kind of limit the unlimited-ness of this universe. I submitted the idea that if we were to travel extreme quantities of light year distances we could eventually find those breaks in frequencies or gravitational fields within this same universe. I'd find another Earth, for example, in which I chose to own a bowling alley instead of becoming a priest."

"One limitless universe, ever expanding with quantum possibilities of the mind."

"That's the idea. I mean, infinite is infinite, right? The universe can take it. Why create other universes when there's no saying what we can find in this one? I don't know… just a thought."

"It's an interesting thought…"

I went on with more of my stupid theories. I kept telling these random and once vivid ideas that I'd forgotten for decades, but that for some reason just came back to me. Matteo woke up someone I thought had died in me a long time ago. I kept talking and listening to myself as a naive young rebel. A time traveling optimist checking on his old tired self. You could say I was in a time loop of me.

But I was only talking to myself in that dark and noiseless basement. I hadn't been talking to Matteo. He'd been cold in my arms for a while.

The first angel to arrive was the little one, Azrael. She came from the shadows as I tended to a barely conscious Zadkiel. She gave me a reassuring smile and stopped in front of Matteo's body. The Black Angel leaned close to extend her hand. Matteo's glowing soul reached out a spectral hand through his chest and touched hers. I witnessed Matteo leaving his body behind. He followed the angel of death into the dark.

Zadkiel tugged my sleeve to get my attention. The basement brightened when a glowing angel dressed in white came down the stairs. I was awestruck by a bloody open wound on her stomach area. She was followed by Yan Fan.

"The cavalry arrives," I said.

The angel immediately used her healing light to properly attach the toy helicopter back over his throat wound. She was unable to cure him, but she could stop his angelic essence from ebbing away.

"Brother, what did you do?"

"You should see the other guy." The P.A. system resonated.

Yan Fan looked at the walls behind her and then back at Zadkiel.

"Is that you coming from the speakers? That's cool! How're you doing it?"

Zadkiel smiled.

"I can hack digital and analog alike. It's an Archangel thing."

"Hold still, please. I'm almost finished," the angel in white said. "You seem rather well considering your obsession with harming yourself unnecessarily."

"Me hitting Sloth, that was very necessary."

I pointed at Matteo's corpse.

"Mr. Tsekalo didn't make it, though."

"That poor man…" the glowing white angel said. And she clasped her hands in a short prayer.

Yan Fan hovered over Matteo and stared at him.

"I'm uploading the recording of his prophecy to your tech suit, Blue. There's a connection between the transients and Lucifer that maybe we could exploit."

"Father," Zadkiel said to me through the P.A. "This is our sister Ricadel. She's taken over Gabriel's ministry. She's doing an amazing job at it, too."

Ricadel gave me a warm hug and smiled at me.

"Many blessings! I have heard so many great things about you, Father!"

"Right. How do you like your coffee? Two sugars? Black? You seem like the hazelnut cream kind."

"I've never tried coffee before. What do you recommend?"

"Forget it. Just a joke."

With Ricadel and my support, Zadkiel stood back up. The speakers resonated again.

"Father, you know what comes next."

"Yes, I do."

Zadkiel was referring to Lucifer. He knew of our last encounter years ago. I'm not getting into the details of it here, but I was left alive, barely breathing at the steps of a cathedral in Madrid, as a message to the Archangels. Lucifer said to them that if I ever got in in his way again he'd make sure to share pieces of me between the seven angels. Since then, they've made sure to keep me away from him.

"You've done enough for all of us. Go back to Santa Cristal. Help your people. We'll take it from here," Zadkiel said.

"I'll arrange for Matteo's transport and try to locate any next of kin," I replied.

Yan Fan approached me.

"Thank you for your help, Father. It's an honor."

"It was very nice meeting you, Ms. Fan. Watch over these screwballs."

It was time for me to call Ramirez and get La Chiringa back in the clouds. I headed to the elevator and as the doors opened, I nodded at the angels.

"Give him hell."

16 SOME PROPHECIES CAN BE ANNULLED

Yan Fan occupied Boy George's body as they jumped across miles at great speed over forest mountains and lakes. Girl George followed them a few miles behind. Yan turned back, grabbing Girl George's hand to keep her closer. They renewed the high jumps.

"We're almost there, girl, try to keep up," Yan said. "Don't want to keep the angels waiting, right?"

Blue spoke to Yan through her helmet speaker.

"Let me get this straight. There was another universe before this one."

"Yes," she replied.

"And Lucifer created the transients there. They're not aliens. They're human prototypes from that universe."

"Yep."

"And they were brought to our universe by Lucifer's twin sister, of whom we didn't know anything about before."

"Yep."

"Okay... And you're saying that my white noise translator works fine, but it was just coded incorrectly because transients communicate in broken math?"

"Right. I think I have a theory to explain that, too. Matteo referred to the other place as the incomplete. It was God's early draft of what would become our world, much like transients are of human beings."

"So the math that wrote that universe wasn't perfected yet?" Blue asked.

"Exactly. I mean, that's not to say that transients actually speak in numbers, but the simple messages coded in math through your white noise box are only understood through incorrect math equations as it made sense to them in that universe."

Blue sighed.

"I don't even know if I can re-program the machine with every faulty math there is. You're talking about an infinity of numeric patterns here."

"What can I say, man? I know."

"And this other previous universe, this changes everything," Blue said. "How we see Lucifer, how we see God... All this time we thought Creation came from God's perfection, but He just had plenty of practice."

"This doesn't change how I see Lucifer just one bit," Yan said. "He's still an ass for taking his daddy issues out on the transients and we need to stop him."

"Speak of the devil, pun intended, Lucifer's ship is hovering over Cali. My sisters Black, Ricadel, Goldie and I are close to Los Angeles to reconvene with my other siblings. It's where we'll make our stand against him. We'll start thinking of a plan while we wait for you."

Yan heard a faint squealing from the communicator channel.

"Is that a—?"

"A pig. It's a winged pig that belongs to Goldie. Can't wait to get off it. Pigs are just not meant to be flown. I hate that I can't walk on my own after fighting Sloth. Anyway, we'll wait for you at the— Oh, my God..."

Yan became concerned.

"What? What's going on Blue?"

"I-I don't think you should see this, Yanhua..." he replied in a somber tone.

"Hold on, Blue. We're coming."

Yan and the transients moved faster. She boosted herself using both of Boy George's feet together, with a technique similar to that of an Olympic long-distance jumper, and the hurdles became longer. Poor Girl George's arm was still being pulled by her brother. She let out a growl and imitated his jumps to keep close to him.

In a couple of hours, they'd reached San Bernandino, and from there they ran to Los Angeles. A trail began to clutter the road close at the city limits. Thousands upon thousands of dead transient babies filled out the highway, scorched infant corpses littering the concrete with viscous colorless liquid spilling from cracked thick membrane bodies. Some of them still twitched. The terrible sight distracted Yan and she lost control of Boy George. The transient pushed her soul out of his body and wailed loudly. He took a few aimless steps among the dead babies. Yan approached him.

"I'm so sorry, boy. I'm so—"

Boy George let out a menacing howl at Yan. Girl George did so, too. They both moved away from the astronaut ghost and began to pick up corpses. Yan took the hint and floated back away from them. She continued moving forward, following the trail of dead transients, but still looking back at the Georges in the distance. They stacked babies on top of each other, like the piles she saw in the caves of Hell Part Two. She wanted to cry and fought her urges to go back and try to ease their pain. But she felt this was an intimate moment for the transients that she needed to respect. She pressed on and turned on her helmet communicator.

"Hey, Blue… I lost the Georges. It'll take me a while to get where you are. Can you send someone to pick me up?"

"Okay, sure. Are you alright?"

"There's thousands of dead transients everywhere. How do you think I am?"

"…I'm sorry."

"Yeah… No. I'm sorry. I didn't mean to be rude. Just send someone, please."

As Yan continued hovering, the freeway background changed from dusty desert areas to greener zones and rows of empty houses built next to each other. She saw more piles of transient corpses along the way with a few other transients tending to their dead; no more than two at a time. Yan wandered on, keeping herself at a safe distance from the transients. She heard a voice yell at her from behind.

"Hey, you Yan Fan?"

Yan turned back to see a red leather clad mohawk sporting punk rocker with fiery wings descend from the sky and land in the middle of the road.

"I'm Isophie. Come to pick you up. I take it you've come up with a way to kill off these things?"

"Kill— What? No! We're not killing any transients. Who are you again? Did Blue send you to get me?"

"Technically, he didn't. They just started debating on who would come get you like they do about everything else and I just took off. You're welcome."

Yan's eyes widened with a sudden horrific realization.

"Did you—Did you kill all these transients?"

"Hold that thought. Be right back."

Isophie ran towards a pair of transients that were mounting a pile of dead transient babies. The creatures noticed the red angel approaching them and let out roars before charging towards her. Isophie took out her sword from her back and it lit up in flames. She swung it horizontally and cut the belly of one of the transients. Its inner infant burst into flames and fell on the ground dead. The other transient stepped back away from Isophie and howled. Yan gasped wide-eyed and floated towards them, placing herself between the Archangel and the remaining transient.

"No! What are you doing? Stop!"

"Get outta my way. This blade can cut through ghosts like you if I want it to."

Blue's voice came through Yan's helmet.

"Yan, be careful. My sister Isophie is headed your way. She can be a handful."

"You don't say! Get off my comm, Blue! Your sister here is about to stab me with her sword!"

"What? Stay away from her! I'm sending help!"

Isophie raised her sword.

"Hey, Casper! I said, get outta my way!"

"These are human beings and you're a mass murderer!" Yan yelled. "You're not killing any more transients!"

"Is that what you think? That nutjob prophet of yours did a real number on you! These things are going to eradicate actual humans if we let them spread! We're dealing with a damn pest problem!"

Yan Fan's instincts took over. She threw a punch at Isophie. As her spectral fist approached the Archangel's face, the transient behind her united with her spirit and the punch that landed on Isophie's chin was the transient's. Isophie's face dropped back and her body followed, falling on her butt. She immediately stood up and held her chin.

"Oh, that's it…"

As Isophie moved in to attack Yan and the transient she occupied, the ground beneath the Archangel's feet receded. Isophie was being sucked into quicksand.

"What the hell?"

A woman wearing an olive halter top and a ceremonial loincloth approached Isophie. Flowers bloomed and butterflies fluttered out from her thick hair.

"Stand down, sister!" Evergreen ordered.

Isophie pointed at Yan with her sword.

"Imma kill that bitch!"

Evergreen locked eyes with Isophie.

"I will not repeat myself."

Isophie's demeanor changed. She nodded at Evergreen and sheathed her sword, but she didn't stop her scornful stare at Yan.

The green Archangel waited until Yan Fan separated from the transient before freeing her sister from the sand trap. The transient ran away from Yan and the angels.

"Sheesh! Who thought it was a good idea to give psycho punk a flaming sword?" Yan asked.

"Hey, I'm doing something! Look around you!" Isophie said to her. "We're up to our necks infested with millions of your little buddies and you're giving me shit for the few thousands I've taken out? It doesn't matter what happened on another time before Creation! We are being invaded now! Even if we get to defeat Lucifer, these transients need to be dealt with! This is it, lady! This is the prophecy coming true!"

"But what if we found a way to work around it?" Yan replied.

"Work around the prophecy?" Evergreen asked.

"Yes. Listen, I've had some breakthrough communicating with the transients. We just need to give Blue a little more time with his translator. If we'd work with them instead of hunt them down, maybe they'd help us fight Lucifer, don't you think?"

Isophie and Evergreen exchanged glances.

"You nerds better pull it off then, 'cause we're going to need all the help we can get against the devil," Isophie said.

Evergreen extended her hand to Yan.

"Come. Let's join the others."

Yan Fan held on to Evergreen's hand as both angels and the ghost took flight. Isophie spread her fire wings and kept her distance from them. Evergeen's wings were feathery, but multi-colored, like that of an exotic bird. Her beauty caught Yan's attention.

"Which one of them are you?" she asked her.

"I am Jophiel... Evergreen. My ministry is nature."

"Oh, great! We sorely need one of those. What with trigger-happy angel back there."

Evergreen did not respond. Yan fan looked down at the infant corpse filled trail on the road below them.

"Dammit. Look how many transients she killed…"

"Most of this was not Isophie's doing, Yan Fan." Evergreen replied. "It was mine. Once we deal with Lucifer, do you have a plan to exile these beings from Earth?"

Yan was taken aback with Evergreen's words. The lack of compassion from Evergreen towards the transients concerned her. Ricadel she was not.

"Blue is working on it. You should check with him."

Evergreen hesitated.

"We are not in speaking terms, my brother and I."

Ah. You're the one that gave your soul to Lucifer, aren't you? Quite the angelic family, you guys make. Yan thought to say this, but she refrained from it.

As they approached their destination, Yan gasped at the sight of the massive golden starship hovering among the clouds. Evergreen and Isophie began their descent towards a forest of tall leafy trees in the middle of a baseball stadium. Yan was puzzled. Evergreen noticed.

"I grew the trees there to use the area as our assembly base."

"Won't Lucifer notice it?"

"We're counting on it. We followed Lucifer's ship to his current location and took over this baseball field. A sky view from the ship will easily reveal the forest in the middle of the field. Our hope is to draw him where there will be the least damage to the humans."

As soon as they arrived at the baseball park's small forest, Yan traversed the trees and headed right to Blue. The angels had set up a simple station with two wooden outdoor tables and benches. The angel Violet sat cross-legged on one of the benches, lotus style. She was focused on her cellphone texting and didn't raise her head to look at Yan Fan, but she greeted her with a simple "Hey."

Blue was sitting at the other bench, fiddling with his small white noise box. He looked a little pale and tired, the toy helicopter still latched to his throat. Some of his body suit's metal chest plates were resting on the table.

There was also an old boom box next to Blue. He clicked it on as soon as he saw Yan, and his voice came through.

"Are you okay?"

"I'm fine. Evergreen came just in time to my rescue. But I left the Georges about four miles south. They were devastated to see so many—"

"I know."

"Are you feeling better? Able to walk yet?"

"I can limp. I'm getting there."

"How's the box going?"

"It's going. I've never uploaded incorrect programing to anything on purpose. I hope I'm doing it right… or wrong, I should say. But we definitely need testing."

Ricadel and the Black Angel approached Blue and Yan Fan. Yan focused to solidify her arms and hugged them both.

"I'm happy to see you're well, Yan," Ricadel said. "Isophie can sometimes be so…"

"Violent? Unhinged? Murdery?" Yan asked.

"All of those, I guess. This incident with the transients, it has stressed a great divide among us that I've suspected has been there for a while."

Yan shook her head, looking around her and noticing how the angels kept themselves apart from each other. Evergreen and Isophie remained outside of the small forest, with the pretext of being on watch. Who knew where Goldie was? Only the Black Angel seemed to partake with all of her siblings with no awkwardness or reservations. Yan took her hand.

"Hey, thank you for helping me with that awful ghost nurse."

Black Angel smiled and nodded.

Loud squealing interrupted the moment. Black Angel, Ricadel, Blue, Violet, and Yan looked up at the trees and saw Goldie's winged pig hop between branches upset. The pig turned into Goldie as she zig-zagged down from the trees. She took off her black top hat and pointed outside of the woods, like a ringmaster presenting the next act of a circus show.

"Stations, everyone! It's show time! Break a leg!"

The Archangels and Yan stepped out of the woods. Blue hobbled with Ricadel's help. They joined Evergreen and Isophie just outside the small forest. Goldie pointed upwards.

"Look!"

They all turned their attention to the golden starship in the sky as a light beam projected down to the baseball field from underneath its smooth metallic center. The beam solidified into a luminous bridge-way. Lucifer steadily descended through it and then walked towards Yan and the seven Archangels. He stopped a few feet across them and studied them.

"Hello. You're all finally here. I don't see you decimating transients anymore, so I gather you've chosen the nobler path. You've probably realized you need my ship to escort them away?"

"That ship was never yours…" Blue challenged him.

Lucifer glanced at Blue's boom box and then back at him, gesturing with his hand that Blue was too chatty.

"Cute. No matter how badly I trash you, Zadkiel, you'll still find a way to talk. You want your spaceship?"

Lucifer took a quick look at his watch. Luminous circle-shaped saucers launched from beneath the starship and legions of transients jumped down from the saucers into the field. Thousands of faceless giants stood behind Lucifer with their golden mothership looming over them.

He calmly clenched his fist and nodded at the seven Archangels.

"Please. By all means. Come and take it."

17 LUCIFER SHUNNED

Up among the clouds, loud bass horns resonated from a golden chariot. Mother called her children, and her children came to her. Just outside a small forest in the outfield of a baseball stadium, seven Archangels stood next to each other against Lucifer. Transients kept amassing behind him, not only those coming from the colossal starship that was once Matilda, but countless more that jumped and ran from many directions, beckoned by the grave siren. Several of them exuded extra limbs, or two heads, as they had come in the middle of reproducing. It was an apocalyptic moment frozen in Yan Fan's eyes. But at the time all she could think of was—

"Pancakes."

Yan's spirit hovered close to an ailing Blue who was immersed in calculations as he struggled to reprogram his white noise box. He was able to stand with help from Ricadel. She took care of her brother, but her eyes were focused on the evil that ages ago took her baby away. It was Yan's uttered random word that broke Ricadel's psychological spell. She turned to her perplexed.

"What did you say?"

"Nothing— It's nothing."

"Are you well?"

"Yeah, I'm fine… I'm just thinking of pancakes for some reason…"

Next to them stood the Black Angel, Violet, and Goldie. The angel of death stared at Lucifer defiant. She took a step forward and then traced a line with the front of her shoe. Violet tapped Black Angel's shoulder.

"Hey! No! Don't make him mad!" she said to her.

"Ya gots that backwards the other way around, see?" Goldie spoke. "He shouldn'a made us mad!"

Goldie took off her black top hat and threw it upwards. The hat twirled and descended, landing in front of two baseball wearing feet. Hers. Goldie's garment changed to that of a nineteen-twenties baseball player. Even her body changed as her belly and cheeks expanded. She looked like a blonde Babe Ruth, and just like babe Ruth, she swung a bat a couple of times before pointing it towards Lucifer.

"Batter up!"

At the other end of the line Evergreen and Isophie also prepared to fight. Isophie lit up her sword and her fire wings spread open making crackling sounds. Gone were Evergreen's butterflies and flowers, replaced by thorny weeds, small rattlesnakes, and large scorpion tails coming from her hair.

"Ricadel, we need you to fight," Evergreen said. "Let young Uriel care for our brother as her ministry of emotions is useless against the transients. Yan Fan, you stay behind, too. I trust that you will find a way to get through to the transients, but we cannot wait any longer."

She leveled her somber gaze on Yan. "Beware, many of them are about to die. If we are to survive this, we must reach Lucifer."

Yan Fan nodded reluctantly.

"Could you at least try to keep the death count to a minimum?"

Evergreen shrugged and gave an empathetic look.

"This is all out of our hands now… Archangels, on my word, we strike together," she ordered.

Isophie broke rank and took flight.

"Wait!" Evergreen yelled.

Isophie flew up higher and higher until only her fiery wings were visible to the naked eye. She watched the transient horde that surrounded and protected Lucifer. They looked like a rattled termite colony after being hit by a stick. Her fire wings shot some of its feathers at the transients like falling tongues of fire.

As Isophie came down to strike Lucifer, some of the transients jumped high between him and the angel, grabbing her legs and pulling her down. She swung her flaming blade and impaled a few of them, but more and more transients kept grabbing her. Lucifer steadily observed and then lifted up his eyebrow at Evergreen. She shook her head and waved her siblings to attack.

The remaining Archangels moved in to fight a wave of transients. Blue kept striking keys on his small metal box. Violet held Blue's elbow and tried to lead them away from the battlefield. Yan stayed close to both of them.

"Dude, having you here was great for posing and stuff, but let's get you out of harm's way," Violet said.

"What she said." Yan retorted.

Blue's voice came through the boom box.

"I just need a little more time with the box."

"OMG! That box got you like—!" Violet said.

"Like what?"

Eight transients barged towards Blue, Violet and Yan Fan. Violet pulled Blue's arm, but there was nowhere to run, as they found themselves surrounded by the transients. Yan immediately entered one of them and jostled the transient closest to her. But the six remaining were already too close to Blue and Violet and were about to attack them.

"Blue!" Yan yelled.

Blue stood in the charging transients' way and spoke into the small box in his hand.

"Here goes nothing… Two plus eight is zero."

The six transients stopped very close to Blue and Violet. They gathered in a circle around the angels.

"Violet, on three, let's move five steps to the right," Blue suggested. "One, two, three."

Both angels moved to the side, and the transients surrounding them followed.

"Whoa! What the hell did you just say to them?" Yan asked.

"It's like you said. They don't really speak in numbers, but they feel at home with broken math. There's something they must understand from it on some level. I just blurted an equation and hoped for the best."

"So what are they doing now?" Violet asked.

"My best guess, if the circle around us is the zero… Did I just tell them to protect us? I think we got an entourage…"

Yan's relief was bittersweet as the moment reminded her of the Georges. They protected her too.

"Violet, would you mind carrying the boombox for me? Thanks, sweetie." Blue said through the boom box without taking his eyes off his box machine. "Good news is I finally got this working… Ladies, I may not seem like much right now, but I'm still the Archangel of science. Now, help me get to that press box over there."

At the outfield, Isophie was drowning in a sea of faceless giants. She slashed through two transients, but another clutched her neck from behind, pulling her back. Other faceless hulks held her arms tight and made it impossible to use her sword again. She felt many massive hands restraining and dragging her.

The ground shook underneath the group of transients that carried Isophie. Quaking roared as edged stone pillars grew from underneath their feet like claws. Some of the transients were pinned in between or through the rocks. Isophie freed herself from the rest of the transients and fell face down to the ground. She looked up. Evergreen stood in front of her. She offered her hand to help Isophie up.

"Even the deadliest snake will be consumed by army ants if their numbers are legion," Evergreen said. "Set your pride aside and fight with us."

"So, what, I'm a snake now?"

Isophie stood up and saw the battleground. The other angels were trying to get to Lucifer, but the transients kept getting in their way, forming together in onion-like ring layers around the Morning Star to both fight and to serve as human shields to protect him. Goldie was the closest to Lucifer, about eight transients away from him. She batted transients left and right, and each transient she hit was knocked out of the park.

"Swing batta batta! Swing!"

Goldie was opening a path through them that Ricadel kept open by shining her potent light that temporarily confused the transients. Evergreen and Isophie followed, but not the Black Angel. She approached Lucifer from the opposite side of Goldie by becoming a dark mist. The mist moved through the transients and quietly dropped them like flies.

"I didn't know she could do that," Isophie said. "That's some Old Testament Exodus shit right there."

Both Evergreen and Isophie raced to the other Archangels and

Lucifer.

When Goldie stood face to face with Lucifer, her body changed back to her true form, but she now wore a golden kung fu kimono and sunglasses. She gestured with her hand to call Lucifer to her.

"I know Kung Fu!"

Sensei Goldie threw martial arts kicks and punches at Lucifer. Isophie flanked him and swung her flaming sword at him. Lucifer didn't waste time with either angel. His body disappeared leaving only a husk of his flesh behind.

He appeared behind both angels and touched their backs, piercing his fingers into their bodies. He let go of both and they slumped flat on the ground unable to move, but they were still conscious. It was as if some conjuring from the Morning Star had paralyzed their bodies.

Lucifer stepped away from the angels as his back was burning. A powerful white light scorched him from behind, dropping him to his knees. Ricadel slowly cooked his skin. She intensified her light, giving everything she could to burn Lucifer alive.

"My light may not kill you, but it will hurt you greatly," Ricadel yelled. "What did you do to my sisters? What did you do to my child?"

"I'm sorry. Which one are you?" he asked.

"You—You do not know who I am?"

She augmented her searing beam. Lucifer was on his knees, his flesh charred black.

"After you stole my child and held me captive in Hell for thousands of years, you do not know who I am?"

Lucifer slowly rose from the ground. His skin shed burn tissues as he moved.

"Ah… I think… I think I remember you now. You've done well for yourself."

His burnt skin crumbled into dust. But he reappeared before her, his skin freshly regenerated, and quickly breached her open stomach wound with his right arm. Ricadel screamed.

"All this time, and you're still looking for your baby?" Lucifer asked.

She fell on her knees in agony. He gave her a dead transient baby he picked up from nearby on the ground.

"Here. Have this one instead."

The dead child in Ricadel's arms shocked her. She let go of it and fell on her back. With trembling hands, she wailed at Lucifer. He approached her and stared down at her with his penetrating black eyes.

"You will never know what befell to your child."

Just as Lucifer said those words, a murder of hungry crows descended on him. The rabid birds pecked at him savagely, tearing away and gulping his flesh. Angered, Lucifer ignited his hands in golden fire and burned them all to the ground. He turned to see Evergreen staring back at him.

"You'd do well to remember who will become your master," he said to her.

"When the day comes, I'll accept my fate. Until then..."

Clouds above Lucifer turned dark gray and hail rained on him. The hail amassed over his body, forming ice layers that suppressed him underneath a glacier. The ground trembled again. This time, it opened and swallowed the ice cage that trapped Lucifer. Evergreen closed the soil over him and as it seemed the earth was resisting its powerful prisoner, she still took a moment to reinforce it.

Evergreen made vast boulder formations that covered the area, sealing Lucifer's prison. She went to help her fallen sisters as Goldie and Isophie both regained their movement. She then held Ricadel's head close to her chest and tried to snap her out of her shock.

"Sister. Ricadel. Come back to us. This is not over yet."

"This prison will not last very long," she said to Isophie. "We need to fight him together."

The stones lodged by Evergreen already showed cracks. Loud thumping noises came from underneath. Little by little, the boulders were being pulverized from within, until Lucifer's hand broke loose and reached the edge of the ground's surface. The angels saw him stand at the edge of the chasm. He took a few steps towards the three Archangels, and they raced to meet him. But a horde of transients, hundreds of them, came from behind Lucifer and overran the angels like an angry mob at a Black Friday sale.

Lucifer winked at Evergreen from a distance.

"See you soon..."

Bored, the Morning Star turned to walk away from the angels. But something caught his attention. He looked over his shoulder. Yan Fan, inhabiting a transient, charged towards him.

"I took you by surprise back on my ship," Lucifer said. "I suppose it won't be so easy this time."

"Not a chance in Hell!" Yan replied.

Lucifer grabbed her neck and lifted, her feet dangled in the air.

"I'm not talking to you."

He tossed her to the side without regard. Yan landed face down on the dirt. She saw the Black Angel, back in her physical form, stepping through the trail of dead transients whose lives she had taken earlier. The dead transients sat up with puppet-like movements, then stood up to closely march behind Black Angel in a creepy parade as she passed by Yan Fan. Black Angel stood at a safe distance from Lucifer while her undead transients launched themselves at Lucifer.

Inside the press box, Violet yelled at Blue as she witnessed the fight from a distance.

"OMG! Zombie transients! Whaaat!"

Blue was too busy interacting with some cables and old control panels.

The dead transients attacked Lucifer, clawing at him from all directions. Lucifer burned and tore them apart, but they kept coming at him unyielding. Lose dead limbs clung to his skin.

"Yan," Blue's voice called through her spectral helmet comm. "We are ready to start. Just say the word."

Yan Fan's transient body stood up from the ground. She released herself from it. Back in her ghost form, she felt the same dizziness she'd experienced when she was inside Lucifer's mothership, but this wasn't the time for her to dwell on that.

"Okay. Patch me through to them."

Back at the press box, Blue clicked a button and a short feedback was heard in all the speakers across the park. The feedback caught the attention of all the transients in the field. They all stood still, facing towards the scattered speakers. Blue spoke through a microphone on the panel.

"Sorry about that. Okay, check! Check! One, two, three. Alright, to the evil gentleman in the red Armani, here's the reason we chose to fight you in this baseball stadium. Yan, you're on."

Yan Fan spoke through her helmet comm. Her voice came out through the speakers of the park.

"This is for Matteo and the crew of the Defiant that you killed. For Matilda, and the Georges… One divided by one equals infinity."

All of the transients faced Yan Fan and began to absorb her spirit into themselves. Her soul multiplied in the hundreds, and then thousands. Each part of her occupied transients. She could see everything through all their bodies. Life from multiple points of view. It took her a moment to get used to her eyes becoming a kaleidoscope of reality. She also felt the membranoid muscles of all her colorless bodies. And she felt their power.

Inside every transient body, Yan could hear masses of babies talking to her in undecipherable broken tongues. But she knew it was the same message spoken to her in unison. The only thought their fear allowed them to convey: Tell me what to do.

"I'll tell you what to do…"

Every single one of the transients piled up on Lucifer, burying him under a mountain of their giant bodies. Using all their strength and weight, they fought to push him against the dirt. Lucifer spread his four wings, freeing himself from the faceless giants. The Archangels joined in the attack, delivering relentless blows. Striking, blasting, conjuring; they threw everything they could at him.

"We can do this all day, Lucifer! You've already lost!" Blue said through the park speakers.

"Is that so?"

Lucifer burst into blinding golden light. The blast incinerated thousands of transients and threw the Archangels back away several yards away from him. Yan Fan felt an abrupt tear in her soul from those transients that died, and she had them retreat away from the devil. The angels all lay unconscious on the ground. Everything around Lucifer was now a perfect circle of black scorched earth.

"Is that it, Zadkiel? Was that the last trick up your sleeve?" Lucifer asked.

He stepped towards the closest transient that was still alive. Blue limped out of the press box without waiting for Violet, who ran behind him.

"Yan!" Blue yelled.

"This is such a letdown," Lucifer said. "This moment played so much better in my mind… And I bet in yours, too. You Archangels and your every move, are so utterly predictable. The only thing I did not see coming, and that I must admit had me confounded for a while is *you*…"

He stretched his arm and opened his hand over the chest of the transient. A golden light shone from his palm and Yan Fan's spirit was sucked out from the faceless giant. Every transient purged the replicated spirits of Yan that inhabited them and, in an instant, the divided souls faded as the spirit that Lucifer caught absorbed them back.

Yan became one again, or at least as whole as she could be having lost many pieces of her soul. Lucifer had her in her grip. She struggled pointlessly to get free from him. Panic and confusion overcame her. Her mind felt heavy and clouded. It was the same sensation she felt back when she was on the mothership.

The closer I get to Lucifer... She couldn't even finish her thought.

"Yan Fan. Since I became aware of you, you became a puzzle to me. You were the one I didn't know what to make of. What was your role in all of this? What were you hoping to accomplish in the little time you have left wandering about?"

"Yan!" Blue cried.

He staggered towards the devil and reached his arms towards Yan, but he stopped when Lucifer shook his head and tightened his grip on her.

"Not another step forward, Zadkiel," Lucifer said.

Violet pulled Blue's arm back.

"Lucifer, please don't kill her," she pleaded.

Lucifer looked again at his watch. And then back at Yan. He released her. Yan floated to Blue for safety. She wanted to touch him, but her mind was too addled.

"It doesn't matter now," Lucifer continued. "All those little episodes of you popping in and out of existence. Ever increasing and more lasting... Don't deny it. I saw it happen when I held you back in my ship. Why didn't you tell her Zadkiel? Don't you think she deserves to know?"

Yan turned her eyes to Blue. He stared at her with sadness and shame.

"Go ahead. Tell her that she will not get to move on because her soul's essence is just moments away from scattering away to nothingness. All those years wasted at that shuttle wreckage on the moon... a peculiar abnormality that now fixes itself. Tell the little fluke that decades disconnected from the afterlife has closed the doors to her. Her fate is now oblivion."

Yan Fan and Blue locked eyes as she began to fade out of existence. With fear in her eyes, she moved her lips trying to say something to Blue.

No sound came from her.

Blue tried to speak, too. He wanted to scream his lungs off. But he had no boom box or stadium speakers at hand. Yan and Blue were about to lose each other forever, with no way of conveying what they felt. Only through their eyes; their love and their sorrow through their eyes.

Violet held Blue tight in her arms as he witnessed Yan's eyes become two black holes and her face wither into a dimming translucent skull. The rest of her body followed. Silent tears rolled down Blue's cheek and he let his body break down with his spirit, her spirit, escaping him. Blue was on his knees, crying, grasping the air and then his own chest.

Yan Fan became nothing.

Lucifer shook his head and fixed his suit.

"I ask you, too, Zadkiel. What were you trying to accomplish? It is insulting that you'd hope for any other outcome than this. This is how you finally learn. I leave you a world infested with transients for you to clean up and decide what to do with. I leave you with proof that everything you thought was right and perfect with God was a lie. His plan is a lie and your existence is pointless. And I leave you without your precious friend Yan Fan. Non-existent. She's what happens when you Archangels dare to dream that humanity can become more."

Lucifer made his way through the defeated angels and approached Blue to whisper in his ear.

"That's the victory I concede to you," he said. "Enjoy."

The devil whistled as he strolled away from the Archangels and the transients in the field. He left behind a mess of wild and confused transient hordes, an abandoned ship hovering the sky, and seven defeated Archangels. He left a devastated Blue, the tear in his heart far worse than the loss of his jaw. Blue wondered if his immense pain was what it felt like to be an angel fallen.

18 UPON A STAR

It took Blue seven minutes to hack into Mother and seven days to end the transient invasion with the help of the other Archangels. City by city, country by country, the ship called transients to it and harbored them. Evergreen created natural terrain paths for the faceless giants to march without causing any damages. Isophie helped too, attracting groups with the bright of her flaming sword, she led them to the golden ship. Ricadel used her light to heal any injured transients hurt by bullets from the military. She also consorted with the Black Angel to sort between humans that perished during the invasion but were meant to live and those that needed to move on. When the Archangels were done combing the entire planet, Goldie took a couple of days to focus and reset reality. Crumbled rubble assembled up in the air as if time went in rewind to restore destroyed buildings and humanity forgot that their visitors ever existed.

Seven days after the angels survived the battle with Lucifer, Mother launched into space.

. . . .

The seven Archangels stood together deep in the crater where space shuttle Defiant's wreckage rested at the moon. Goldie contained the area within a golden dome with breathable air, gravity, and warm temperature, even though none of the angels needed it. They half-circled around a heavy-looking cream-colored seat, moving it from deep in the caverns to an open area where light rays reflected and turned to shades of bright gold. Blue took a few steps closer to the chair. There was silence for a while. A funeral for Yan Fan was taking place. Only Earth and an infinity of stars served as witnesses.

"I'm pretty sure this was the seat where she sat."

Blue had a few days to update his armor. It was a darker cobalt chromium suit than the one damaged by his fight with Lucifer, tightly fitted with slicker platinum plaques on his chest and shoulders. The newest upgrade was an exterior skeleton-like metal spine that covered his throat up in a row of plasmid discs. The discs glowed in bluish hues at different sections of his gullet as his angelic essence flowed intermittently through him. He also built a new metallic jaw for himself with movements limited to that of a bone jaw. There were two small round discs at each side of his jaw that allowed its movement, but also contained potent amps that voiced his thoughts at will. But out of all the changes in his appearance, his siblings noticed his buzzcut the most.

Black Angel, sported a black lace over her ragged gray dress and black school shoes. She clutched Ricadel's dress with hands trembling. Suppressing her panic took a lot of will, but this would be the last goodbye to Yan so she insisted to be brought back to space. She let go of the gown and moved over to Blue. Wrapping her arms around his thigh, she leaned her head on him.

Goldie was the first to speak, or rather sing. Wearing a black suit, shirt, and veiled hat, along with a gold tie and a small golden heart pendant on the upper left side of her chest; she poured champagne from a bottle. Three back up male singers in black suits appeared behind her. Their harmonies meshed well with her voice as she sang Peter Gabriel's *I Grieve*.

"*...So hard to move on. Still loving what's gone... They say life carries on. Carries on and on, and on, and on...*"

As soon as the song ended, the backup singers disappeared. Goldie hugged Blue, tilted her head and gave him a wink with a smile.

"Celebrate her."

Evergreen, her hair adorned with stargazer lilies, set a funeral crown next to the seat.

"She spoke for an entire species when no one else did. That is admirable."

The angel of nature intended to return to her place in the semi-circle, but Blue's fingers briefly touched hers, even though his gaze escaped Evergreen's. This was the first time he'd acknowledge her since the movie theater in Downtown Phoenix.

Violet pulled back her dark purple hoodie and crunched the ground with her black boots as she strode over to the chair.

"I could like, sense the sheer terror those transients felt. It infected me. When Yan shared their bodies, it made them better. In a way, she kind of completed their hearts? She mattered to them and stuff."

Isophie wore black shades, many silver chains on her pierced face, and a black leather jacket and tights. She grabbed the champagne bottle from Goldie and took a big gulp. Stepping forward, she spilled the rest all over the chair and drew her blazing sword.

"She got in my face. Lady's got balls, I'll give her that."

The red angel handed her flaming blade to Blue and got out of his way. He held the sword and stared at the empty wet seat. He moved the blade close to the chair and it lit up. Crackling cindered sparks floated from the burning seat and faded in the air. The pyre blazed high and the angels stood before it silent for a while. Tearful, Ricadel held Blue from behind. He held her hands tight.

"Aaand another veil has been placed on reality," Isophie said. "Humanity is once again oblivious that they almost kicked the bucket. What Uriel said before about this apocalypse, she was right. We just swept everything under a rug. How long can we keep this up?"

"Until they are ready to accept our existence and that of—"

"Yeah, but when will that be?"

Ricadel, wearing her usual glowing white gown, had a black band on her arm. She glanced at Isophie and then turned to face the other angels.

"Brother. Sisters. There is doubt in us after all that we have witnessed. We are no longer sure that our actions make a difference… and we fear to be abandoned by God. Let us remember Yan Fan and people like her. Through their selfless acts, they remind us of what we fight for. The universe is bigger now, we are no longer alone. But God's plan— our plan, remains the same. Lucifer is still out there and one day we will defeat him. We are protectors of Creation and humanity. Let us not forget that we are still angels."

"How can you say that?" Evergreen asked. "You who have lost more to him than all of us?"

Ricadel stepped forward with angered eyes.

"Because I refuse to let things be the way he wants them to be; in misery and pain for all but him. I'll tell you this. The deeper I've fallen to darkness, the brighter I see the light I need to reach. Heed my words. Lucifer will fall. This I swear. His day will come. And I hope you will all join me on that day."

"Amen!" Goldie exclaimed. "Preach it, sister!"

Evergreen raised her eyebrow. Antlers grew out from her hair.

Black Angel clenched her fist and nodded.

Isophie smirked.

"Oorah!"

"One day…" Violet said.

Waiting for their brother to speak, the Archangels looked at Blue. He took a moment to gaze back at everyone in his family.

"I'll be there."

Blue turned and treaded away from the bonfire.

"But tonight I have a long trip ahead of me. Hey, Goldie, please make sure get everyone home safely. I'll see you all soon."

. . . .

Mother's space voyage was quiet. The once golden behemoth, now irradiated a blueish luminosity. Blue made some adjustments to the ship, but couldn't bring himself to reprogram its main frame. Countless sections of the transport remained unexplored. Every night he stared at distant galaxies from the glass hallway at the far side of the ship. Crystal walls and floors brought him closer to the stars than he had ever been. It was the only thing he appreciated about the monstrosity that Matilda had become.

Blue strolled through the extensive incubator hangar where millions of transients stood immobile next to each other. Double-checking the chamber's temperature, he made sure they were comfortable in their stasis. He also ran over the specs of every planet on each galaxy he visited looking for the perfect living conditions for the transients. He reviewed coordinates and changed course a few times, just to go back to the original traced trajectory.

After finishing all his chores, he finally returned to the glass hallway.

Blue swiped the air and a holo-screen hovered him. With soundless finger taps, he activated a few apps and listened to Yan Fan's recordings.

Day 140

I remember dreaming of myself standing naked on a red star. I'm sure it was a star; it definitely wasn't Earth. That one was vivid. I think you were in that dream, too. It was so cold and I was walking for what felt was years on the star's dark red flames. The sky was red, too. I saw you descend and open your arms to me. Your wings were made of light. I stepped closer and you embraced me. I never saw your face, so I couldn't swear it was really you, but you felt warm. You felt safe… It must have been you.

Blue paused the message teary-eyed. He saw a comet passing by leaving a gleaming trail of white and pink in its path.

"Oh, she would've loved to see that."

Blue noticed a small light blinking on his screen. He picked up the call and a familiar voice spoke to him.

"Hey, Blue."

. . . .

Almost two weeks before Blue's journey to space, during the transient world invasion, the Archangel of science just beaten demon prince Sloth. Only a few minutes passed after Father Anselmo left the basement of the mental hospital at Ithaca, New York. Ricadel and the Black Angel helped Blue take a few slow painful steps forward. Yan Fan hovered behind him. Blue touched his helicopter toy neck brace, just readjusted by his sister. He felt a slight discomfort, but he did his best to pretend he was fine. Ricadel still noticed.

"Brother, I appreciate you needed to defeat Sloth," she said to him. "But now you are in no condition to fight Lucifer."

Blue's floating holo-screen displayed words.

couldnt face him even at my best

need to find another

"Another what?" Yan asked.

Blue did not respond. His eyes were fixated on a text notice that appeared on his holo-screen. He opened a palm-sized monitor from his suit's chest plate to read the message. It was from Father Anselmo:

Spaceboy, beware. Before he died Matteo told me he foresaw that Ms. Fan will not make it out of this. He said her soul won't be able to move on.

Blue halted. He spoke to Ricadel through his screen.

ricadel need a moment

will catch up

"I'm not leaving you alone, brother."

azrael and yan will look out for me

please

Ricadel stared at Blue. She noticed a change in his eyes.

"Very well. I'll wait for you outside. Please know that you can trust me to help with whatever troubles you."

Blue nodded and hugged Ricadel. After the angel left, he bent down to the Black Angel and showed her the text.

Blue's screen floated close to the angel of death.

think I can save her

but she belongs to your ministry

need your blessing

"Guys, what's going on?" Yan Fan asked.

Black Angel bowed and walked away. Blue turned to face Yan.

"Dude, what is it?"

need to talk

please hold still

A faint buzzing began as Blue turned on the small rotator on his throat. His eyes looked tired; weak with the feeling of a part of himself slowly escaping him. Yan saw a small fraction of Blue's angelic essence flowing to her.

. . . .

Blue stood at the glass hallway of Mother, looking at the stars. He heard Yan's voice speak to him through his suit's comm.

"How did you know this would work?"

"I didn't. I just hoped. I've been thinking about it for sure. When I was in a coma and I remembered Leo— But I didn't know…"

"Leo?"

"Ah, yeah. We met in the fifteenth century. You've read about him. His name was Leonardo da Vinci. He was a young polymath. An inventor's mind with the heart of an artist and a very opinionated and progressive man. We discussed politics, science, history, architecture, religion… Our relationship was— We were two colleagues that deeply respected each other's ideas… with benefits."

"Wait, you dated Leonardo da Vinci?"

"I did. He amazed me every moment I spent with him. Leo came up with these amazing designs. A mechanical lion that moved and roared just like a live one; an ethereal canvas to capture wandering spirits in some of his paintings, like the Mona Lisa; human wings to reach the stars; even a time travel chamber, or what he called the room with three doors, one for yesterday, one for today, one for tomorrow. They all worked! Some of these inventions I guarded so humanity wouldn't discover them before their time. There were days I truly believed that he'd change the world for the better."

Blue sighted.

"Eventually we parted ways. The world was on the brink of a renascent industrial evolution and I needed to focus on my ministry of science. I trusted he'd be fine going back to his creations. But even though his mind and soul were so uniquely strong, his heart wasn't. We hadn't seen each other for two years when I realized he was agonizing after suffering several heart attacks. He was in his twenties still, barely hanging on the heart of a ninety-year-old. I couldn't let him die. So, I did the only thing I could to save him—"

"You did to him what you did to me."

"Yes."

"You made him a saint."

"Yes. Patron saint of innovation."

"Did it work? What happened then?"

"It worked. He lived on and continued to invent and research."

"He died in France, right? His heart finally gave out?"

"No. That's what the world was made to believe. But he was murdered. When I found him, his heart was torn out of his body, and a pair of special goggles I gifted him was also missing. It was the only possession stolen from him."

"Oh, God! I'm so sorry, Blue."

"I searched for years, but I never found the murderer. And Leo wasn't the only one. Other saints have been assassinated throughout the centuries, with organs or artifacts removed. That's why I had doubts when I thought of making you a saint. But when Father Anselmo texted me what Matteo had foreseen, I had to try to circumvent the prophecy anyway I could. We got lucky."

"Lucky?" Yan said. "You sainted me to anchor my soul with yours and then we made Lucifer think I faded out of existence! That's crazy! Do you know how weird it is to be a ghost faking her death?"

"Ha! If you put it like that, it sounds a bit ridiculous, yeah. What can I say? Some prophecies can be annulled, others can be sidestepped. By the way, that was amazing, that thing you did with your face. Making it look like a skull."

"Hee, yeah! It's so weird the things I can do now."

"When you were 'dying', what is it that you said to me when your voice went out?"

"Pancakes! It's our emotional safe word!"

Blue shook his head and laughed.

"Have you told Ricadel yet?"

"Not yet. Only Black Angel knows. I think Violet suspects. Can't hide my feelings from her. But I want to keep your existence a secret to protect you. If Lucifer knew—"

"Fine. But you need to tell Ricadel. She's my friend and she needs to know!"

"Alright, I will."

"So, come on. Tell me all about it! What did Lucifer say?" Yan asked.

"Oh, you know, typical Lucifer stuff. 'Ooh! I'm Lucifer, the light bringer, and you're all little pieces of walking shit! Fear me!' "

"Hahaha!"

"I guess my question to you is, Yan Fan, how does it feel to be the saint of space exploration?"

"It feels great, really. I have no more flash-outs. I feel whole. I'm more in control of myself. And... I can sense your presence. I mean, I know you're hundreds of light years away from me, but I can look up to the stars and point where you are."

"Same here. We're connected now."

"We've always been connected, Blue," Yan said. "Ever since that first time I saw you on the Defiant."

There was a brief silence. *She remembered*, Blue thought.

"Anyway, listen! I think I found it! You're not going to believe this. I'm sending you my coordinates. You need to come now!"

. . . .

Mother traversed through several galaxies. Stars, planets, nebulas, asteroid belts, all speeding to the golden ship's rearview. Weeks passed before Blue arrived at his destination. He couldn't believe his eyes. It was a giant red sun in the center of a solar system. Seventeen planets orbited it, all of them habitable for humans according to the ship's readings. There was an eighteenth planet detected and that's where Yan waited for Blue. The coordinates were correct, but Blue was confused. The eighteenth planet was the red star itself.

As Mother got closer to the mighty red giant, Blue noticed that its northern hemisphere was layered in crystalized land unlike anything he'd seen before. The cobalt ship approached the eighteenth planet and flew over its glass mountainous layout. Blue found a clear zone to land Mother.

After taking time to study the landscape, he deemed it safe to release the transients.

The Archangel tracked and found the small round saucer he'd given Yan Fan to travel. Yan was close by, but she wasn't wearing her bulky space suit. Instead, she seemed very relaxed in a cosmonaut overall as she collected samples of minerals from the ground. She hovered over to Blue and they hugged.

"Isn't it wonderful?" she asked him. "This is so vast! About twenty times the size of Earth."

"Twenty-two."

"That's great! And I haven't even had the time to explore the other planets in this system. Is it true? Readings on my saucer could be wrong."

"They're not!" he said excited. "Humans will be able to live here one day when they're ready to travel the stars."

"Well, they can keep the other seventeen planets. This red star is for the transients."

"Deal!" Blue laughed.

"Oh, man! Blue, this is it. Check this out."

Yan hovered upwards to the top of a crystal hill. Blue followed. They stood on crystal soil and could clearly see crimson star flares thousands of miles underneath their feet. Under a red sky, Blue felt he was in a dream, the one from Yan's recordings. It was a dream now shared between a human and an angel. Staring at the transients spread out in the distance, he knew they'd be well fed with nutrients that the rich beautiful world provided. They would be sheltered in beautiful diamond-hard glass caves and far away from harm. Just like Yan always wanted. This was where she lived, too.

"This place. You get the honor of naming it." Blue said to her.

"Roger that," she replied. "A perfect place like this... I'll call it Heaven..."

Blue smiled at the astronaut ghost.

"Part Two."

AFTERWORD

When Lucifer visited the book store in chapter 6 of this novel, you most likely noticed I referenced a few very specific book titles that the devil browsed before finding the one he wanted. Did they sound appealing to you? If they did, just don't try to order them on Amazon...yet. In truth, these titles were made up as a tribute to three very talented authors that are currently working on their own incredible fictional worlds.

Back in 2017, I was losing my ongoing lazy battle with the demon Sloth for reasons that we don't need to get into here. But suffice to say that coming from a comic book and film making background, I'm used to a collaborative artistic process. Writing a novel got very lonely for me without receiving immediate feedback from another creative mind to bounce ideas from. It took me two years to finish the first draft of *Violet Descends* because of this. And also, Netflix. (They're killing me with all those recommended comedy specials and shows!) So there was very little writing I accomplished at the time and I was about to give up on completing the Seven Lights story. I thought of maybe moving on to other things, but I'd lost my inspiration to create anything.

Enter Sally Blue, a fantasy writer who reached out to other creators through Meetup. She wanted to establish a writers workshop with a small focused group of about 4 or 5 people. Each writer would submit novel chapters of about 5,000 words to be discussed in bi-weekly meetings. I got to see her Meetup posting by accident. I was really looking to join a group to talk Star Wars or whatever. But I saw her posting and I figured I'd try it. To join, you needed to submit a chapter and I'd already written something almost a year before that I thought was decent enough.

Our first meeting was in the month of May and 9 people were allowed to attend after handing in their fantasy scripts. But Sally said she'd pick only half of them to move forward by the end of the meeting. Everyone else that tried to get in were either too late after deadline or didn't follow the submission requirements. But these 9 people did and I got to read their chapters and give them feedback. I was very delighted and a little intimidated after reading the stories because most of them were very good. It made me doubt that they'd picked mine, and I kind of felt like the non-flirty girl at *The Bachelor* that you know wouldn't get the rose at the end of the first episode. (I'm sorry if I screwed up the metaphor. I don't really watch that show)

Sally did pick my chapter along with Amy Joscelyn's and Tom Mortensen's. I was floored and thrilled to be chosen. But now we needed to continue our work. Again, I went from not writing anything in 18 months to submitting a chapter every two weeks. And that's what we've done for a year, give or take, as of this writing. Overcoming obstacles from everyday life, dealing with day jobs, our families, health issues; we've persevered through all of it and will continue to do so. Because the thing about being a writer is that you need to write. It's the only way to get the writing part done. So we write and we don't stop.

We call ourselves the Novelmobile.

Transient of the Stars is the first novel published from the Novelmobile sessions, and I'm super proud of it. It only took 10 months to complete. That's about 20 meetings right there. And I've already started on the next book.

In your face, Sloth!

Without giving too much away from their stories:

Sally's tale is a modern fantasy dealing with dreams that combines magical forests and urban city settings. Hers is a story you experience through emotions. She can put feelings into words like no one I've ever read. She's amazing in bringing out the humanity in all her characters, even if they're not human. Beware: Sally will make you care for little Smurf-like creatures and then she'll make you cry for them!

Amy's book has stories that span the lifetime of the queen of an imaginary kingdom. When it comes to her descriptions and dialogues, the word that comes to my mind is *precise*. Striking like a ninja, she can tell you so much about a character or a place with just a few words. Amy is also a wordsmith with the ability to come up with the weirdest words and ancient poetry. She will make your stomach growl with the best food descriptions ever. And she sings in a choir, too.

And bringing up the rear…

Tom's story is about a woman that time-travels every time she blacks out and wakes up as a younger version of herself. It's laugh-out-loud funny and full of great character moments and pop culture references. Tom is very observant of details, specially when it comes to characters. He's also been trained by Navy SEALs to detect story clichés, a very useful skill that has served us all. We talk about Star Wars, so I get to have the proverbial cake and eat it too!

I'm very lucky to be a part of this group of writers. They inspire me with their work and their constructive criticism has made my craft infinitely better narrative-wise. I just wish I'd met them when I was writing *Violet Descends*.

This is a big thank you to Sally, Amy, and Tom. I'm honored to be working with you and to have you as friends. I can't wait to see what great ideas you come up with next and for the world to share the pleasure I've had reading your amazing tales.

Thank you for reading.

-Angel

#savemarcus

ABOUT THE AUTHOR

Angel Fuentes is a writer from Puerto Rico who has authored several short stories and screenplays. His most notable work, *Santa Cristal*, was made into an independent film. He also founded and served as publisher of RBA Comics, where he wrote several comic book titles. Mr. Fuentes is currently living and writing in the Big Apple.

Transient of the Stars is the second volume of a series of fantasy books and a sequel to *Violet Descends: A Seven Lights Novel*, his first novel.